ALSO EDITED BY MAXIM JAKUBOWSKI
FROM CLIPPER LARGE PRINT

The Best British Mysteries Volume I
The Best British Mysteries Volume II
The Best British Mysteries Volume III

The Best British Mysteries IV

The Best British Mysteries IV

Edited by
Maxim Jakubowski

W F HOWES LTD

This large print edition published in 2007 by
W F Howes Ltd
Unit 4, Rearsby Business Park, Gaddesby Lane,
Rearsby, Leicester LE7 4YH

1 3 5 7 9 10 8 6 4 2

First published in the United Kingdom in 2006
by Allison & Busby Limited

A CIP catalogue record for this book is available
from the British Library

ISBN 978 1 84632 869 5

Typeset by Palimpsest Book Production Limited,
Grangemouth, Stirlingshire
Printed and bound in Great Britain
by Antony Rowe Ltd, Chippenham, Wilts.

CONTENTS

INTRODUCTION

Already our fourth volume presenting the best crime and mystery short stories written by British authors and it's another veritable cornucopia of thrills, dirty deeds, clever plots, evil villains, determined sleuths, psychological torment, confounding puzzles, and almost every shenanigan under the sun (or, in many instances, the moon . . .).

The ingenuity of crime writers never ceases to amaze me as they plumb the hidden depths of the human psyche and explore that tenuous territory that sometimes separates good and evil in which characters much like you and me can sometimes get away with it, or not, as the case may be. Murder, deceit and wrongdoing are fertile grounds, though, for splendid entertainment, as a recent statistic confirmed, showing that British library readers now read more mysteries than romance; the first time this has historically happened. Whether you read crime books for the intellectual crime-solving element, or for its often fascinating insight into human nature or, more simply, for the sheer pleasure of a good read where the plot effortlessly goes from A to Z with many a roadside attraction during the journey, there is no more satisfying form of entertainment and the mystery short story embodies all these virtues in a concentrated format which proves a challenge to good writers and a particular delight to readers. And, forgive me for just a touch of gentle chauvinism, British crime and mystery writers certainly rule the roost in this regard.

A scintillating, if murderous menu . . .

Enjoy the fruits of their crimes.

Maxim Jakubowski

ACKNOWLEDGEMENTS

'The Jane Case' by Michael Z Lewin © 2005 by Michael Z Lewin. First appeared in *Alfred Hitchcock's Mystery Magazine*. Reprinted by permission of the author.

'Retrospective' by Kevin Wignall © 2005 by Kevin Wignall. First appeared in *Greatest Hits*, edited by Robert Randisi. Reprinted by permission of the author and his agent, Curtis Brown Limited.

'The Spiteful Shadow' by Peter Tremayne © 2005 by Peter Tremayne. First appeared in *The Mammoth Book of New Historical Whodunits*, edited by Mike Ashley. Reprinted by permission of the author and his agent, AM Heath & Co Limited.

'Blue Christmas' by Peter Robinson © 2005 by Peter Robinson. First appeared as a chapbook from Crippen & Landru. Reprinted by permission of the author.

MICHAEL Z LEWIN

THE JANE CASE

The Old Man was huffing and puffing, but for once it was a physical thing and not a litany of complaint about how people do things these days and not like they used to. This time the complaining was not his, it was Mama's.

'Use it or lose it,' she said to him. And so now here he was whirling the pedals of a so-called bicycle. But how could it be a bicycle if it didn't go anywhere? Huh!

And, for that matter, what was the 'it' he might *lose* if he didn't do all this going nowhere? Mama spelled it out with talk, talk, talk, but now he couldn't remember. Just that was because he rested sometimes when he climbed the stairs to the flat. Two flights, that climb. Twenty-eight steps, plus a few more at the doorway. So now and then he turned into Angelo and Gina's kitchen half-way up and sat in a chair. So what? You get a little tired, you sit, plus they were his son and daughter-in-law, who might be home, or their children, or the others. Sitting in a chair doesn't mean you're about to fall over and die, God help you. If it did, who'd be left standing? Huh!

1

And so what, he watched more television now? What else was it for? And was there a law? Only now, it seemed, there was. Mama couldn't prohibit, but after an hour, or half an hour, she could start to talk at him. And not stop. 'Do this. Do that. Do *something*.'

So maybe that *was* it. In the family business there was less and less something for him to do, him, the *head* of the family, no matter who ran the day-to-day. All of a sudden it's not like he founded the Lunghi Detective Agency and taught them everything they knew. All of a sudden it's not like he can observe and follow and record and *detect* anymore. No wonder he gained a few pounds. What else should he do?

'You want to work more? Show them how fit you are,' Mama said. 'Get rid of some inches.'

'What, become shorter? I'll do that anyway, getting older.'

'Don't be stupid.' And she turned away.

Now he was stupid, too, with everything else?

But, in the end, he did what she wanted because she was delicate and would get upset if he didn't. So here he was. Thursday in the second week of it, at the YMCA gym. On a so-called bike that went nowhere. Soon on a so-called treadmill that had nothing to tread. How many of them here knew from grapes? Huh!

'And after a few weeks,' the Y's Guru Mick said, 'I'll start you on some weights. You're really going to hate me then.'

I should have to wait till then? the Old Man thought. Guru Mick, with his big muscles, took him into a little room and did a 'personal evaluation' and gave a 'personal programme.' All smiles and calling him 'buddy' and saying 'I'm going to be your exercise guru.' Huh!

The Old Man wiped his face with a towel and saw he had seven more minutes of going nowhere.

'I'm so worried about Papa,' Mama said to her daughter-in-law over plates of salad at lunch time. 'So much he sits.'

Midday meetings for lunch were unusual, and today it seemed to Gina that Mama had sought her out because something was on her mind. 'Well, Papa's not as young as he used to be,' Gina said. 'He's entitled to some rest.'

Mama put down her fork. 'It's not entitlement, Gina. It's prison. He hates it.'

'I thought he liked watching TV.' Gina tried to remember the programmes her father-in-law had mentioned at the dinner table. There were the police and detective shows to be pulled to pieces, but wasn't there also some words and numbers game each day in the afternoon? She couldn't pull back its name.

'What he *wants* to do is work.' Mama held up her hands. 'I know, I know. I asked for less for him, but too much less is not enough. I wouldn't interfere, Gina, God knows, but if you and Angelo have cases he could help with then he'd be happy,

3

I'd be happy. Some surveillance without cars, maybe. Or shoplifters, or even serving papers. Anything.'

'If that's what you want, Mama.' Gina pursed her lips and reviewed what was on the agency's agenda at the moment. Other than the routine work for solicitors, there was an industrial, but would *that* be appropriate?

'Meanwhile all he can think to do is go to the gym, that's how desperate he is,' Mama said.

'Papa goes to the *gym*?'

'To be doing, not sitting. He started at the YMCA last week on Monday, so eleven days now. He's determined to lose a few inches, to show you and Angelo how fit he still is. This inch-losing is good for the health too. He should be rewarded for effort, I think. Don't you?'

'Are you waiting for a treadmill?'

The Old Man turned to the voice to find it belonged to one of those musclemen. 'What?'

'The one on the end is free.'

'I'm watching this runner, this red vest,' the Old Man said.

The muscleman looked at the runner the Old Man pointed at. Red Vest was pounding away on a treadmill in front of them.

'You see that?' the Old Man said. 'How his heels kick out sideways?'

The man looked at the runner on the treadmill.

'Kicking out doesn't go forward. This Red Vest

can be as fit as he likes, but in a race he'd lose inches. More if it's longer.'

'Oh.' The man frowned. 'So . . . you're not waiting for a treadmill, then?'

This muscleman wanted a machine, not an education. The Old Man waved him to it and turned back to Red Vest. The kicking out was extremely pronounced. It even looked un-comfortable, like he could twist his ankles with the kicking.

How old was this Red Vest? Older than David, the Old Man's grandson, but how much? Fifteen? Maybe twenty? Young enough to learn? To correct his ways? Perhaps, if he really wanted to.

The Old Man's running days were long gone, but he'd done enough on tracks and across the foothills of his youth. And then he found himself thinking of the great Emilio Lunghi, who won a silver medal running in the Olympics of 1908, beating the German, Braun, but losing to the American, Sheppard, in the 800 meters. Not a relative, this Emilio, but a famous namesake. And if he had found only a few more inches . . .

'Did he steal *your* mobile too?'

This time the questioner was a young woman. A girl, only. Was *everybody* so young now? Maybe the age of Maria, his granddaughter, this one. But who can tell these days? 'What?'

'I saw you watching that bastard on the treadmill.'

'He's a bastard?' The Old Man glanced with sympathy at Red Vest.

'He stole my mobile phone.'

'He *stole* it?' Now no sympathy. The Old Man had little sympathy to spare for thieves.

'I was on Saracen Street talking to my brother and *that* bastard came up behind me and pulled my arm down from my ear, grabbed the phone out of my hand and ran away with it.'

'How long ago was this stealing?'

'Monday. Then I came in here to train on Tuesday, and there he was. I couldn't believe it. He was running on a treadmill, just like today.'

'And this phone stealer, did he give it back?'

'Did he, hell. He just laughed in my face and said he never did it and he could prove it. But he *did* do it. He absolutely did.' The look on the young woman's face was one of pure hatred.

The Old Man considered what he'd been told about the theft. She was talking. The bastard came up behind her . . . 'You didn't see him coming, so you saw him going?' he asked.

'Not his face. He had on a green waterproof with a hood.'

'So . . . ?' The Old Man spread his hands. At home, in the family, at a meal like they would have tonight, everyone would know he was asking for elucidation with the gesture, for explanation. But this young girl just looked from one hand to the other, so he spelled it out. 'You didn't see his face yet you're sure you know it's him? How can this be?'

6

'Look at the way he runs,' the young woman said. 'See how he kicks out his heels?'

'"Dishing" they call it, in horses,' the Old Man said at the dinner table. 'Jane told me.'

'Horses?' Salvatore said. 'Did I miss something?'

Thursday night was one of three times a week that the Lunghis made an effort to eat together. This time even Salvatore, Mama and the Old Man's eldest child, was there. He was the only member of the immediate family who did not live in the family's connected properties on Walcot Street.

'This girl, this Jane, she rides horses. So she recognised the stealer by his gait.'

'Dishing? Well, who wants another *dish* of curry?' This was Rosetta, the youngest of the senior Lunghis' three children. She cooked on Thursdays, often her trademark curry. 'I'm getting up anyway. Papa?'

Normally the Old Man complained that curry wasn't Italian, and then ate more. But today the three hands that went up for seconds did not include his.

Angelo, the younger son who ran the family business, tapped the side of his cheek as he tried to digest his father's story. 'Am I understanding right, Papa? You're telling us because you want us to take this Jane as some kind of client?'

'It's injustice this thief can dish at the YMCA with impunity,' the Old Man said. 'He dished on

Tuesday the day after he stole the poor girl's phone, and laughed in her face. Then today he dishes again, right in front of her.'

'But a *client*, Papa? Is she paying?'

'She has no money to pay,' the Old Man said. 'She's a dropout, to work with horses, though she builds strength in the gym to be a jockey one day.'

'So . . . *not* paying?' Angelo said.

'What did I just say? Huh!'

There was a silence at the table to mark the moment. This was because it was unprecedented for the Old Man to suggest that the agency work without a paying client. He could have invented, 'Show me the money,' it was so unprecedented.

Angelo looked around the table, catching the eyes of each of the adults. 'For myself,' he said, 'I'm happy to see if we can help. But, Papa, I never thought I'd hear *you* say we should take on work for free.'

'You can think too much about money,' the Old Man said. 'More than a certain amount, who needs more?'

All their lives the Lunghi siblings had listened to their father ask, 'Who's paying?' For him the answer had never before been, 'Us.'

When dinner was over and the dishes dealt with, the middle generation of Lunghis retired to the living room. Angelo brought a bottle of wine.

'What's with Papa?' Salvatore asked for them all.

'I never in my life thought I'd hear about him going to a *gym*.'

Rosetta said, 'He didn't want seconds, and it wasn't because Mama nagged him.'

Angelo said, 'He wants us to work for free.'

Gina, who could have pulled the strands together, kept quiet while the others talked. Maybe they would work it out for themselves.

'It sounds like he's been to the Y every day since Monday last week,' Salvatore said. 'Did it sound that way to you?'

'Maybe he's trying to lose weight, and get fit,' Rosetta said. 'But why now?'

'He wants us to work for free,' Angelo said.

There was a pause.

Gina said, 'Do any of you mind working for free on this?'

No one did.

'So let's think about the case. *Is* there anything we can do?'

'For horsey Jane?' Salvatore said. 'Lots of kids have their phones stolen, don't they?'

'Lots,' Rosetta said.

'What do the thieves do with the phones they steal? Make phone calls?'

'They sell them on to foreign countries.'

'Really, Rose?'

'Places where there aren't so many phones or so many high-tech ones. But there's a market here too. They replace the SIM card and clean them out with a computer so they can be resold as legitimate second-hand.' Rosetta only rarely participated actively in investigations, but she was the family's accountant and expert on things technical.

'So,' Salvatore said, 'this dishing thief will be selling to a middle-man. We could crack a whole ring here.'

'For free?' Angelo's voice was faint.

'But you can see why the police aren't interested yet,' Rosetta said. 'How do you convince a jury with identification evidence that's from the back and just because of the way somebody runs?'

'If she's a pretty girl,' Salvatore said, 'if she bats her eyelashes, she could convince a jury.'

'You and pretty girls,' Rosetta said. Salvatore's success with pretty girls was the stuff of family legend. Rosetta's bad luck with men was legend too.

'It would never come to trial without a lot more evidence,' Gina said.

'And that's where we come in, is it?' Salvatore asked. 'I guess I could make some time.'

'Wouldn't it be better,' Gina said, 'to think about what Papa could do to find more evidence?'

Salvatore and Rosetta studied Gina as they considered this. Gina turned to her husband and pointed a finger as he was about to open his mouth. 'Angelo, if you say 'For free?' one more time, I'm going to hit you.'

'You heard them,' the Old Man said. 'All they think is money. Huh!'

10

'That's not what I heard,' Mama said. 'You want your blanket in that chair?'

'What am I, a dog, with a blanket?'

'I just asked. You might be cold. Sometimes you're cold.'

'All right, all right. I'll be cold. I'll have the blanket and be a dog if that makes you happy. Woof woof.'

Mama passed the Old Man the blanket he usually kept in his lap while watching television at night. 'What *I* heard,' she said, 'was that they agreed it was OK to work for this Jane for free.'

'Who needs agreeing? Can they stop me if I want to do something for injustice?' He patted the blanket into place. 'Where is the pointer? Do you see the pointer?'

Mama looked around for the TV remote. 'You want to do it for this Jane all by yourself, or do you want help?'

The Old Man considered. 'Help, of the right kind . . . could help.'

'What kind is right?'

'When they don't think they always know better than I do. No do this, do that.'

'There it is.' Mama pointed to the remote control device on the table beside him.

'Thank you. Thank you.' He pushed a button. The television burst into life. 'Huh! So loud. Why is it always so loud?'

'So make it quiet.'

The Old Man muted the sound. 'It's like with

mobile phones themselves. People always shout. Is that the way people are now? Everybody shouts?'

'Maybe they're all deaf from loud music.' Mama picked up her knitting.

'I'll be deaf, if I don't watch out.' He turned the sound back on. 'So loud! Huh!'

In the morning Gina went upstairs after the children left for school.

The Old Man was surprised to see her. 'Look at this, Mama. We have a visitor today.' He looked at his wrist. 'Shouldn't you be in the office, Gina?'

'So charming you are,' Mama said. 'Tea for you, Gina? Or coffee?'

'No thanks. I *am* here on business.'

The Old Man frowned. 'What business that's not in the office?'

'After you and Mama came back up last night, we all talked about the mobile phone thief.'

'*After?*' the Old Man said. 'Huh!'

'We wondered what your plan is.'

'My plan?'

'It's your case. We all want to help if you'll tell us what to do.'

'So how did it go?' Angelo asked when Gina came back downstairs and crossed over to the office.

'He's going to talk with Charlie. See for himself what the police position is. All Horsey Jane told him was that they weren't interested.'

Angelo nodded. 'There could be more to it.'

'Even if they're not ready to raid the YMCA gym, I'd have thought the police would be interested that a thief has been identified.'

'If one has.'

'Meaning?'

'If you were a police officer, how much weight could you give to an identification from the back of how somebody runs?'

Charlie, a computer officer at Bath's Manvers Street police station, rose to greet the Old Man when he was ushered in. 'Welcome to crime central, Mr Lunghi. We don't see enough of you.'

'More help you need?' The murder of Charlie's father was the only murder case the Lunghi family had ever investigated. It was the Old Man who solved it.

'I was thinking more that we don't see enough of you socially, but if you have something in the way of business that you'd like to share . . .'

'I have a thief,' the Old Man said, 'but I don't want to share. You can have him all.'

The Old Man sat and told Charlie about the phone-thief who dished when he ran.

'What's the victim's name?' Charlie asked when the story was done.

'Jane Winchester.'

'Let me look up who she talked to.' Charlie turned to his computer.

'*This* is your computer?' the Old Man said. 'This little thing?'

'Yes. Why?'

'Boxes I thought they were. Screens with big tubes at the back and no room on a desk for anything else.'

'Technology moves on, Mr L.'

While Charlie studied his flat monitor the Old Man considered technology. Getting fit in the gym was one thing, but the modern technology, he could use some of that too, to show his effectiveness.

Charlie said, 'We get a lot of phone thefts in Bath, you know, because of all the students and tourists we have. And your Jane Winchester . . .' Click, click, click. 'She talked with D.C. Potter. But the officer in charge . . .' More buttons. Keys, they called them. The Old Man knew *that* much. '. . . is D.S. Joseph. Let me just check whether she's in the station.' Charlie picked up the phone.

'You're back,' Mama said.

'I'm back. I'm also front and side-by-side.' The Old Man felt jaunty because he'd learned things he didn't know before. He dropped his jacket on a chair. 'I'll go out again in a few minutes.'

Mama didn't know why this precluded his hanging the garment on a hook, but she rode with it in the circumstances. 'Of course,' she said. 'You're working.'

'I'm working,' the Old Man said, 'but—'

'But maybe you'd like a cup of tea?'

14

'Good idea. I'll take a minute off.' In an instant he was at his place at the small table in their kitchen.

'You saw Charlie?'

'And he found a detective for me. Not the one in charge of the case but the underling, the one who talked with the Jane when she reported the disher's theft in the first place.' The Old Man thought for a moment, then got up to retrieve his notebook from a jacket pocket.

While she filled the kettle and put teabags in two cups, Mama decided not to point out how much easier getting the notebook out would have been had the jacket been hanging. These were delicate times and needed discretion.

'This so-called detective,' the Old Man said when he was in place at the table. 'This Potter. You wouldn't believe. He wouldn't detect sugar in a biscuit.'

'You want a biscuit?'

'Twist my arm.'

'So you didn't like Potter the detective. What did he say?' Mama got out the Rich Teas.

'He said the Jane was stupid, expecting an arrest from a thief running away. But I say it doesn't take stupid to recognise from the back and from the feet. It takes clever.'

'So Potter wasn't interested.'

'He thought the Jane wasted his time. But I say he wastes my time.'

'And what did Charlie say?'

The Old Man looked up with a pleased expression. 'Charlie said that if I believed the Jane, then chances were she should be believed.'

Good for Charlie, Mama thought. Perhaps she could cook something for him.

'And he said he would get together information about phone thefts over the last year. I should expect a call.'

'So now you sit here by the telephone?'

'Now? Now I wait for my tea. But then I go to the gym.'

'Good,' Mama said. '*Good.* Mustn't let all this work get in the way of the fitness.'

But when he got to the YMCA, the Old Man did not change clothes or begin his warm-up routine. First he checked to see if the red vested disher was on a treadmill. He wasn't, so the Old Man sought out Guru Mick.

'How you doing, buddy?' Guru Mick said.

'I need to know about one of your members,' the Old Man said. 'When he comes in, who he is.'

'That sort of thing is confidential, buddy. Sorry.'

'It's to help my grandson, David. David wants muscles. He thinks he's too spindly for the girls.'

'Well we can certainly help him with that,' Guru Mick said.

'But the boy is so shy. He wants to come when there's someone closer to his age. Another boy, or young man. One who runs. One who uses a treadmill, say.'

'Oh yes?'

'Yesterday there was one who was perfect.' The Old Man pointed. 'On that treadmill. He wore a red vest.'

'I don't remember exactly who you mean, buddy.'

'About eleven in the morning. You can't look?' The Old Man gestured to the gym computer. 'Find out when he comes in, if it's regular. I can come then too, ask for a name myself. That's confidential enough, isn't it?'

There was a payphone in the reception area of the YMCA. The Old Man fiddled with change, then got help from the bearded man at the desk. It was all a palaver. This must be why so many people talked into mobile phones all the time. Everywhere you saw them. And they were ringing if they weren't already talking. A noise, a nuisance. But, still, to be able to make a call without palaver . . .

The number he called was the one he'd been given by Jane Winchester. But he got a machine instead. 'I want to meet about the disher,' he told the Jane's machine. 'I want to tell you what I've learned so far. Talk about what to do. Can you come to Walcot Street between four and five? I'll be there.' And he left the address, but it was for the family flat, not the agency office. Who would want to interrupt Gina or Angelo in the office?

★   ★   ★

The Old Man was waiting in the lower kitchen when David came home from school. 'Hi Grandpa.'

'David, you're home.'

David dropped his school bag on the floor and opened the refrigerator. But then he looked back. 'Do you want me to call Mum?'

'No. No. I'm just waiting.'

David took out the bowls of curry and of rice left over from the night before. He got a clean plate from the dishwasher but then turned to his grandfather. 'I'm hungry.'

'So eat.'

'You want some?'

The Old Man looked at his watch, which read quarter to four. 'Why not? A taste.'

David dished out servings onto each of two plates. While the first was in the microwave he found cutlery.

'Thank you,' the Old Man said, when his grandson brought the steaming plate to him.

'You're welcome,' David said. 'I've been all day in the kitchen trying to get it just right.'

The Old Man mixed up the curry with the rice and took a forkful. He blew on it. Not pasta, not Italian, but not bad. Huh!

They ate for awhile in silence. Then David said, 'Did you get tired on the way upstairs, Grandpa?'

'That's not me anymore.'

'It isn't?'

'Now I go to the gym and get aerobic and strong. Maybe you will too.'

'The *gym*? Me?'

'There's something wrong with all those healthy exercises? Huh! Your generation is obese from sitting around.'

'I'm not obese,' David said.

'You *look* thin, but inside who knows? All those hours you sit at your computer . . .'

'I do PE at school.'

'And tell me, this PE, do you go running, by any chance?'

Horsey Jane rang the downstairs bell just after four-thirty. David answered the door. The fact that she was pretty, and short, left him momentarily speechless. She also looked younger than he'd expected if she was out of school and working with horses.

Jane tilted her head. 'Do I have the right place?'

'If your name is Jane Winchester you do.'

David led her up to the kitchen where the Old Man was rinsing his plate. 'Ah, Jane.'

'Hi, Mr Lunghi.'

'Too late for curry but sit. You want some tea? I'm having tea.'

'Tea would be nice. Thanks.' She sat.

'David, make us some tea, will you? Jane, this is my grandson, David.'

'Me David, you Jane,' David said.

Jane blinked, then finally smiled.

David turned to the kettle, his face flushing.

'I want to report on your case,' the Old Man said.

'Have you found out something?'

The Old Man paused a moment for effect. 'Only that I think I know who this disher is.'

'It can't hurt for me to see who was in the gym at eleven,' Guru Mick had said. 'How old did you say the guy on the treadmill was?'

The Old Man watched as Guru Mick clicked through various screens, cross-referencing members who were fifteen to twenty five with those who were male and in the gym the previous day at eleven.

It was all too fast for the Old Man to read a single thing on a single screen. He tried, but failed. Did these computer people have special computer eyes? Was that part of high-tech? Was there an operation for it, maybe? Huh!

Click click click.

The Old Man's gaze wandered around the room and stopped with a woman on an exercise bike. Why did they face such bikes at the walls with the backs to the room? Did they know what they made the people on them look like? If Mama came here she would change such thing in a minute. Huh!

'OK,' Guru Mick said, 'we're down to three. Tell me, buddy, what build did the guy you're trying to find have?'

'Build?'

'Body shape.'

'He was . . . normal.'

'So not *big*.'

'Not muscles like you, or fat like the woman on the bike.'

'So that,' Guru Mick said, 'rules out Lennie and . . .' More clicks. 'And it rules out Darren.' Clicks and a flourish. 'Oh I know him.'

'You do?'

'Quiet lad. Three, four times a week. Yeah, a runner.' Guru Mick turned to the Old Man. 'Now, you do know, Mr Lunghi, that because of the Data Protection Act I can't tell you *any* of the information we have stored here.'

'I know.'

'But I've just noticed that one of the water coolers needs a new bottle. That will take me a couple of minutes.' Guru Mick walked away.

'Alistair Balson,' the Old Man said.

'Alistair Balson . . .' Jane shook her head. 'Never heard of him.'

'You don't know the name, but why should you? His address I have as well, and that he comes in Tuesday and Thursday. Other days too, but not so regular. And the time can be ten-thirty like yesterday or later.'

'What are you going to do, Grandpa?' David asked. 'Confront him at the gym on Tuesday morning?'

The Old Man wagged his finger at David. 'Confront is what this Jane already did and he laughed. The police don't laugh, but they say

21

Jane's identification is not enough. What we need is new evidence.'

David was getting excited. 'We could wait till he's in the gym and then, when he comes out, I could walk along in front of him and put my phone up to my ear like I'm talking on it and see if he tries to snatch it – only I'll have it on a cord. It would be like a sting.'

'Or a string,' the Old Man said. 'But with a string all we have is another his word against ours.' He looked at Jane. 'This Balson runs fast?'

'Yes.'

'And he does train at it, even though he loses seconds. So we won't catch him by running after. But . . .' He held up a finger.

'What, Grandpa?'

'We could catch him a different way.'

'Surveillance can be really boring,' David said as he walked Jane down the stairs to the street. 'I know. I've done a lot of it.'

'Really?'

'What with it being a family business and all. I'm older and more experienced than my years.'

Although Jane didn't react, David thought she looked interested, maybe even impressed. But just as they neared the front door, it burst open and Marie pushed past them both. Then she stopped and turned. 'Who's the girlie, maggot-face? Not your *girlie*friend?' Chuckling, Marie ran up the stairs, leaving her blushing brother and the family's puzzled pro bono client to look after her.

'Who's *that*?' Jane asked.

'My half-witted sister. A sad story really.'

After dinner the Old Man came downstairs to find Gina and Rosetta in the kitchen. 'Ah, Rose,' he said. 'Just the person.'

The women exchanged glances. 'What can I do for you, Papa?' Rosetta said.

'I want to check out some high tech.'

'Check it out?'

'For use, on the Jane case. I need mobile phones, two. And camcorder, one. The agency has them, yes?'

'We have them . . .' Rosetta said looking at Gina.

'Good.' He waited.

'What's the camcorder for, Papa?' Rosetta said.

'For camcording, of course. Huh!'

'I mean, what will you be taking images of?'

'I don't understand what's so hard. Do you keep me waiting or do I get my equipment?'

'Come on through to my office, Papa,' Rosetta said. 'Let me show you what we have.'

The Old Man sat in his chair reading an instruction book. Mama knitted as she watched him. 'What?' he said.

'Nothing.'

Click, click, click . . .

However, eventually he said, 'When will you be done?'

'With what?'

He waved a hand. '*That.*'

'This pullover?'

'Your knitting. Whatever it is.'

Mama considered. 'Probably in about ten days I'll be finished.' This is not what her husband was asking, which she knew full well.

The Old Man returned to the booklet, his glasses, the camera. He turned the camera upside down. Then he turned it over. He sighed. He sighed again.

Mama took pity on him and put down her knitting. She pulled a chair up close. 'It's a camera. You use cameras. What's so hard?'

'This camera takes videos.'

'It does?'

'It saves a camcorder and is smaller and easier, Rosetta said. She showed me, but I don't quite remember up the stairs.'

'You want to go back down?'

'If I wanted to go down, I would go down. Huh!'

Mama considered the camera. Then she saw there was a second. 'Two cameras you have?'

'One is for David.'

'David?'

'Tomorrow we go out.'

'And does he already know how to use his camera?'

The Old Man shrugged. Then, 'You think I should get him up here?'

If anyone in the family could work out how to

operate something with a battery, it was David. Mama picked up her knitting. 'Can't hurt,' she said. Click, click, click.

Because it was a Saturday David was able to leave the house early without anybody asking where he was going. He found his grandfather waiting, as agreed, in the café on Walcot Street, Doolally's. 'Hi, Grandpa.'

'Have you had breakfast?' the Old Man said. 'You want to order something?' But he had already risen from his chair.

They walked to the steps that lead from Walcot Street up to the Crescent Paragon. More steps up even than to the flat, but the Old Man climbed them with comparative ease. Clear improvement, and after only ten days. But by the time they were climbing Lansdown Hill he felt the strain. Without saying anything, he slowed down.

Without saying anything, David slowed too.

It was more than half an hour before they got to Upper Hedgemead Road. The address for Alistair Balson was a two storey house in a terrace of six.

'So that's where he lives, Grandpa?'

'It doesn't look like flats, this house,' the Old Man said, 'but you should go up to the door to confirm.'

'*I* should?'

'He's seen me at the gym, this Balson. He might

25

remember. If you get caught say you're looking for your dog. He's lost. Poor Rover.'

David hesitated.

'Or your cat. Go. I'll be . . .' The Old Man saw a bench across the street where Lower Hedgmead Road split off from Upper to form the north boundary of Hedgemead Park. 'I'll be on the bench.' He crossed the street, leaving David to gaze at Balson's building.

The bench turned out to be in a good position. They could keep watch on Balson's door in comparative comfort, if they were in for a long wait. The day was not too hot or cold, and was impossible to tell. And who knew if he would come or go or when.

The problem with this Balson was that the Old Man was by no means sure of recognising him. Unless he was running away, of course. That image was clear for him. Like with Jane.

The police were stupid not to accept her identification. Perhaps when the case was resolved he could have a word with Charlie, or other officers, and convince them. Maybe it would lead to a whole new branch of forensic science. The gaits of suspects. The cops could make them run away. That the suspects wouldn't mind. Huh!

David was beaming when he rejoined his grandfather. 'It *is* flats. *And* Balson lives in the basement. There are three bells and the bottom one says, 'Balson and Coates: Cyberlocity.'

'Cyberlocity? What is this Cyberlocity?'

David shook his head. 'Maybe some internet business?'

The Old Man gazed across the street, taking in the whole row of buildings. Not what *he'd* call suitable for dividing into flats. Or for locating a business. He shook his head, but said nothing. Who'd have thought when he began to buy property in Walcot Street that the area would become commercial and fashionable?

'Grandpa?'

'What?'

'If it's flats, how will we know who to follow if someone comes out?'

'A young man.' The Old Man looked at David. 'Older than you, but not so much. How many can there be in one house?'

David looked at the house. It wasn't large but if all three flats were let to students . . .

'A young man comes out,' the Old Man said, 'and what you do is chase him. Shout, say he owes you money. When he runs away I can identify him.'

But in the event they were half-lucky. Less than an hour after they settled themselves on the bench, two young men came out of the house. Both were dressed in clothes that could be appropriate for the gym, but the clincher was that they came up a flight of stairs from below ground level rather than through the building's front door. They could only be coming from the basement flat of Balson and Coates.

'I didn't realise the stairs were used,' David said.

As he said it, the young men pushed bushy branches out of their way and unlocked a chain on the gate to the stairwell.

'Whatever,' the Old Man said. 'These two we follow.'

David rose. 'Do you know which is Balson?'

The Old Man squinted at the pair as they relocked the gate. Could he recall hair colour, build . . . ? But from the distance the two young men looked about the same. All he recalled was the red vest, but both these suspects wore green waterproof jackets. So he said, 'If they split up, we take one each. But this is background surveillance remember, with cameras.'

David had already taken a picture of the young men. He'd taken pictures of several things as he passed time on the bench with his grandfather.

'No risks,' the Old Man said. 'Even if we have the luck and see our Balson steal a dozen phones, we don't interfere. That's why we have the cameras. That's why we have the phones to keep in touch.'

The walk back down the hill was much easier than the walk up, and not just because of the slope. Adrenaline was flowing now. Both David and the Old Man felt it.

At the bottom of Lansdown Road the suspects

crossed the street. Then, at the corner of George and Broad, they touched fists and separated. One maybe-Balson went right, toward Milsom Street, pulling up the hood of his green jacket. The other headed a few steps down Broad and turned into the newsagent's there.

The Old Man pointed for David to take the first of the two. David grinned and lifted the camera suspended from his neck to show that it was ready for action. He gave a wave and headed down George Street past the Royal York Hotel.

David's camera reminded the Old Man to get his out too, and turn it on. Position it to be handy to take a picture. Just point and push the button. Not like the old days, with light meter and focus. Pictures were easy now with the high tech. And digital – though always you used your fingers, so it was an odd name for them to choose. Plus there was the video feature so who needed a camcorder?

The Old Man moved to the door of the newsagent's, ready to go in. But instead he had to stand back and make way as his maybe-Balson came out with a *Chronicle*. This maybe-Balson turned toward town and didn't even say thank you. Huh!

But then, only a couple of shops down the street, the young man turned left into an alley. The Old Man followed, though he already knew what the shortcut led to. The entrance of the YMCA.

David felt simultaneously obvious and invisible as he followed his maybe-Balson. If the guy had *any* awareness of the people around him as he turned down Milsom Street, he'd *have* to know that David was tailing him. But at the same time there were tons of young people out on the pavements – it *was* a Saturday in Bath, after all, and Milsom Street was famous for shopping. So why should anyone single him out?

'Hey, Davy!'

What? What? 'What?'

'I said hello.' The speaker was Linzi, a girl from school. One of Marie's friends.

'Hi, hi, Linzi.'

'What are you up to, little man? Hey, *look* at me when I'm talking to you.'

'Sorry, sorry. But I'm working.' David strained to find his maybe-Balson down the street.

Linzi was not tiny in any case, but seeing that David was looking past her, she moved to obstruct his view. 'You. *Working*? At what?'

David moved again and was able to see that his suspect had also stopped walking. Maybe-Balson appeared to be making a call. 'You know what our familydoes,' David said to Linzi. 'I'm working on a case with my grandfather. I'm sorry. Really I am. But I have to go.' He stepped past the surprised girl.

But then David stopped. Linzi *was* Gwenny Morton's older sister, and Gwenny was *fit. And* she laughed at his joke in maths on Friday. He turned back to Linzi, trying to think of some additional way to save the situation. He wouldn't want

Linzi telling Gwenny something to make her think badly of him.

But Linzi now had her phone out and was dialling. When she saw David look back at her she waved it at him. 'I'm calling Marie. I'm going to tell her you were *so rude*.' She turned her back.

David was stricken. He twisted to find his may be-Balson, who was still nearby, talking to someone. Then back to Linzi. But finally he decided that Linzi must be sacrificed. He was at work, after all.

The Old Man followed his own maybe-Balson through the YMCA's automatic doors, and down the stairs that led to the Health and Fitness Studio. He watched as the young man presented his membership card to the gym's scanner and it was beeped in. Then the maybe-Balson went to the locker board and took the key to locker 41. He left his card in the slot on the board that matched it, and headed for the changing rooms.

The Old Man felt a hand on his shoulder. He turned and found Guru Mick. 'How you doin', buddy?'

'Me? Doing?'

'Not working out today?'

'Uh, no.'

'So what can we do for you?' Guru Mick touched the camera hanging from the Old Man's neck. 'Taking pictures of us? So your grandson can see what it's like here?'

31

'That's it.'

'Wouldn't it be easier to bring him in?'

'You might not be here for him to see.'

'So, you want a picture of me?'

'Who else?' the Old Man said. 'Plus, my wife, who sent me here to become a muscleman. She should see who makes it happen.'

Guru Mick stepped back and struck a pose.

The Old Man lifted the camera, pointed it at Guru Mick, and clicked the button.

The flash attracted attention from the staff and members nearby. 'Come on!' Guru Mick called. 'Get in a picture.'

The Old Man watched in silence as a tableau of sweat, muscles and Lycra posed itself before him. Then, just as it was all about ready, a young man emerged from the changing rooms. He was wearing a red vest.

'Hey, Alistair,' Guru Mick called. 'Get into the picture!'

Alistair hesitated but Guru Mick dragged him to a position at the front of the group. 'On your knees, buddy.'

Alistair knelt.

'Now,' Guru Mick said, 'everybody say "cheese." Or is that not what you say in Italy, Mr L?'

'We say *formaggio*,' the Old Man said, his spirits suddenly high. He was about to have a picture of red vest Alistair's face. He couldn't have asked for better from this visit to the gym.

'*Formaggio*,' Guru Mick said. 'On three, then, everybody. Ready? One. Two . . .'

Click.

David was absolutely stricken. 'I am *so* sorry, Linzi.'

'Why are *you* sorry, David Lunghi? *You* didn't steal my phone – that perv did.' She wrinkled her face and glanced up the slope in the direction the thief had run.

David's eyes followed hers. The thief was gone. David lowered his camera.

'My dad is going to be *so* pissed off,' Linzi said. 'He tells me and tells me to be careful when I use it.' She shook her head. 'It was a birthday present.'

David couldn't think how to explain it all to her. Besides, his mind was on what he'd just witnessed.

'Although I must say,' Linzi said, turning her eyes on him, 'it didn't help that while I was trying to get through to Marie you were taking my picture.'

'It was a video.'

'You were *videoing* me?'

'Not you. It was—'

'I *know* when there's a camera pointed at me, David Lunghi. So do you secretly *looove* me? Is that it? Because *I* thought it was our Gwenny you fancy. *She* certainly thinks so. She told me all about the way you look at her during maths, how you're always offering to help her. What was it you wanted to *help* her with, little Davy?' Linzi laughed.

For all that he could tell Linzi's laughter was because she was upset, David felt his face flush like a beacon. 'Maybe . . .' he said. 'Well, I mean it's possible, maybe . . . I might be able to get it back for you.'

'Get what back?' Linizi frowned. 'My phone? How the hell could you do that?' She waved a hand behind her. 'He's gone. *It's* gone. I'm toast.'

'Well, the thing is, did you happen to notice the way he ran?'

'You are *so* weird.'

And then David's mobile phone began to ring. For Linzi that was just rubbing her nose in her loss. She turned away in a huff.

'Hello?' David said.

'David,' the Old Man said, 'you'll never believe.'

'Me too, Grandpa.'

'I have a picture, of the face.'

David frowned. 'Whose face?'

'Alistair Balson. He posed for my camera.'

'Where, Grandpa? Where are you?'

'The YMCA gym.'

'He's there *now*?' David tried to figure out how that could be. The YMCA was not far, and there *was* an alleyway shortcut, past the Vintage to Vogue second-hand clothes shop, but still . . .

'How else do I take a picture? Of course he's here, ever since I followed him.'

'Grandpa, are you saying that the guy *you* followed is Alistair Balson?'

'Is something wrong with your ears? I just said. Huh!'

'Because, Grandpa, I'm on Milsom Street.'

'Good. Not far.'

'And I've just seen *my* Balson steal a phone.'

'Your Balson stole?'

'And he ran away, Grandpa. And he was dishing as he ran. I've never seen *anybody* run like that before.'

David and his grandfather stood together, watching the treadmills. 'You see?' the Old Man said. 'You see how he runs?'

'Yes,' David said.

'This one knocks his knees but he's no disher.'

'My Balson was definitely the disher,' David said.

The Old Man nodded in agreement. When David arrived at the gym he'd played the short video he'd made with his digital camera. The whole thing was only about thirty seconds, and some of it was blurry from the excitement of reacting to a theft that was happening before his very eyes. But for four or five seconds David had caught images of the fleeing thief that were clear enough to confirm the weird style of running.

'So what do we do now, Grandpa?' David asked as they watched the gym Alistair Balson.

'Guru Mick called this knock-knee Alistair, but not Balson. Could there be two Alistairs?'

'Good thought,' David said.

The Old Man considered. Then he said, 'Come,' and he led David away from the treadmills to the locker board. He took out the card that was slotted beneath the hook marked 41. 'Huh!'

'What, Grandpa?'

'Look for yourself.'

David looked. It was the membership card for 'Jeremy Coates'. 'Grandpa?'

'Yet Guru Mick calls this runner, "Alistair."'

It took a few minutes to prise Guru Mick away from a blonde who was doing lat pulldowns. When they did, he greeted David with enthusiasm. 'So this is your grandson, Mr L? Hi, buddy. Want to put a few muscles on? Impress the girls?' Guru Mick patted David on a shoulder.

The idea of building muscles struck David silent momentarily.

'Shy, eh?' Guru Mick said. 'Your grandpa told me about that.'

The Old Man said, 'For now, it's something else we're here for.'

'What's that, Mr L?'

'The red vest on that treadmill.' The Old Man pointed across the gym. 'You called him Alistair.'

'Yeah, Alistair . . . Balson.' Guru Mick's face lit up. 'Oh, right. Alistair Balson is the name we found yesterday, isn't it?' He looked at David. 'A gym pal for you, buddy.'

'It's the name,' the Old Man said, 'but not the same person. Because his locker he leaves the card of somebody else.' The Old Man showed Guru Mick the card he had taken from the slot for locker 41.

'But I know Alistair's a member,' Guru Mick said. 'I processed his membership myself.' He looked at the card. 'Jeremy Coates. Well, Jeremy's a member too. They came in together.' He looked across the gym to where the red vested runner was knocking his knees on a treadmill. He scratched his head. 'He's using Alistair's card?'

From his silence, David suddenly burst into life. 'I've got it, Grandpa. I've got it!'

Saturday night was not usually a meal at which the whole of the Lunghi family gathered, but Mama was so proud that she summoned everyone and made this Saturday an exception. Even Salvatore came, although later he had a date with a model.

Over pizzas from Bottelino's Gina, Angelo and Rosetta sat rapt as Mama drew out the story that led to the arrests that had followed David's deduction. Even Marie paid attention.

'So from the YMCA you went where?' Mama said.

'To the police station,' David said. 'And from there they took us along when they went to the flat in Upper Hedgemead Road.'

'We were the only ones who could identify,' the Old Man said. 'Since these police don't identify from running, no matter how you explain it to them.'

'But they made us stay in a car while they raided the flat,' David said.

'And how many arrests from your work on the Jane case?' Mama asked rhetorically, and with pride.

'Two, Grandma,' David said. 'Alistair Balson and Jeremy Coates.' He glanced at his grandfather. 'Balson was the disher. Coates knocked his knees.'

'Two arrests so far,' the Old Man said. 'But they'll talk, these phone thieves. They'll implicate the people they sell the phones on to.'

'They were raising money for equipment,' David said. 'They had a band.'

'Cyber . . . elastic, or something,' the Old Man said. 'Huh! They've never heard of work for money?'

'*My* men know about work,' Mama said. 'Good work.'

'So did the police recover the phone that started all this?' Rosetta asked.

'Not Jane's,' the Old Man said.

'But four others,' David said. He glanced at Marie. 'Including Linzi's. She won't get it back right away, but she will eventually.'

'And I bet you want to be the one to ring and tell her,' Marie said.

David flushed. 'She was very upset. It's a matter of common courtesy, really.'

'Pity about the pimple on your nose, little David. Gwenny won't be impressed by that.'

David felt his nose. Marie laughed. Mama asked, 'Who is this Gwenny?'

'Nobody,' David said.

'*You're* the nobody,' Marie said.

'Hush, Marie,' Gina said. 'It's been a good day. David and his grandfather did well.'

'So tell me about the gym,' Salvatore said, looking to his father. 'These thieves each trained at the gym, but used the other's membership card when they went?'

'Their idea was it would give an alibi,' the Old Man said. 'Suppose someone thinks he recognises a thief who runs away. With the card scanned at the YMCA, the thief can say, "I was at the gym when your phone was stolen." He can say, "I can prove it." That's what the disher said to Jane.'

'The computer at the Y shows whose card was scanned and the time,' David said. 'But there's no way to tell whether you're scanning in your *own* card.'

'They go to the gym, these thieves,' the Old Man said. 'They always wear red vests. So who can tell this one rather than that one among so many exercising people?'

'Hardly cast iron,' Angelo said.

'But when they were stealing they wore jackets with hoods,' David said. 'That would make it harder for someone to see a face anyway.'

'It ends up one person's word against another's,' the Old Man said, 'and then the computer alibi could make the difference. Who would prosecute? Who would convict without other evidence?'

'Plus,' David said, 'when one was out stealing,

the other was running on the treadmill, to keep in training for running away.'

Angelo scratched his head. 'But they never figured somebody would identify the way they *ran*. Well . . . Well done, Papa.'

'And well done the Jane,' the Old Man said. 'She did it first.'

'And well done David, who got it on the camera,' Rosetta said.

'So, little Davy,' Marie said, 'you going to call Jane too? Tell her the good news?'

David flushed more deeply than ever. 'Well, it really would be no more than common courtesy.'

KEVIN WIGNALL

RETROSPECTIVE

There was more death and misery in this room than was fit for any civilized place. Mutilated bodies, the diseased and the starving, the fearful and the grief-stricken; and all those empty eyes, the haunted and expressionless faces – it was all here, and it was all his.

Tomorrow night, the Dorchester Street Gallery would open its doors and the celebrities and art world players would get their vicarious thrills as they socialised and flirted and exchanged business cards over wine and morsels amid the horror of his life's work.

Most of his life's work, at any rate; the landscape photographs of recent years had been shunted off into one small side gallery. He didn't mind that, either, conscious of the fact that the landscapes hadn't earned him this retrospective.

When people thought of Jonathan Hoyle, they thought of the images that had been used to fill both the two large gallery spaces and the big fat accompanying catalogue. For nearly twenty years, he'd produced these iconic photographs of the world's war zones and he suspected he was alone in seeing what he'd done. Far from exposing the truth, he'd reduced human tragedy to the level of pornography, or worse, for pornographers were at least honest.

He heard a noise behind him and turned to see the young gallery assistant approaching. Her name was Sophie, he thought, and she looked pretty and mousy in the moneyed way of gallery assistants. If he were a different type of photographer, he'd be trying to seduce her into sitting for him.

'Having a final look around, Mr Hoyle?'

He wasn't sure how to respond, so he said, 'Please, call me Jon.'

'Thank you.' She blushed, and again, he thought maybe he should move from his current obsession to the landscape of the female body. 'It's a bit cheeky of me, I know, but do you think you could sign my copy of the catalogue?'

He looked at the catalogue in her hand and his thoughts crumbled into dust. There was the dead Palestinian boy whose picture had once appeared on newspaper front pages the world over. The gallery had offered him a choice of two photographs for the cover and he'd opted for this one without a second thought, but it still depressed him to see it.

'Of course.' He took the catalogue and the pen she proffered. 'It's Sophie, isn't it?' She nodded and he wrote a simple inscription, thanking her for all her help.

She studied it, apparently happy with the

personal touch, then looked at the cover and said, 'It's such a beautiful picture, incredibly moving.' She looked up at him again and said, 'Why did you stop . . . I mean, why didn't you take anymore war photography after this one?'

He sighed. These questions would always haunt him. The life he'd lived, the person he'd been, out there on the ragged edges of the world, it would always get in the way of the simpler things. You're a pretty girl, he wanted to say, I'd like to go for a drink with you and talk about art, and I'd like to see you naked. But she was right, the Palestinian boy had been the last.

'I stopped because I'd finally captured the truth; there was nothing left to say after that.'

She smiled, uncertain, as if she feared he might be teasing her. 'But your photographs are *all* about the truth.'

'Are they?' She didn't know how to respond. 'Goodnight, Sophie, I'll see you tomorrow evening.' He drifted toward the door, enigma intact, almost self-satisfied.

It was already dark and there was a cold wind picking up, but he decided to walk back to the hotel, wanting to clear his head out there on the streets. As he stepped outside though, he was faced with a black Range Rover, tinted windows, a young guy in a suit waiting by one of the rear doors.

'Evening, Mr Hoyle. Your car.' He was Australian, like most of the people keeping London's service economy afloat. The guy opened the door in readiness for him.

Jon was about to tell him that he felt like walking, but stopped himself and said, 'My car? No one ordered a car for me.'

If he'd had a moment longer he might have figured that the guy's suit was a little too expensive to suggest a chauffeur. He didn't have time though. Before he'd even finished speaking, the guy had produced a gun from somewhere, a silencer already attached. He was pointing it at Jon, but holding it in a casual, almost non-threatening way.

'Get in the car, mate. I don't wanna have to kill you here, but I will.'

The thought of running had died even before it was fully formed. He remembered seeing that French journalist getting shot in Somalia, remembered how sudden and arbitrary it had been – one minute talking to the soldiers, the next crumpled in the dust, oozing blood. There was no running, and he felt bad because, right at this moment, he couldn't remember that French journalist's name, even though he'd drunk with him a couple of times.

Jon got in the back of the Range Rover and the young guy got in after him, closing the door.

'OK, let's go.' Another guy was in the driving seat but it was soon clear the car belonged to the gunman. They lurched forward, nearly clipping another parked car, and the Australian said, 'Mate, if you scratch my bloody paintwork!' He turned to Jon then and said, 'Gotta blindfold you.' He put the blindfold on, tying it behind Jon's head, surprisingly gentle. 'How's that feel?'

'OK, I suppose, under the circumstances.'

'Yeah, sorry about that. The name's Dan, Dan Borowski.' Bizarrely, Jon felt him take his hand and shake it like he was introducing himself to a blind man. And it was bizarre mainly because he knew this was it; whoever they were, they were going to kill him.

I don't wanna have to kill you here, that's what the guy had said, and he'd given his full name, which meant he saw no danger because he was talking to a dead man. He couldn't help but be amused by the irony of it, that he'd travelled unscathed through every impression of hell the world had to offer, only to die in London.

'You're gonna kill me.'

He waited for the voice, and when it came it was a little regretful. 'Yeah. Client wants to meet you first, but your number's up. I'm sorry.'

'Why? I mean, why does he want me dead?'

'Didn't say.' His tone was casual again. 'Gotta be something to do with your work though, don't you think?'

Jon nodded. He was surprised how calm he felt. He wondered if experienced pilots felt like this when their planes finally took a nosedive, if they serenely embraced the void, knowing they'd defied it too long already.

Jon didn't want pain, but he could imagine this guy, Dan, making it easy for him anyway; he was clearly a professional killer, not like some of the monstrous amateurs he'd seen parading around in their makeshift uniforms. He didn't want to die either, but he'd tap-danced around death for so long, he could hardly complain now as it reached out to rest its hand upon his shoulder.

He was curious though, trying to think which aspect of his work had angered someone so much that, even now, a few years after he'd stopped being a war photographer, they were still determined to kill him for it. It couldn't be for offending some cause or other.

He could only imagine this being a personal bitterness, the result of a photograph that had so intruded on someone else's grief or suffering that this seemed a justifiable retribution. That ruled out the landscapes, but not much else.

He supposed a lot of the people who knew and loved the subjects of his photographs would have killed him if they'd had the means. The fact that this person clearly had been able to hire a contract killer perhaps narrowed it down a little further. It made the Balkans, the Middle East and Central America more likely as the source. It hardly mattered though; whoever it was, whichever photograph, they were striking a blow for all the unknown families.

'You *are* a contract killer, I take it.'

'Among other things,' said Dan.

Jon was already getting attuned to having no visuals to fall back on, and although Dan had fallen silent again, he could sense that he had more to say. Sure enough, after a couple more beats, a stop at traffic lights, a left turn, Dan spoke again.

'You know, in a way, you and I are a lot alike. Our jobs, anyway.'

Jon laughed and said, 'I'm cynical about the work I do, but that's a bit rich. I photograph death. In a strange way, I think I sanitize it, but at least I can hold my hands up and say I've never caused it.'

There was a slight pause, during which Jon realized he'd talked in the present tense, even though it was a while now since he'd photographed the overspill of war. Dan seemed fixed on something else, the distraction audible in his voice as he said, 'I'm picking up some negative vibes here, like you're dismissing the work you've produced. I've gotta tell you, Jon, you're wrong about that. You're a great photographer, and it's a document of our times, good or bad.'

'Well, we'll have to agree to differ on that.'

'No way!' He laughed as if they were old friends disagreeing over favourite teams or dream dates. 'Seriously, I'm such a fan of your work. I've even got the book of landscapes. It was one of the reasons I agreed to this job.'

It was Jon's turn to laugh. 'You agreed to kill me for money because you're such a fan of my work! Well thanks, I'm touched.'

Another pause, and Dan's response was subdued, even a little hurt. 'The contract would have gone to someone else, anyway. I took the job because I wanted to meet you, and I wanted to make sure it was done right.'

He couldn't ignore the final point because it was what he'd hoped for, that he wouldn't let him suffer. And maybe another man, certainly one in another profession, wouldn't have looked at his own killer's intentions in quite the same way, but Jon *was* touched by the sentiment now that he thought about it.

'Thanks, Dan. I do appreciate that, and I know if it hadn't been you, it would have been someone else.'

'Yeah, it's too bad.'

'You didn't say how we were similar.'

He was relaxed again, almost cheery as he said, 'I just meant the way we go into areas, not just geographical areas, you know, areas of the human condition that most people don't ever experience. We drop in, I do what I've been paid to do, you get your picture, and we're back out again, onto the next little screw-up.'

'I still don't see it. From my point of view, you're part of the problem. I may not be part of the solution, but at least I'm letting the world know what's really happening.'

Dan laughed and said, 'See, we're already getting somewhere; you're looking at your own work in a more positive light.' The car stopped and the engine was turned off. For the first time, Jon felt a nervous twitching in his stomach. 'We're here.'

Dan helped him out of the car, a brief reminder of the cold night air, a coldness he wanted to savour, to fill his lungs with it like he was about to swim underwater for a long time. They walked through a door and it was still cold but no longer fresh, then up several flights of stone steps.

At the top, they walked through another door and then Dan took off the blindfold. They were in a large loft which looked as if it had only recently stopped being used as a factory or workspace. No doubt its next reincarnation would be as a couple of fabulous apartments, and neither of the new owners would ever imagine that it had been the scene of an execution.

There were two chairs in the middle of the floor, facing each other, a few yards apart. He noticed too, over to one side, what looked like a picture under a sheet, resting against a pillar. Jon wondered if that was it, the evidence of his crime, the photograph that had cost him his life.

He'd seen that happen to other photographers, their determination to get the ultimate shot drawing them too far into the open. It felt now like a stray bullet had hit him sometime in the last twenty years, the day he'd taken that picture, whatever it was, and ever since, he'd simply been waiting to fall.

'Take a seat. We shouldn't have to wait long.'

'Will you do it here?' Dan looked around the

room as if weighing up its suitability. He nodded. Jon pointed at the picture under the sheet. 'Is that the photograph under there? Is that why he wants me dead?'

'I don't know, but you'll find out soon enough. Best you just sit down.'

Dan sat on one of the chairs so Jon took the other. He took a good look at Dan now. He looked young but he was probably thirty, maybe older, good looking in that healthy Australian way, and his face was familiar somehow, but then, Jon had seen so many faces in his life, they all ended up looking a little familiar.

Suddenly, he thought of the blindfold. He had no idea which part of London they were in, though they hadn't driven far. But if he was definitely to be killed, he couldn't understand why he'd had to be blindfolded.

'Does this guy definitely want me dead? There's no way out of it?'

Dan shook his head regretfully and said, 'Why do you ask?'

'The blindfold. If he definitely wants me dead, I can't understand why I had to be blindfolded.'

'He's just really cautious. And he doesn't know that when I bring someone in, they stay in.'

'How much is he paying you?'

Dan smiled and offered the briefest shake of his head. He stared at Jon for a while then, still smiling, intrigued, and finally said, 'I don't suppose you recognize me?'

50

'Your face is vaguely familiar, but I don't know where from.'

'You took my picture once.' He could see the look of surprise on Jon's face and waited for it to sink in before adding, 'Not only that – it's in the exhibition.'

'I . . . I don't remember.'

'Yes you do. Near the Congo-Rwandan border. You were taking pictures of the refugees escaping the fighting. Remember, there were thousands of them, just this silent broken river of people pouring over the border. I walked past you, didn't think anything of it. Then I see the picture, all those refugees walking towards the camera, me walking away from it.'

Jon shook his head, astonished, because he did remember now. He'd been taking shots for an hour or more, never quite feeling he'd captured what he was after. Then a Western soldier had walked past him in black combats, heavily armed but still looking suicidally ill-equipped for where he was heading, a war zone of mind-altering barbarity. That was his picture, another one which had been dubbed iconic.

And the amazing thing was, he'd seen him again, five days later, back in the hotel. He'd recognized him just from the easy confident gait of his walk, from his build, the cut of his hair. Jon had asked someone who he was and he'd been told he was a mercenary, that he'd gone in for the German government and brought out some aid workers who'd been taken by the guerrillas. It had always intrigued him, that a man could walk so casually into hell and still come back.

'You saved those German aid workers.'

Dan shrugged and said, 'I saved three of them. One had already been killed by the time I got there. Another died on the way out.'

'I've always wondered about that. Weren't you scared at all, going in there, knowing what was happening?'

'No,' he said, smiling dismissively.

'I've been to some pretty freaky places, but I would have been scared going in there.'

'That's because you only had a camera. I was armed; I knew I could handle it. I didn't know I could get them out alive, I was nervous about that, but I knew I could handle a few drug-crazed guerrillas.'

'So you're not just a contract killer.'

'No, like I said, I do all kinds of stuff. But don't paint me like Mother Theresa – I got paid more for bringing those people out of the jungle than you probably got paid in five years.'

'At least you brought them out. You saved someone; it's more than I ever did.'

'It wasn't your job to save people.'

'It wasn't my job, but it was my duty as a human being. I used to look at some of these people and think they were savages, and yet I'd watch people dying and worry about things like light and exposure.' Dan was shaking his head, the blanket disagreement of a true fan. 'Tell me something, if you'd been in the jungle and stumbled across those hostages, would you have left them there to die? It wouldn't have been your job to save them, no payment, but would you?'

'Yeah, I probably would have had a go.'

'That's the difference, Dan. You may be a cold-blooded killer, but you're still human. I never saved anyone.'

Dan seemed to turn it over for a few seconds and then said, 'You know, certain times of year, if a croc finds a baby turtle on the river bank, it'll scoop it up in its mouth, take it down to the water and let it go. See, they're programmed to help newly hatched crocs, so they just help anything small that's moving toward the water. Six months later, that croc, he'll still kill that turtle.'

Jon wondered if that was true, but was struck then by something else.

'I don't follow. What's your point?'

Dan laughed and said, 'I have absolutely no bloody idea!'

Jon laughed too and then they were both silenced as the street door down below opened and closed and heavy steps worked laboriously toward them. Jon expected to feel nervous again, but if anything, their conversation had left him even more prepared. Maybe the nerves would come again later, but with any luck, he wouldn't have too long to think about it.

Dan stood up now, but gestured for Jon to stay

where he was, and as if the approaching man were already in earshot, he said quietly, 'You know, if there'd been any other way . . .'

'Don't. And I'm glad I met you, too. I was always curious about the guy in that photograph.'

Dan nodded and walked over to the door as it opened and a heavy-set guy in his fifties walked in. He was balding, wearing an expensive grey suit, an open collar. At first, Jon had him down as an Eastern European, but he quickly realised the guy was an Arab.

The guy looked across, a mixture of disdain and satisfaction, but spoke to Dan for a minute or two in hushed tones. Their conversation seemed relaxed, as if they were filling each other in on what had happened recently, and when it was over, Dan nodded and left.

The client walked across the room without looking at him, picked up the picture under its sheet and placed it on the chair facing Jon. He walked around the chair and stood behind it, finally allowing himself to make eye contact.

'You are Jonathan Hoyle.' His voice was deep, the accent giving it an added gravitas. 'May I call you Jonathan?'

'People call me Jon.'

He gave a little nod and said, 'So, Jon, do you know anyone called Nabil?' Jon shook his head. 'It's my name. I am Nabil. It was also my son's name. I know you don't have children, so I also know that you don't understand what it is to lose a child. And I know you don't understand what it is for your dead child's photograph to be made into a piece of art, bought and sold, put on the covers of books. I know you don't understand any of this.' There was no anger in his words; they were no more than statements of fact. And Jon couldn't question them so he remained silent. 'That is what I know about you. And this is what I know about me. I know that killing you tonight will not bring my son back and will not ease my pain. Indeed, the pain may become worse because your death will bring even more interest to your work, but still, I must insist on your death. First, I want you to look again at my son's photograph, knowing his name, knowing . . .'

He stopped, suddenly overcome, and took a deep breath. Jon lowered his gaze slightly, not wanting to stare at this man who was still so visibly torn by grief. He heard the sheet being pulled away, saw it drop to the floor, and a part of him didn't want to look up, because he had a feeling he knew which picture it would be, and the memory of it was already making him feel sick.

'Look at my son, Mr Hoyle. Jon, look at my son.'

He looked up. There was the print of the Palestinian boy, blown-up life-size. His name had been Nabil and he'd been fourteen years old and now Jon could think of no good reason why he shouldn't die tonight.

The boy's father wasn't crying but he had the

look of a man who had no more tears left, a man who'd been beaten by life and was spent. Jon thought of all the times over the last four years that this man had chanced upon that picture and had the wound torn afresh.

Jon knew something of that, because he'd experienced it too. He'd seen the picture pulled from image libraries and used to illustrate newspaper and magazine stories – no context, no explanation, just a cynical, exploitative pathos.

He'd been fêted for that photograph; and yet, as ambivalent as he'd been about it, as much as its appearance had made jagged shards of his memory, he'd never once given thought to the boy's family. He could see it now, of course, how they'd probably come to hate him even more than the unknown Israeli soldier whose bullet had killed Nabil that day in Gaza.

'Do you have anything to say?'

'That was the last photograph I ever took in a war zone.'

Nabil laughed a little, incredulous as he said, 'That's not much of a defence.'

'I don't have any defence. It isn't right for you to kill me, but I can make no sound argument for sparing me. If it means anything, if it offers any comfort, I'm sorry.'

Nabil nodded once, almost like a bow of his head. Jon wanted it over with now, he wanted Dan to come back into the room and end it, but Nabil looked contemplative, as if he was still dwelling upon something and wanted to ask another question. He suddenly became grim and determined though, and started toward the door.

Jon felt his stomach tighten into a spasm, his blood spinning out of control with adrenaline, a mixture of fear and of self-loathing, knowing that it was wrong to leave it like this, without at least telling him the truth. 'Nabil.' Nabil stopped and turned to look at him. Jon felt ashamed because he knew it looked like he was stalling, and he wasn't; his nerves were for something else, for the things he wanted to say for the first time. He wanted to offer this man something more than a trite apology, and he wanted to get something off his own conscience before he died. 'Before you call Dan back in, I want to tell you something about the day your son died. It won't change anything, but I want to tell you anyway.'

Nabil's expression was unyielding, but he walked back toward the chair and stood a few paces behind it. 'Go on.'

Jon took a couple of deep breaths, looked at the photograph again, then at Nabil. 'I took a lot of good photographs that day, and in the days before. You remember how volatile it was at that time, almost like there was something unstable in the air.'

'I remember.'

'So I was there, and there were Palestinian boys, young men, throwing stones at an Israeli patrol. I saw your son.'

Nabil prickled defensively and said, 'Yet you have no pictures of him throwing stones.'

'Because he wasn't throwing stones. Like a lot of people those days, he was just trying to get from one place to another without getting caught up in it. He didn't look scared, he just looked like a kid who was used to it, confident, almost carefree.' He looked at the photograph in front of him and wished as he had many times, that he'd captured that carefree face as a counterpoint. 'I wasn't even wasting film at that point. Stone throwing, that was just becoming routine. Then someone started firing on the soldiers and one of them got hit. They fired back and one of the stone throwers took a bullet in the shoulder. I got some good pictures of his friends helping him, this hive of activity and this dazed, strangely calm kid in the middle of it all. There were a couple of other photographers with me. And within another ten minutes it was all over. I was walking away on my own when I saw blood on the floor. I walked around the corner, into the yard of a house that had been bombed the week before, and I saw the body lying there. I recognized him right away, the kid I'd seen earlier. I guessed he'd been hit by a stray bullet, had managed to drag himself into the yard. He looked so young, and all the clichés were there – he looked peaceful, his face angelic, and the only thing that went through my mind at that moment, was that I knew this photograph would make front pages all around the world. I took it, just one shot, and I knew I'd got it, the bloody hole in the side of his chest, the angelic face. I felt satisfied. I'm ashamed to say that, but I did, I felt like I'd found that day's star prize. And then the strangest thing happened. I kept looking through the lens, looking at his face, and I just knew something wasn't right, somehow. It took a moment, but I saw it in the end.' He got up out of his chair and walked toward the picture. Nabil glanced at the door, as if ready to shout, but Jon kept his course. He picked up the picture and turned it for Nabil to see. 'This is the truest photograph I ever took, and it's a fake. It shows a dead Palestinian boy, your son, but when this photograph was taken, the boy wasn't dead.'

Nabil looked at him, surprised and yet wary, as if suspecting an attempt to earn his forgiveness. Jon didn't want that though, and wasn't even sure whether it was in this Nabil's power to grant it. He wanted only to tell the truth of how this photograph had been taken.

'Remember, I told you this won't change anything. The circumstances matter to me, but it doesn't change a thing.'

'Please, continue.'

Jon nodded and said, 'I knelt down beside him and checked for a pulse, but I didn't need to. As soon as my hand touched his neck, his eyes opened, and he started to mutter something, very quietly, like he was afraid we'd be overheard. I knew he was really bad.' Jon shook his head, the

59

memory of his own helplessness briefly overpowering him again. 'I just didn't know what to do, and in the distance I could hear the Israeli armoured cars and I thought, if I could just get out to them, they'd have a medic with them, or there might be an ambulance. I put my camera down and I went to leave, but he grabbed my arm and I couldn't understand what he was saying but I could see it in his face, that he didn't want me to go, and I knew he was dying and there was nothing I could do. The injury was bad. He'd lost a lot of blood. And he looked so alone – I'd never noticed that before. So I just held his hand and I looked at him. I was muttering back to him, telling him I was still there.' Jon could feel tears in his eyes, but they weren't stacked up enough to run down onto his cheeks, and he didn't want them to because he didn't want any sympathy. 'I couldn't save him. All the horrors I've witnessed, all the death and mutilation, but I didn't know how to save that boy.'

Nabil was staring at him blankly, overcome with the onslaught of new information about his son's death.

'You stayed with him? Till he died?'

'It wasn't long after that. It was almost like he'd been waiting for someone to find him, so that he didn't die alone. And he didn't die alone, I gave him that much, but another person could have saved him, I'm sure of it. That's why I stopped being a war photographer.'

'Because you watched my son die?'

'I've seen plenty of kids die. No, it was because I had the illusion of detachment snatched away from me, and once you've lost that, you never get it back.' Jon put the picture back on the chair and took one last look at it. He was glad it was over. 'You can call Dan in now. I'm ready.'

Without looking at him, Nabil walked across to the door and opened it. Jon could see Dan sitting on the top step outside. He jumped up and by the time he came into the room, his gun was already in his hand. It would be quick, Jon told himself, and it would be done.

Dan looked at Nabil, surprised that he was still there, and said, 'Wouldn't you prefer to leave first?'

'No, but there's no need for the gun. You can take him back.'

Dan shrugged, expressing no emotional response, no disappointment, no relief, and said simply, 'You do realise this doesn't change anything?'

He was talking about the fee and Nabil nodded and said, 'Of course, and I'm sorry if I've wasted your time.'

'Time's never wasted,' said Dan, smiling.

Nabil finally looked at Jon again. 'It's some comfort that you were with my son in his final moments, but that isn't why I'm sparing you. I was determined to kill the man who took that picture because I knew he had absolutely no understanding of what he'd done by taking it. I was wrong. I see now, you did understand.'

'That once, I understood. But there are thousands of mothers and fathers out there to whom I could offer no answers, none at all.'

The grieving father in front of him said no more. He offered Jon his hand, and when he shook it, he was surprised to find his own palm clammy and Nabil's dry as parchment. Nabil must have given some slight signal then, because Dan touched Jon on the elbow and the two of them left.

He looked back before descending the stairs. Nabil was sitting in the chair he'd occupied himself, and he was staring at the picture of his son, broken, the universe refusing to reform itself around him. Jon wished he could go back in there and say something else to comfort him, but he'd already given him everything he had.

The driver had gone, and Dan drove back with Jon in the passenger seat. He still didn't recognise this part of London. At first neither of them spoke, but after a few minutes, Dan said, 'What the bloody hell happened back there?'

'I don't know.' Jon tried to think back, but all he could think of was Dan coming in with his gun already drawn, then his insistence on getting his fee. 'You would have killed me, wouldn't you? I mean, you wouldn't have given it a second thought.'

'Of course. But I thought I explained all of that.

I wouldn't have been killing *you*, Jonathan Hoyle, I just would have been hitting a target.'

Jon smiled. He could imagine this guy being completely untroubled by what he did, sleeping well, walking lightly through the world. He'd been like that himself once, and maybe Dan's moment would also come, but he doubted it somehow.

He'd killed people, he'd saved people, he'd inhabited the same world as Jon, and on at least one occasion, they'd even crossed paths. But Dan Borowski was a natural in that world, someone who wore death easily and saw it for what it was.

No doubt if Dan had found the young Nabil dying in the ruins, he'd have known what to do. If the boy could have been saved, Dan would have left him and gone for help. If he couldn't, Dan would have stayed with him, just as Jon had, but when it was all done, he'd have left it behind.

'When you were talking earlier, about our jobs being similar, you missed something.'

Dan glanced over, casually curious, and said, 'What's that?'

'The need to detach what you're doing from the individual on the end of it – your target, my subject.'

Dan nodded, and at first it didn't look like he'd respond further, but then he said, 'I wonder how many people around the world have died since I picked you up earlier. Hundreds? Thousands? It doesn't matter. None of those lives matter to us. If I'd killed you tonight, the vast majority of the world's population wouldn't have even known about it. If I die tomorrow, it won't matter to anyone. So you see, it's just not worth thinking about. I live well, and that's enough for me. Should be enough for you too.'

Jon nodded, even though he felt like he needed a few minutes to work out what Dan had just said – on first pass, it wasn't much clearer than the crocodile story. Then he realized that they'd turned into Dorchester Street and a moment later Dan had pulled up outside the gallery.

'Oh, God, sorry mate, I've brought you back to the gallery. I'll take you to the hotel.'

'No, this is fine, really. After everything that's happened, I could use the fresh air.'

Dan laughed and said, 'I bet!' He looked serious then as he added, 'It's been a pleasure, Jon, and for what it's worth, I think you handled yourself really bloody well. Not many people would've stayed calm like that.'

'I had nothing to lose.' He smiled and said, 'So long, Dan.'

'You take care now.'

Jon got out of the car and watched as Dan pulled away. He heard his name then and turned to see Sophie coming out of the gallery, her coat on, bag over her shoulder, catalogue under one arm. She managed to lock the door without putting anything on the floor, then walked over to him.

'Hi, what are you still doing here?'

'Long story. I was somewhere else, and then I

got dropped off here by mistake.' She smiled, showing interest, the slightly awkward way people did when they felt they had to be interested but weren't really. 'Sorry, don't let me keep you. I'm sure you wanna get home.'

'No, it's fine. I don't have anything to rush back for.' Maybe he needed to go back to photographing people in some form or other because it seemed he'd read her completely wrong.

'Well, I'm only heading back to the hotel – would you like to come back for dinner?'

She looked staggered, maybe even suspecting he wasn't serious, as she said, 'I'd love to, but do you mind? The general word is that you don't care for company.'

'I never used to.'

They started to walk and he couldn't help but smile. A contract killer named Dan Borowski had shot him in the head this evening, a death he'd accepted, even embraced – from now on, everything else was a gift.

PETER TREMAYNE

THE SPITEFUL SHADOW

'It is so obvious who killed poor Brother Síoda that it worries me.'

Sister Fidelma stared in bewilderment at the woe-be-gone expression of the usually smiling, cherubic features of Abbot Laisran.

'I do not understand you, Laisran,' she told her old mentor, pausing in the act of sipping her mulled wine. She was sitting in front of a blazing fire in the hearth of the abbot's chamber in the great Abbey of Durrow. On the adjacent side of the fireplace, Abbot Laisran in his chair, his wine left abandoned on the carved oak table by his side. He was staring moodily into the leaping flames.

'Something worries me about the simplicity of this matter. There are some things in life that appear so simple that you get a strange feeling about them. You question whether things can be so simple and, sure enough, you often find that they are so simple because they have been made to appear simple. In this case, everything fits together so flawlessly that I question it.'

Fidelma drew a heavy sigh. She had only just

arrived at Durrow to bring a Psalter, a book of Latin psalms written by her brother, Colgú, King of Cashel, as a gift for the abbot. But she had found her old friend Abbot Laisran in a pre-occupied frame of mind. A member of his community had been murdered and the culprit had been easily identified as another member. Yet it was unusual to see Laisran so worried. Fidelma had known him since she was a little girl and it was he who had persuaded her to take up the study of *Anruth*, one degree below that of *Ollamh*, the highest rank of learning, it had been Laisran who had advised her to join a religious community on being accepted as a *dálaigh*, an advocate of the Brehon Court. He had felt that this would give her more opportunities in life.

Usually, Abbot Laisran was full of jollity and good humour. Anxiety did not sit well on his features for he was a short, rotund, red-faced man. He had been born with that rare gift of humour and a sense that the world was there to provide enjoyment to those who inhabited it. Now he appeared like a man on whose shoulders the entire troubles of the world rested.

'Perhaps you had better tell me all about it,' Fidelma invited. 'I might be able to give some advice.'

Laisran raised his head and there was a new expression of hope in his eyes.

'Any help you can give, Fidelma . . . truly, the facts are, as I say, lucid enough. But there is just something about them . . .' He paused and then shrugged. 'I'd be more than grateful to have your opinion.'

Fidelma smiled reassuringly.

'Then let us begin to hear some of these lucid facts.'

'Two days ago, Brother Síoda was found stabbed to death in his cell. He had been stabbed several times in the heart.'

'Who found him and when?'

'He had not appeared at morning prayers. So my steward, Brother Cruinn, went along to his cell to find out whether he was ill. Brother Síoda lay murdered on his bloodstained bed.'

Fidelma waited while the abbot paused, as if to gather his thoughts.

'We have, in the abbey, a young woman called Sister Scáthach. She is very young. She joined us as a child because, so her parents told us, she heard things. Sounds in her head. Whispers. About a month ago, our physician became anxious about her state of health. She had become . . .' He paused as if trying to think of the right word. 'She believed she was hearing voices instructing her.'

Fidelma raised her eyes slightly in surprise.

Abbot Laisran saw the movement and grimaced.

'She has always been what one might call eccentric but the eccentricity has grown so that her behaviour has become bizarre. A month ago I placed her in a cell and asked one of the apothecary's assistants, Sister Sláine, to watch over her. Soon after Brother Síoda was found, the steward and I went to Sister Scáthach's cell. The door was always locked. It was a precaution we had recently adopted. Usually the key is hanging on a hook outside the door. But the key was on the inside and the door was locked. A bloodstained robe was found in her cell and a knife. The knife, too, was bloodstained. It was obvious that Sister Scáthach was guilty of this crime.'

Abbot Laisran stood up and went to a chest. He removed a knife whose blade was discoloured with dried blood. Then he drew forth a robe. It was clear that it had been stained in blood.

'Poor Brother Síoda,' murmured Laisran. 'His penetrated heart must have poured blood over the girl's clothing.'

Fidelma barely glanced at the robes.

'The first question I have to ask is why would you and the steward go straight from the murdered man's cell to that of Sister Scáthach?' she demanded.

Abbot Laisran compressed his lips for a moment.

'Because only the day before the murder Sister Scáthach had prophesied his death and the manner of it.

'She made the pronouncement only twelve hours before his body was discovered, saying that he would die by having his heart ripped out.'

Fidelma folded her hands before her, gazing thoughtfully into the fire.

'She was violent then? You say you had her placed in a locked cell with a Sister to look after her?'

'But she was never violent before the murder,' affirmed the abbot.

'Yet she was confined to her cell?'

'A precaution, as I say. During these last four weeks she began to make violent prophecies. Saying voices instructed her to do so.'

'Violent prophecies but you say that she was not violent?' Fidelma's tone was sceptical.

'It is difficult to explain,' confessed Abbot Laisran. 'The words were violent but she was not. She was a gentle girl but she claimed that the shadows from the Otherworld gave her instructions; they told her to foretell the doom of the world, its destruction by fire and flood when mountains would be hurled into the sea and the seas rise up and engulf the land.'

Fidelma pursed her lips cynically.

'Such prophecies have been common since the dawn of time,' she observed.

'Such prophecies have alarmed the community here, Fidelma,' admonished Abbot Laisran. 'It was as much for her sake that I suggested Sister Sláine make sure that Sister Scáthach was secured in her cell each night and kept an eye upon each day.'

'Do you mean that you feared members of the community would harm Sister Scáthach rather than she harm members of the community?' queried Fidelma.

The abbot inclined his head.

'Some of these predictions were violent in the extreme, aimed at one or two particular members of the community, foretelling their doom, casting them into the everlasting hellfire.'

'You say that during the month she has been so confined, the pronouncements grew more violent.'

'The more she was constrained the more extreme the pronouncements became,' confessed the abbot.

'And she made just such a pronouncement against Brother Síoda? That is why you and your steward made the immediate link to Sister Scáthach?'

'It was.'

'Why did she attack Brother Síoda?' she asked. 'How well did she know him?'

'As far as I am aware, she did not know him at all. Yet when she made her prophecy, Brother Síoda told me that she seemed to know secrets about him that he thought no other person knew. He was greatly alarmed and said he would lock himself in that night so that no one could enter.'

'So his cell door was locked when your steward went there after he had failed to attend morning prayers?'

Abbot Laisran shook his head.

'When Brother Cruinn went to Síoda's cell, he found that the door was shut but not locked. The key was on the floor inside his cell . . . this is the frightening thing . . . there were blood-stains on the key.'

'And you tell me that you found a bloodstained robe and the murder weapon in Sister Scáthach's cell?'

'We did,' agreed the abbot. 'Brother Cruinn and I.'

'What did Sister Scáthach have to say to the charge?'

'This is just it, Fidelma. She was bewildered. I know when people are lying or pretending. She was just bewildered. But then she accepted the charge meekly.'

Fidelma frowned.

'I don't understand.'

'Sister Scáthach simply replied that she was a conduit for the voices from the Otherworld. The shadows themselves must have punished Brother Síoda as they had told her they would. She said that they must have entered her corporeal from and used it as an instrument to kill him but she had no knowledge of the fact, no memory of being disturbed that night.'

Fidelma shook her head.

'She sounds a very sick person.'

'Then you don't believe in shadows from the Otherworld?'

'I believe in the Otherworld and our transition from this one to that but . . . I think that those who repose in the Otherworld have more to do than to try to return to this one to murder people. I have investigated several similar matters where shadows of the Otherworld have been blamed for crimes. Never have I found such claims to be true. There is always a human agency at work.'

Abbot Laisran shrugged.

'So we must accept that the girl is guilty?'

'Let me hear more. Who was this Brother Síoda?'

'A young man. He worked in the abbey fields. A strong man. A farmer really, not really one fitted in mind for the religious life.' Abbot Laisran paused and smiled. 'I'm told that he was a bit of a rascal before he joined us. A seducer of women.'

'How long had he been with you?'

'A year perhaps a little more.'

'And he was well behaved during this time? Or did his tendency as a rascal, as you describe it, continue?'

Abbot Laisran shrugged.

'No complaints were brought to me and yet I had reason to think that he had not fully departed from his old ways. There was nothing specific but I noticed the way some of the younger *religieuse* behaved when they were near him. Smiling, nudging each other . . . you know the sort of thing?'

'How was this prophecy of Brother Síoda's death delivered?' she replied, ignoring his rhetorical question.

'It was at the midday mealtime. Sister Scáthach had been quiet for some days and so, instead of eating alone in her cell, Sister Sláine brought her to the refectory. Brother Síoda was sitting nearby and hardly had Sister Scáthach been brought into the hall than she pointed a finger at Brother Síoda and proclaimed her threat so that everyone in the refectory could hear it.'

'Do you know what words she used?'

'I had my steward note them down. She cried out: "Beware, vile fornicator for the day of reckoning is at hand. You, who have seduced and betrayed, will now face the settlement. Your heart will be torn out. Gormflaith and her baby will be avenged. Prepare yourself. For the shadows of the Otherworld have spoken. They await you." That was what she said before she was taken back to her cell.'

Fidelma nodded thoughtfully.

'You said something about her having to know facts about Brother Síoda's life that he thought no one else knew?'

'Indeed. Brother Síoda's came to me in a fearful state and said that Scáthach could not have known about Gormflaith and her child.'

'Gormflaith and her child? Who were they?'

'Apparently, so Brother Síoda told me, Gormflaith was the first girl he had ever seduced when he was a youth. She was fourteen and became pregnant with his child but died giving birth. The baby, too, died.'

'Ah!' Fidelma leant forward with sudden interest. 'And you say that Brother Síoda and Sister Scáthach did not know one another? How then did she recognise him in the refectory?'

Abbot Laisran paused for a moment.

'Brother Síoda told me that he had never spoken to her but of course he had seen her in the refectory and she must have seen him.'

'But if no words ever passed between them who told her about his past life?'

Abbot Laisran's expression was grim.

'Brother Síoda told me that there was no way that she could have known. Maybe the voices she heard were genuine?'

Fidelma looked amused.

'I think I would rather check out whether Brother Síoda had told someone else or whether there was someone from his village here who knew about his past life.'

'Brother Síoda was from Mag Luirg, one of the Uí Ailello. No one here would know from whence he came or have any connection with the Kingdom of Connacht. I can vouch for that.'

'My theory is that when you subtract the impossible, you will find your answers in the possible. Clearly, Brother Síoda passed on this information somehow. I do not believe that wraiths whispered this information.'

Abbot Laisran was silent.

'Let us hear about Sister Sláine,' she continued. 'What made you choose her to look after the girl?'

'Because she worked in the apothecary and had some understanding of those who were of bizarre humours.'

'How long had she been looking after Sister Scáthach?'

'About a full month.'

'And how had the girl's behaviour been during that time?'

'For the first week it seemed better. Then it became worse. More violent, more assertive. Then it became quiet again. That was when we allowed Sister Scáthach to go to the refectory.'

'The day before the murder?'

'The day before the murder,' he confirmed.

'And Sister Sláine slept in the next cell to the girl?'

'She did.'

'And on that night?'

'Especially on that night of her threat to Síoda.'

'And the key was always hung on a hook outside the cell so that there was no way Sister Scáthach could have reached it?'

When Abbot Laisran confirmed this, Fidelma sighed deeply.

'I think that I'd better have a word with Sister Scáthach and also with Sister Sláine.'

Fidelma chose to see Sister Scáthach first. She

was surprised by her appearance as she entered the gloomy cell that the girl inhabited. The girl was no more than sixteen or seventeen years old, thin with pale skin. She looked as though she had not slept for days, large dark areas of skin showed under her eyes that were black, wide and staring. The features were almost cadaverous, as if the skin was tightly drawn over the bones.

She did not look up as Fidelma and Laisran entered. She sat on the edge of her bed, hands clasped between her knees, gazing intently at the floor. She appeared more like a lost waif than a killer.

'Well, Scáthach,' Fidelma began gently, sitting next to the girl, much to the surprise of Laisran who remained standing by the door, 'I hear that you are possessed of exceptional powers.'

The girl started at the sound of her voice and then shook her head.

'Powers? It is not a gift but a curse that attends me.'

'You have a gift of prophecy.'

'A gift that I would willingly return to whoever cursed me with it.'

'Tell me about it.'

'They say that I killed Brother Síoda. I did not know the man. But if they tell me that it was so then it must be so.'

'You remember nothing of the event?'

'Nothing at all. So far as I am aware, I went to bed, fell asleep and was only awoken when the steward and the abbot came into my cell to confront me.'

'Do you remember prophesying his death in the refectory?'

The girl nodded quickly.

'That I do remember. But I simply repeated what the voice told me to say.'

'The voice?'

'The voice of the shadow from the Otherworld. It attends me at night and wakes me if I slumber. It tells me what I should say and when. Then the next morning I repeat the message as the shadows instruct me.'

'You hear this voice . . . or voices . . . at night?'

The girl nodded.

'It comes to you here in your cell?' pressed Fidelma. 'No where else?'

'The whispering is at night when I am in my cell,' confirmed the girl.

'And it was this voice that instructed you to prophesy Brother Síoda's death? It told you to speak directly to him? Did it also tell you to mention Gormflaith and her baby?'

The girl nodded in answer to all her questions.

'How long have you heard such voices?'

'I am told that it has been so since I was a little girl.'

'What sort of voices?'

'Well, at first the sounds were more like the whisperings of the sea. We lived by the sea and so I was not troubled at first for the sounds of the sea have always been a constant companion. The sounds were disturbing but gentle, kind sounds. They came to me more in my head, soft and sighing. Then they increased. Sometimes I could not stand it. My parents said they were voices from the Otherworld. A sign from God. They brought me here. The abbey treated me well but the sounds increased. I was placed here to be looked after by Sister Sláine.'

'I hear that these voices have become very strident of late.'

'They became more articulate. I am not responsible for what they tell me to say or how they tell me to say it,' the girl added as if on the defensive.

'Of course not,' Fidelma agreed. 'But it seems there was a change. The voice became stronger. When did this change occur?'

'When I came here to this cell. The voice became distinct. It spoke in words that I could understand.'

'You mention voices in the plural and singular. How many voices spoke to you?'

The girl thought carefully.

'Well, I can identify one.'

'Male or female.'

'Impossible to tell. It was all one whispering sound.'

'How did it become so manifest?'

'It was as if I woke up and they were whispering in a corner of the room.' The girl smiled.

'The first and second time it happened, I lit a candle and peered around the cell but there was no one there. Eventually I realised that as strong as the voices were they must be in my head. I resigned myself to being the messenger on their behalf.'

'And the voice instructed you to do what?'

'It told me to stand in the refectory and pronounce their messages of doom.'

Abbot Laisran learnt forward in a confiding fashion.

'Sometimes these messages were of violence against the whole community and at other times violence against individuals. But it was the one against Brother Síoda that was the most specific and named events.'

Fidelma nodded. She had not taken her eyes from the girl's face.

'Why do you believe this voice came from the Otherworld?'

The girl regarded her with a puzzled frown.

'Where else would it be from? I am a good Christian and say my prayers at night. But still the voice haunts me.'

'Have you heard it since the warning you were to deliver to Brother Síoda?'

The girl shook her head.

'Not in the same specific way.'

'Then in what way?'

'It has gone back to the same whispering inconsistency, the sound of the sea.'

Fidelma glanced around the cell.

'Is this the place where you usually have your bed?'

The girl looked surprised for a moment.

'This is were I normally sleep.'

Fidelma was examining the walls of the cell with keen eyes.

'Who occupied the cells on either side?'

'On that side is Sister Sláine who looks after this poor girl. To the other side is the chamber occupied by Brother Cruinn, my steward.'

'But there is a floor above this one?'

'The chamber immediately above this is occupied by Brother Torchán, our gardener.'

Fidelma turned to the lock on the door of the cell.

Abbot Laisran saw here peering at the keyhole.

'Her cell was locked and the key on the inside when Brother Cruinn and I came to this cell after Brother Síoda had been found.'

Fidelma nodded absently.

'That is the one puzzling aspect,' she admitted.

Abbot Laisran looked puzzled.

'I would have thought it tied everything together. It is the proof that only Scáthach could have brought the weapon and robe into her cell and therefore she is the culprit.'

Fidelma did not answer.

'How far is Brother Sída's cell from here?'

'At the far end of this corridor.'

'From the condition of the robe that you

showed me, there must have been a trail of blood from Brother Sída's cell to this one?'

'Perhaps the corridor had been cleaned,' he suggested. 'One of the duties of our community is to clean the corridors each morning.'

'And they cleaned it without reporting traces of blood to you?' Fidelma was clearly unimpressed by the attempted explanation. Fidelma rose and glanced at the girl with a smile.

'Don't worry, Sister Scáthach. I think that you are innocent of Brother Síoda's death.' She turned from the cell, followed by a deeply bewildered Abbot Laisran.

'Let us see Sister Sláine now.'

At the next cell, Sister Sláine greeted them with a nervous bob of her head.

Fidelma entered and glanced along the stone wall that separated the cell from that of Sister Scáthach's. Then she turned to Sister Sláine who was about twenty-one or -two, an attractive looking girl.

'Brother Síoda was a handsome man, wasn't he?' she asked without preamble.

The girl started in surprise. A blush tinged her cheeks.

'I suppose he was.'

'He had an eye for the ladies. I presumed that you were in love with him, weren't you?'

The girl's chin came up defiantly.

'Who told you?'

'It was a guess,' Fidelma admitted with a soft

smile. 'But since you have admitted it, let us proceed. Do you believe in these voices that Sister Scáthach hears?'

'Of course not. She's mad and has now proved her madness.'

'Do you not find it strange that this madness has only manifested itself since she was moved into this cell next to you?'

The girl's cheeks suddenly suffused with crimson.

'Are you implying that . . . ?'

'Answer my question,' snapped Fidelma, cutting her short.

The girl blinked at her cold voice. Then, seeing that Abbot Laisran was not interfering, she said, 'Madness can alter, it can grow worse . . . it is a coincidence that she became worse after Abbot Laisran asked me to look after her. Just a coincidence.'

'I am told that you work for the apothecary and look after sick people? In your experience, have you ever heard of a condition among people where they have a permanent hissing, or whistling in the ears?'

Sister Sláine nodded slowly.

'Of course. Many people have such a condition. Sometimes they hardly notice it while others are plagued by it and almost driven to madness. That is what we thought was wrong with Sister Scáthach when she first came to our notice.'

'Only at first?' queried Fidelma.

'Until she started to claim that she heard voices being articulated . . . words that formed distinct messages which, she also claimed, were from the shadows of the Otherworld.'

'Did Brother Síoda ever tell you about his affair with Gormflaith and his child?' Fidelma changed the subject so abruptly that the girl blinked. It was clear from her reaction that Fidelma had hit on the truth.

'Better speak the truth now for it will become harder later,' Fidelma advised.

Sister Sláine was silent for a moment, her eyes narrowed as she tried to penetrate behind Fidelma's inquisitive scrutiny.

'If you must know, I was in love with Síoda. We planned to leave here soon to find a farmstead where we could begin a new life together. We had no secrets from one another.'

Fidelma smiled softly and nodded.

'So he did tell you?'

'Of course. He wanted to tell me all about his past life. He told me of this unfortunate girl and her baby. He was very young and foolish at the time. He was a penitent and sought forgiveness. That's why he came here.'

'So when you heard Sister Scáthach denounce him in the refectory, naming Gormflaith and relating her death and that of her child, what exactly did you think?'

'Do you mean, about how she came upon that knowledge?'

'Exactly. Where did you think Sister Scáthach obtained such knowledge if not from her messages from the Otherworld?'

Sister Sláine pursed her lips.

'As soon as I had taken Sister Scáthach back to her cell and locked her in, I went to find Brother Síoda. He was scared. I thought at first that he had told her or someone else apart from me. He swore that he had not. He was so scared that he went to see Abbot Laisran . . .'

'Did you question Sister Scáthach?'

The girl laughed.

'Little good that did. She simply said it was the voices. She had most people believing her.'

'But you did not?'

'Not even in the madness she is suffering can one make up such specific information. I can only believe that Síoda lied to me . . .'

Her eyes suddenly glazed and she fell silent as if in some deep thought.

'Cloistered in this abbey, and a *conhospitae*, a mixed house, there must be many opportunities for relationships to develop between the sexes?' Fidelma observed.

'There is no rule against it,' returned the girl. 'Those advocating celibacy and abstinence have not yet taken over this abbey. We still live a natural life here. But Síoda never mixed with the mad one, never with Scáthach.'

'But you have had more than one affair here?' Fidelma asked innocently.

'Brother Síoda was my first and only love,' snapped the girl in anger.

Fidelma raised her eyebrows.

'No others?'

The girl's expression was pugnacious.

'None.'

'You had no close friends among the other members of the community?'

'I do not get on with women, if that is what you mean.'

'It isn't. But it is useful to know. How about male friends?'

'I've told you, I don't . . .'

Abbot Laisran coughed in embarrassment.

'I had always thought that you and Brother Torchán were friends.'

Sister Sláine blushed.

'I get on well with Brother Torchán,' she admitted defensively.

Fidelma suddenly rose and glanced along the wall once more, before turning with a smile to the girl.

'You've been most helpful,' she said abruptly, turning for the door.

Outside in the corridor, Abbot Laisran was regarding her with a puzzled expression.

'What now?' he demanded. 'I would have thought that you wanted to develop the question of her relationships?'

'We shall go and see Brother Torchán,' she said firmly.

Brother Torchán was out in the garden and had to be sent for so Fidelma could interview him in his cell. He was a thickset, muscular young man whose whole being spoke of a life spent in the open.

'Well, Brother, what do you think of Sister Scáthach?'

The burly gardener shook his head sadly.

'I grieve for her as I grieve Brother Síoda. I knew Brother Síoda slightly but the girl not at all. I doubt if I have seen her more than a half a dozen times and never spoken to her but once. By all accounts, she was clearly demented.'

'What do you think about her being driven to murder by voices from the Otherworld?'

'It is clear that she must be placed in the care of a combination of priests and physicians to drive away the evilness that has compelled her.'

'So you think that she is guilty of the murder?'

'Can there be any other explanation?' asked the gardener in surprise.

'You know Sister Sláine, of course. I am told she is a special friend of yours.'

'Special? I would like to think so. We often talk together. We came from the same village.'

'Has she ever discussed Sister Scáthach with you?'

Brother Torchán shifted uneasily. He looked suspiciously at Fidelma.

'Once or twice. When the abbot first asked her to look after Sister Scáthach, it was thought that it was simply a case of what the apothecaries call tinnitus. She heard sounds in her ears. But then Sláine said that the girl had become clearly demented saying that she was being woken up by the sound of voices giving her messages and urging her to do things.'

'Did you know that Sláine was having an affair with Síoda?' Fidelma suddenly said sharply.

Torchán coloured and, after a brief hesitation, nodded.

'It was deeper than an affair. She told me that they planned to leave the abbey and set up home together. It is not forbidden by rule, you know.'

'How did you feel about that?'

Brother Torchán shrugged.

'So long as Síoda treated her right, it had little to do with me.'

'But you were her friend.'

'I was a friend and advised her when she wanted advice. She is the kind of girl that attracts men. Sometimes the wrong men. She attracted Brother Síoda.'

'Was Brother Síoda the wrong man?'

'I thought so.'

'Did she ever repeat to you anything Brother Síoda told her.'

Torchán lowered his eyes.

'You mean about Gormflaith and the child? Sister Sláine is not gifted with the wisdom of silence. She told me various pieces of gossip. Oh . . .' he hesitated. 'I have never spoken to Scáthach, if that is what you mean.'

'But, if Sláine told you, then she might well have told others?'

'I do not mean to imply that she gossiped to anyone. There was only Brother Cruinn and myself whom she normally confided in.'

'Brother Cruinn, the steward, was also her friend?'

'I think that he would have liked to have been something more until Brother Síoda took her fancy.'

Fidelma smiled tightly.

'That will be all, Torchán.'

There was silence as Abbot Laisran followed Fidelma down the stone steps to the floor below. Fidelma led the way back to Sister Scáthach's cell, paused and then pointed to the next door.

'And this is Brother Cruinn's cell?'

Abbot Laisran nodded.

Brother Cruinn, the steward of the abbey, was a thin, sallow man in his mid-twenties. He greeted Fidelma with a polite smile of welcome.

'A sad business, a sad business,' he said. 'The matter of Sister Scáthach. I presume that is the reason for your wishing to see me?'

'It is,' agreed Fidelma easily.

'Of course, of course; a poor, demented girl. I have suggested to the abbot here than he should send to Ferna to summon the bishop. I believe that there is some exorcism ritual with which he is acquainted. That may help. We have lost a good man in Brother Síoda.'

Fidelma sat down unbidden in the single chair that occupied the cell.

'You were going to lose Brother Síoda anyway,' she said dryly.

Brother Cruinn's face was an example of perfect self-control.

'I do not believe I follow you, Sister,' he said softly.

'You were also losing Sister Sláine. How did you feel about that?'

Brother Cruinn's eyes narrowed but he said nothing.

'You loved her. You hated it when she and Brother Síoda became lovers.'

Brother Cruinn was looking appalled at Abbot Laisran as if appealing for help.

Abbot Laisran wisely made no comment. He had witnessed too many of Fidelma's interrogations to know when not to interfere.

'It must have been tearing you apart,' went on Fidelma calmly. 'But instead you hid your feelings. You pretended to remain a friend, simply a friend to Sister Sláine. You listened carefully while she gossiped about her lover and especially when she confided what he had told her about his first affair and the baby.'

'This is ridiculous!' snapped Brother Cruinn.

'Is it?' replied Fidelma as if pondering the question. 'What a godsend it was when poor Sister Scáthach was put into the next cell to you. Sister Scáthach was an unfortunate girl who was suffering, not from imagined whispering voices from the Otherworld, but from an advance cause of the sensation of noises in the ears. It is not an uncommon affliction but some cases are worse than others. As a little child, when it developed, silly folk – her parents – told her that the whistling and hissing sounds were the voice of lost souls in the Other world trying to communicate with her and thus she was blessed.

'Her parents brought her here. She probably noticed the affliction the more in these conditions than she had when living by the sea where the whispering was not so intrusive. Worried by the worsening affects, on the advice of the apothecary, Abbot Laisran placed her in the cell with Sister Sláine, who knew something of the condition, to look after her.'

Fidelma paused, eyes suddenly hardening on him.

'That was your opportunity, eh, Brother Cruinn? A chance to be rid of Brother Síoda and with no questions asked. A strangely demented young woman who was compelled by voices from another world to do so would murder him.'

'You are mad,' muttered Brother Cruinn.

Fidelma smiled.

'Madness can only be used as an excuse once. This is all logical. It was your voice that kept awakening poor Sister Scáthach and giving her these messages which made her behave so. At

91

first you told her to proclaim some general messages. That would cause people to accept her madness, as they saw it. Then, having had her generally accepted as mad, you gave her the message to prepare for Síoda's death.'

She walked to the head of his bed, her eye having observed what she had been seeing. She reached forward and withdrew from the wall a piece of loose stone. It revealed a small aperture, no more than a few fingers wide and high.

'Abbot Laisran, go into the corridor and unlock Sister Scáthach's door but do not open it nor enter. Wait outside.'

Puzzled, the abbot obeyed her.

Fidelma waited and then bent down to the hole.

'Scáthach! Scáthach! Can you hear me, Scáthach? All is now well. You will hear the voices no more. Go to the door and open it. Outside you will find Abbot Laisran. Tell him that all is now well. The voices are gone.'

She rose up and faced Brother Cruinn, whose dark eyes were narrowed and angry.

A moment later they heard the door of the next door open and a girl's voice speaking with Abbot Laisran.

The abbot returned moments later.

'She came to the door and told me that the voices were gone and all was well.'

Fidelma smiled thinly.

'Even as I told her to do so. Just as that poor

influenced girl did what you told her to, Brother Cruinn. This hole goes through the wall into her cell and acts like a conduit for the voice.'

'I did not tell her to stab Brother Síoda in the heart,' he said defensively.

'Of course not. She did not stab anyone. You did that.'

'Ridiculous! The bloodstained robes and weapon were in her cell . . .'

'Placed there by you.'

'The door was locked and the key was inside. That shows that only she could have committed the murder.'

Abbot Laisran sighed.

'It's true, Fidelma. I went with Brother Cruinn myself to Sister Scáthach's cell door. I told you, the key was not on the hook outside her door but inside her cell and the door was locked. I said before, only she could have taken the knife and robe inside and locked herself in.'

'When you saw that the key was not hanging on the hook outside the door, Laisran, then did you try to open the door?' Fidelma asked innocently.

'We did.'

'No, did *you* try to open the door?' snapped Fidelma with emphasis.

Abbot Laisran looked blank for a moment.

'Brother Cruinn tried the door and pronounced it locked. He then took his master keys, which he held as steward, and unlocked the door. He had to wriggle the key around in the lock. When the door was open the key was on the floor on the inside. We found it there.'

Fidelma grinned.

'Where Brother Cruinn had placed it. Have Cruinn secured and I will tell you how he did it later.'

After Brother Cruinn was taken away by attendants summoned by Abbot Laisran, Fidelma returned to his chamber to finish her interrupted mulled wine and to stretch herself before the fire.

'I'm not sure how you resolved this matter,' Abbot Laisran finally said, as he stacked another log on the fire.

'It was the matter of the key that made me realise that Brother Cruinn had done this. Exactly how and, more importantly, why, I did not know at first. I realised as soon as Sister Scáthach told me how she was awoken by the whispering voice at night that it must have come from one of three sources. The voice must have come from one of the three neighbouring cells. When she showed me where she slept, I realised from where the voice had come. Brother Cruinn was the whispering in the night. No one else could physically have done it. He also had easy access to Brother Síoda's locked cell because he held the master keys. The problem was what had he to gain from Brother Síoda's death? Well, now we know the answer – it was an act of jealousy, hoping to eliminate Brother Síoda so that he could pursue his desire for Sister Sláine. That he was able to convince you that the cell door was locked and that he was actually opening it, was child's play. An illusion in which you thought that Sister Scáthach had locked herself in her cell. Brother Cruinn had placed the key on the floor when he planted the incriminating evidence of the bloodstained weapon and robe.

'In fact, the door was not locked at all. Brother Cruinn had taken the robe to protect his clothing from the blood when he killed Síoda. He therefore allowed no blood to fall when he came along the corridor with the robe and knife to where Sister Scáthach lay in her exhausted sleep. Remember that she was exhausted by the continuous times he had woken her with his whispering voice. He left the incriminationg evidence, left the key on the floor and closed the door. In the morning, he could go through the pantomime of opening the door, claiming it had been locked from the inside. Wickedness coupled with cleverness but our friend Brother Cruinn was a little too clever.'

'But to fathom this mystery, you first had to come to the conclusion that Sister Scáthach was innocent,' pointed out the abbot.

'Poor Scáthach! It is her parents who should be put on trial for filling her susceptible mind with this myth about Otherworld voices when she is suffering from a physical disability. The fact was Scáthach could not have known about Gormilaith. She was told. If one discounts voices from the Otherworld, then it was by a human agency. The question was who was that agency and what was the motive for this evil charade.'

Abbot Laisran gazed at her in astonishment.

'I never cease to be amazed at your astute mind, Fidelma. Without you, poor Sister Scáthach might have stood condemned.'

'On the contrary, Abbot Laisran, without you and your suspicion that things were a little too cut and dried, we should never even have questioned the guilt or innocence of the poor girl at all.'

PETER ROBINSON

BLUE CHRISTMAS

A *three day holiday*. Banks sat down at the breakfast table and made some notes on a lined pad. If he was doomed to spend Christmas alone this year, he was going to do it in style. For Christmas Eve, Alastair Sims' *A Christmas Carol*, black and white version, of course. For Christmas Day, *Love, Actually*. Mostly it was a load of crap, no doubt about that, but it was worth it for Bill Nighy, and Keira Knightley was always worth watching. For Boxing Day, *David Copperfield*, the one with the Harry Potter actor in it, because it had helped him through a nasty hangover one Boxing Day a few years ago, and thus are traditions born.

Music was more problematic. Bach's *Christmas Oratorio* and Handel's *Messiah*, naturally. Both were on his iPod and could be played through his main sound system. But some years ago, he had made a Christmas compilation tape of all his favourite songs, from Bing's 'White Christmas' to Elvis's 'Santa Claus is Back in Town' and 'Blue Christmas', The Pretenders' '2000 Miles' and Roland Kirk's 'We Free Kings'. Unfortunately, that had gone up in flames along with the rest of his music collection. Which meant a quick trip to HMV in Eastvale that afternoon to pick up a few seasonal CDs so he could make a playlist. He had to go to Marks and Spencer's, anyway, for his frozen turkey dinner, so he might as well drop in at HMV while he was in the Swainsdale Centre. As for wine, he still had a more than decent selection from his brother's cellar – including some fine Amarone, Chianti Classico, Clarets and Burgundies – which would certainly get him through the next three days without any pain. Luckily, he had bought and given out all his Christmas presents earlier – what few there were: money for Tracy, a Fairport Convention box-set for Brian, chocolates and magazine subscriptions for his parents, and a silver and jet bracelet for Annie Cabbot.

Banks put his writing pad aside and reached for his coffee mug. Beside it sat a pristine copy of Sebastian Faulks's *Human Traces*, which he fully intended to read over the holidays. There should be plenty of peace and quiet. Brian was with his band in Europe and wouldn't be able to get home in time. Tracy was spending Christmas with her mother Sandra, stepdad Sean and baby Sinead, and Annie was heading home to the artists' colony in St Ives, where they would all no doubt be having a good weep over *A Junkie's Christmas*, which, Annie had told him, was a Christmas staple among her father's crowd. He had seen it once, himself, and he had to admit that it wasn't bad, but it hadn't become a tradition with him.

All in all, then, this Christmas was beginning to feel like something to be got through with liberal doses of wine and music. Even the weather was refusing to cooperate. The white Christmas everyone had been hoping for since a tentative sprinkle in late November had not materialised, though the optimists at the meteorological centre were keeping their options open. At the moment, though, it was uniformly grey and wet in Yorkshire. The only good thing that could be said for it was that it wasn't cold. Far from it. Down south people were sitting outside at Soho cafés and playing golf in the suburbs. Banks wondered if he should have gone away, taken a holiday. Paris. Rome. Madrid. A stranger in a strange city. Even London would have been better than this. Maybe he could still catch a last minute flight.

But he knew he wasn't going anywhere. He sipped some strong coffee and told himself not to be so maudlin. Christmas was a notoriously dangerous time of year. It was when people got depressed and gave in to their deepest fears, when all their failures, regrets and disappointments came back to haunt them. Was he going to let himself give in to that, become a statistic?

He decided to go into town now and get his last minute shopping over with before it got really busy. Just before he left, though, his phone rang. Banks picked up the receiver.

'Sir? It's DC Jackman.'

'Yes, Winsome. What's the problem?'

'I'm really sorry to disturb you at home, sir, but we've got a bit of a problem.'

'What is it?' Banks asked. Despite having to spend Christmas alone, he had been looking forward to a few days away from the Western Area Headquarters, if only to relax and unwind after a particularly difficult year. But perhaps that wasn't to be.

'Missing person, sir.'

'Can't someone else handle it?'

'It needs someone senior, sir, and DI Cabbot's on her way to Cornwall.'

'Who's missing?'

'A woman by the name of Brenda Mercer. Forty-two years old.'

'How long?'

'Overnight.'

'Any reason to think there's been foul play?'

'Not really.'

'Who reported her missing?'

'The husband.'

'Why did he leave it until this morning?'

'He didn't. He reported it at 6pm yesterday evening. We've been looking into it. But you know how it is with missing persons, sir, unless it's a kid. It was very early days. Usually they turn up, or you find a simple explanation quickly enough.'

'But not in this case?'

'No, sir. The husband's getting frantic. Difficult.

Demanding to see someone higher up. And he's got the daughter and her husband in tow now. They're not making life any easier. I've only just managed to get rid of them by promising I'd get someone in authority to come and talk to them.'

'All right,' Banks said, with a sigh. 'Hang on. I'll be right in.'

Major Crimes and CID personnel were thin on the ground at Western Area Headquarters that Christmas Eve, and DC Winsome Jackman was the one who had drawn the short straw. She didn't mind, though. She couldn't afford to visit her parents in Jamaica, and she had politely passed up a Christmas dinner invitation from a fellow member of the potholing club, who had been pursuing her for some time now, so she had no real plans for the holidays. She hadn't expected it to be particularly busy in Major Crimes. Most Christmas incidents were domestic and, as such, they were dealt with by the officers on patrol. Even criminals, it seemed, took a bit of time off for turkey and Christmas pud. But a missing person case could turn nasty very quickly, especially if she had been missing for two days now.

While she was waiting for Banks, Winsome went through the paperwork again. There wasn't much other than the husband's report and statement, but that gave her the basics.

When David Mercer got home from work on 23rd December at around 6 p.m., he was surprised to find his wife not home. Surprised because she was always home and always had his dinner waiting for him. He worked in the administration offices of the Swainsdale Shopping Centre, and his hours were fairly regular. A neighbour had seen Mrs Mercer walking down the street where she lived on the Leaside Estate at about a quarter past four that afternoon. She was alone and was wearing a beige overcoat and carrying a scuffed brown leather bag, the kind with a shoulder-strap. She was heading in the direction of the main road, and the neighbour assumed she was going to catch a bus. She knew that Mrs Mercer didn't drive. She said hello, but said that Mrs Mercer hadn't seemed to hear her, had seemed a bit 'lost in her own world.'

Police had questioned the bus-drivers on the route, but none of them recalled seeing anyone matching the description. Uniformed officers also questioned taxi drivers and got the same response. All Mrs Mercer's relatives had been contacted, and none had any idea where she was. Winsome was beginning to think it was possible, then, that someone had picked Mrs Mercer up on the main road, possibly by arrangement, and that she didn't want to be found. The alternative, that she had been somehow abducted, didn't bear thinking about, at least not until all other possible avenues had been exhausted.

Winsome had not been especially impressed by David Mercer – he was the sort of pushy, aggressive white male she had seen far too much of over the past few years, puffed up with self-importance, acting as if everyone else were a mere lackey to meet his demands, especially if she happened to be black and female. But she tried not to let personal impressions interfere with her reasoning. Even so, there was something about Mercer's tone, something that didn't quite ring true. She made a note to mention it to Banks.

The house was a modern Georgian-style semi with a bay window, stone cladding and neatly kept garden, and when Banks rang the doorbell, Winsome beside him, David Mercer opened it so quickly he might have been standing right behind it. He led Banks and Winsome into a cluttered but clean front room, where a young woman sat on the sofa wringing her hands and a whippet-thin man in an expensive, out-of-date suit paced the floor. A tall Christmas tree stood in one corner, covered with ornaments and lights. On the floor were a number of brightly wrapped presents and one ornament, a tiny pair of ice skates, which seemed to have fallen off. The radio was playing Christmas music faintly in the background.

'Have you heard anything?' David Mercer asked.

'Nothing yet,' Banks answered. 'But, if I may, I'd like to ask you a few more questions.'

'We've already told everything to her,' he said, gesturing in Winsome's direction.

'I know,' said Banks. 'And DC Jackman has discussed it with me. But I still have a few questions.'

'Don't you think you should be out there on the streets searching for her?' said the whippet-thin man, who was also turning prematurely bald.

Banks turned to face him slowly. 'And you are?'

He puffed out what little chest he had. 'Claude Mainwaring, solicitor. I'm Mr Mercer's son-in-law.'

'Well, Mr Mainwaring,' said Banks, 'it's not normally my job, as a detective chief inspector, to get out on the streets looking for people. In fact, it's not even my job to pay house calls asking questions, but as it's nearly Christmas, and as Mr Mercer here is worried about his wife, I thought I might bend the rules just a little. And believe me, there are already more than enough people out there trying to find Mrs Mercer.'

Mainwaring grunted as if were unsatisfied with the answer, then he sat down next to his wife. Banks turned to David Mercer, who finally bade him and Winsome to sit, too. 'Mr Mercer,' Banks asked, thinking of the doubts that Winsome had voiced on their way over, 'can you think of anywhere your wife might have gone?'

'Nowhere,' said Mercer. 'That's why I called you lot.'

'Was there any reason why your wife might have gone away?'

'None at all,' said Mercer, just a beat too quickly for Banks's liking.

'She wasn't unhappy about anything?'

'Not that I know of, no.'

'Everything was fine between the two of you?'

'Now, look here!' Mainwaring got to his feet.

'Sit down and be quiet, Mr Mainwaring,' Banks said as gently as he could. 'You're not in court now, and you're not helping. I'll get to you later.' He turned back to Mercer and ignored the slighted solicitor. 'Had you noticed any difference in her behaviour before she left, any changes of mood or anything?'

'No,' said Mercer. 'Like I said, everything was quite normal. May I ask what you're getting at?'

'I'm not getting at anything,' Banks said. 'These are all questions that have to be asked in cases such as these.'

'Cases such as these?'

'Missing persons.'

'Oh God,' cried the daughter. 'I can't believe it. Mother a missing person.'

She used the same tone as she might have used to say 'homeless person', Banks thought, as if she were somehow embarrassed by her mother's going missing. He quickly chided himself for being so uncharitable. It was Christmas, after all, and no matter how self-important and self-obsessed these people seemed to be, they *were* worried about Brenda Mercer. He could only do his best to help them. He just wished they would stop getting in his way.

'Has she ever done anything like this before?' Banks asked.

'Never,' said David Mercer. 'Brenda is one of the most stable and reliable people you could ever wish to meet.'

'Does she have any close friends?'

'The family means everything to her.'

'Might she have met someone? Someone she could confide in?'

Mercer seemed puzzled. 'I don't know what you mean. Confide? What would Brenda have to confide? And if she did, why would she confide it someone else rather than in me? No, it doesn't make sense.'

'People do, you know, sometimes.'

'Not Brenda.'

This was going nowhere fast, Banks thought, seeing what Winsome had meant. 'Do you have any theories about where she might have gone?'

'Something's happened to her. Someone's abducted her, obviously. I can't see any other explanation.'

'Why do you say that?'

'It stands to reason, doesn't it? She'd never do anything so irresponsible and selfish as to mess up all our Christmas plans and cause us so much fuss and worry.'

'But these things, abductions and the like, are much rare than you imagine,' said Banks. 'In most cases, missing persons are found healthy and safe.'

Mainwaring snorted in the background. 'And the longer you take to find her, the less likely she is to be healthy and safe,' he said.

Banks ignored him and carried on talking to David Mercer. 'Did you and your wife have any arguments recently?' he asked.

'Arguments? No, not really.'

'Anything that might upset her, cause her to want to disappear.'

'No.'

'Do you know if she has any male friends?' Banks knew he was treading on dangerous ground now, but he had to ask.

'If you're insinuating that she's run off with someone,' Mercer said, 'then you're barking up the wrong tree. Brenda would never do that to me. Or to Janet,' he added, glancing over at the daughter.

Banks had never expected his wife Sandra to run off with another man, either, but she had done. No sense in labouring the point, though. If anything like that had happened, the Mercers would be the last people to tell him, assuming that they even knew themselves. But if Brenda had no close friends, then there was no one else he could question who might be able to tell him more about her. All in all, it was beginning to seem like a tougher job than he had imagined.

'We'll keep you posted,' he said, then he and Winsome headed back to the station.

Unfortunately, most people were far too absorbed in their Christmas plans – meals, family visits, last minute shopping, church events and what have you – to pay as much attention to local news stories as they did the rest of the time, and even that wasn't much. As Banks and Winsome whiled away the afternoon at Western Area Headquarters, uniformed police officers went from house to house asking questions and searched the wintry Dales landscape in an ever-widening circle, but nothing came to light.

Banks remembered, just before the shops closed, that he had things to buy, so he dashed over to the Swainsdale Centre. Of course, by closing time on Christmas Eve it was bedlam, and everyone was impatient and bad-tempered. He queued to pay for his turkey dinner because he would have had nothing else to eat otherwise, but just one glance at the crowds in HMV made him decide to forgo the Christmas music for this year, relying on what he had already and what he could catch on the radio.

By six o'clock he was back at home, and the men and women on duty at the police station had strict instructions to ring him if anything concerning Brenda Mercer came up.

But nothing did.

Banks warmed his leftover lamb curry and washed it down with a cold beer. After he'd finished the dishes, he made a start on *Human Traces*, then he opened a bottle of claret and took it with him into the TV room. There, he slid the shiny DVD of *A Christmas Carol* into the player, poured himself a healthy glass and settled back.

108

He always enjoyed spotting the bit where you could see the cameraman reflected in the mirror when Scrooge examines himself on Christmas morning, and he found Alastair Sims's over-the-top excitement at seeing the world anew as infectious and uplifting as ever. Even so, as he took himself up to bed around midnight, he still had a thought to spare for Brenda Mercer, and it kept him awake far longer than he would have liked.

The first possible lead came early on Christmas morning, when Banks was eating a soft-boiled egg for breakfast and listening to a King's College Choir concert on the radio. Winsome rang to tell him that someone had seen a woman resembling Mrs Mercer in a rather dazed state wandering through the village of Swainshead shortly after dawn. The description matched, down to the coat and shoulder-bag, so Banks finished his breakfast and headed out.

The sky was still like iron, but the temperature had dropped overnight, and Banks thought he sniffed a hint of snow in the air. As he drove down the dale, he glanced at the hillsides, all in shades of grey, their peaks obscured by low-lying cloud. Here and there a silver stream meandered down the slope, glittering in the weak light. Whatever was wrong with Brenda Mercer, Banks thought, she must be freezing if she had been sleeping rough for two nights now.

Before he got to Swainshead, he received

another call on his mobile, again from Winsome. This time she told him that a local train driver had seen a woman walking aimlessly along the tracks over the Swainshead Viaduct. When Banks arrived there, Winsome was already waiting on the western side along with a couple of uniformed officers in their patrol cars, engines running so they could stay warm. The huge viaduct stretched for about a quarter of a mile across the broad valley, carrying the main line up to Carlisle and beyond, into Scotland, and its twenty or more great arches framed picture-postcard views of the hills beyond.

'She's up there, sir,' said Winsome, pointing as Banks got out of the car. Way above him, more than a hundred feet up, a tiny figure in brown perched on the edge of the viaduct wall.

'Jesus Christ,' said Banks. 'Has anyone called to stop the trains? Anything roaring by her right now could give her the fright of her life, and it's a long way down.'

'It's been done,' said Winsome.

'Right,' said Banks. 'At the risk of stating the obvious, I think we'd better get someone who knows about these things to go up there and talk to her.'

'It'll be difficult to get a professional, sir, on Christmas Day.'

'Well, what do you . . . ? No. I can read your expression, Winsome. Don't look at me like that. The answer's no.'

'But you know you're the best person for the job, sir. You're good with people. You listen to them. They trust you.'

'But I wouldn't know where to begin.'

'I don't think there are any set rules.'

'I'm hardly the sort to convince someone that life is full of the joys of spring.'

'I don't really think that's what's called for.'

'But what if she jumps?'

Winsome shrugged. 'She'll either jump or fall if someone doesn't go up there soon and find out what's going on.'

Banks glanced up again and swallowed. He thought he felt the soft, chill touch of a snowflake melt on his eyeball. Winsome was right. He couldn't send up one of the uniformed lads – they were far too inexperienced for this sort of thing – and time was of the essence.

'Look,' he said, turning to Winsome, 'see if you can raise some sort of counsellor or negotiator, will you? In the meantime, I'll go up and see what I can do.'

'Right you are, sir.' Winsome smiled. Banks got back in his car. The quickest way to reach the woman was drive up to Swainshead station, just before the viaduct, and walk along the tracks. At least that way he wouldn't have to climb any hills. The thought didn't comfort him much, though, when he looked up again and saw the woman's legs dangling over the side of the wall.

★　　★　　★

111

'Stop right there,' she said. 'Who are you?'

Banks stopped. He was about four or five yards away from her. The wind was howling more than he had expected, whistling around his ears, making it difficult to hear properly, and it seemed colder up there, too. He wished he was wearing something warmer than his leather jacket. The hills stretched away to the west, some still streaked with November's snow. In the distance, Banks thought he could make out the huge rounded mountains of the Lake District.

'My name's Banks,' he said. 'I'm a policeman.'

'I thought you'd find me eventually,' she said. 'It's too late, though.'

From where Banks was standing, he could only see her in profile. The ground was a long way below. Banks had no particularly fear of heights, but even so, her precarious position on the wall unnerved him. 'Are you sure you don't want to come back from the edge and talk?' he said.

'I'm sure. Do you think it was easy getting here in the first place?'

'It's a long walk from Eastvale.'

She cast him a sidelong glance. 'I didn't mean that.'

'Sorry. It just looks a bit dangerous there. You could slip and fall off.'

'What makes you think that wouldn't be a blessing?'

'Whatever it is,' said Banks, 'it can't be worth

this. Come on, Brenda, you've got a husband who loves you, a daughter who needs—'

'My husband doesn't love me, and my daughter doesn't need me. Do you think I don't know? David's been shagging his secretary for two years. Can you imagine such a cliché? He thinks I don't know. And as for my daughter, I'm just an embarrassment to her and that awful husband of hers. I'm the shop-girl who married up, and now I'm just a skivvy for the lot of them. That's all I've been for years.'

'But things can change.'

She stared at him with pity and shook her head. 'No they can't,' she said, and gazed off into the distance. 'Do you know why I'm here? I mean, do you know what set me off? I've put up with it all for years, the coldness, the infidelity, just for the sake of order, not rocking the boat, not causing a scene. But do you know what it was?'

'No,' said Banks, anxious to keep her talking. 'Tell me.' He edged a little closer so he could hear her voice above the wind. She didn't tell him to stop. Snowflakes started to swirl around them.

'People say it's smell that sparks memory the most, but it wasn't, not this time. It was a Christmas ornament. I was putting a few last minute decorations on the tree before Janet and Claude arrived and I found myself holding these tiny, perfect ice skates I hadn't seen for years. They sent me right back to a particular day, when I was a child. It's funny because it didn't seem like just a memory. I felt as if I was *really* there. My father took me skating on a pond somewhere in the country. I don't remember where. But it was just getting dark and there were red and green and white Christmas lights and music playing – carols like 'Silent Night' and 'Away in a Manager' – and someone was roasting chestnuts on a brazier. The air was full of the smell. I was . . . My father died last year.' She paused and brushed tears or melted snowflakes from her eyes with the back of her hand. 'I kept falling down. It must have been my first time on ice. But my father would just pick me up, tell me I was doing fine, and set me going again. I don't know what it was about that day, but I was so happy, the happiest I can ever remember. Everything seemed perfect and I felt I could do anything. I wished it would never end. I didn't even feel the cold. I was just all warm inside and full of love. Did you ever feel like that?'

Banks couldn't remember, but he was sure he must have. Best to agree, anyway. Stay on her wavelength. 'yes,' he said. 'I know what you mean.' It wasn't exactly a lie.

'And it made me feel worthless,' she said. 'The memory made me feel that my whole life was a sham, a complete waste of time, of any potential I once might have had. And it just seemed that there was no point in carrying on.' She shifted on the wall.

'Don't!' Banks cried, moving forward.

She looked at him. He thought he could make

out a faint smile. She appeared tired and drawn, but her face was a pretty one, he noticed. A slightly pointed chin and small mouth, but beautiful hazel eyes. 'It's all right,' she said. 'I was just changing position. The wall's hard. I just wanted to get more comfortable.'

She was concerned about comfort. Banks took that as a good sign. He was within two yards of her now, but he still wasn't close enough to make a grab. At least she didn't tell him to move back. 'Just be careful,' he said. 'It's dangerous. You might slip.'

'You seem to be forgetting that's what I'm here for.'

'The memory,' said Banks. 'That day at the pond. It's something to cherish, surely, to live for?'

'No. It just suddenly made me feel that my life's all wrong. Has been for years. I don't feel like *me* any more. I don't feel anything. Do you know what I mean?'

'I know,' said Banks. 'But this isn't the answer.'

'I don't know,' Brenda said, shaking her head. 'I just feel so sad and so lost.'

'So do I,' said Banks, edging a little closer. 'Every Christmas since my wife left me for someone else and the kids grew up and moved away from home. But it does mean that you feel something. You said before that you felt nothing, but you do, even if it is only sadness.'

'So how do you cope?'

'Me? With what?'

115

'Being alone. Being abandoned and betrayed.'

'I don't know,' said Banks. He was desperate for a cigarette, but remembered that he had stopped smoking ages ago. He put his hands in his pockets. The snow was really falling now, obscuring the view. He couldn't even see the ground below.

'Did you love her?' Brenda asked.

The question surprised Banks. He had been quizzing her, but all of a sudden she was asking about him. He took that as another good sign. 'Yes.'

'What happened?'

'I suppose I neglected her,' said Banks. 'My job . . . the hours . . . I don't know. She's a pretty independent person. I thought things were OK, but they weren't.'

'I'm sure David thinks everything is fine as long as no one ruffles the surface of his comfortable little world. Were you unfaithful?'

'No. But she was. I don't suppose I blame her now. I did at the time. When she had a baby with him, that really hurt. It seemed . . . I don't know . . . the ultimate betrayal, the final gesture.'

'She had a baby with another man?'

'Yes. I mean, we were divorced and they got married and everything. My daughter's spending Christmas with them.'

'And you?'

Was she starting to feel sorry for him? If she did, then perhaps it would help to make her see that she wasn't the only one suffering, that suffering was a part of life and you just had to put up with it and get on with things. 'By myself,' he said. 'My son's abroad. He's in a rock group. The Blue Lamps. They're doing really well. You might even have heard of them.'

'David doesn't like pop music.'

'Well . . . they're really good.'

'The proud father. My daughter's a stuck-up, social-climbing bitch who's ashamed of her mother.'

Banks remembered Janet Mainwaring's reaction to the description of her mother as missing: an embarrassment. 'People can be cruel,' he said.

'But how do you cope?'

Banks found that he had edged closer to her now, within a yard or so. It was almost grabbing range. That was a last resort, though. If he wasn't quick enough, she might flinch and fall off as he reached for her. 'I don't know,' he said. 'Christmas is a difficult time for all sorts of people. On the surface, it's all peace and happiness and giving and family and love, but underneath . . . You see it a lot in my job. People reach breaking point. There's so much stress.'

'But how do *you* cope with it alone? Surely it must all come back and make you feel terrible?'

'Me? I suppose I seek distractions. *A Christmas Carol. Love, Actually* – for Bill Nighy and Keira Knightley – and *David Copperfield*, the one with the Harry Potter actor. I probably drink too much as well.'

'Daniel Radcliffe. That's his name. The Harry Potter actor.'

'Yes.'

'And I'd watch *Love, Actually* for Colin Firth.' She shook her head. 'But I don't know if it would work for me.'

'I recommend it,' said Banks. 'The perfect antidote to spending Christmas alone and miserable.'

'But I wouldn't be alone and miserable, would I? That's the problem. I'd be with my family and miserable.'

'You don't have to be.'

'What are you suggesting?'

'I told you. Things can change. You can change things.' Banks leaned his hip against the wall. He was so close to her now that he could have put his arms around her and pulled her back, but he didn't think he was going to need to. 'Do it for yourself,' he said. 'Not for them. If you think your husband doesn't love you, leave him and live for yourself.'

'Leave David? But where would I go? How would I manage? David has been my life. David and Janet.'

'There's always a choice,' Banks went on. 'There are people who can help you. People who know about these things. Counsellors, social services. Other people have been where you are now. You can get a job, a flat. A new life. I did.'

'But where would I go?'

'You'd find somewhere. There are plenty of flats available in Eastvale, for a start.'

'I don't know if I can do that. I'm not as strong as you.' Banks noticed that she managed a small smile. 'And I think if I did, I would have to go far away.'

'That's possible, too.' Banks reached out his hand. 'Let me help you.' The snow was coming down heavily now, and the area had become very slippery. She looked at his hand, shaking her head and biting her lip.

'*A Christmas Carol*?' she said.

'Yes.'

'I always preferred *It's a Wonderful Life*.'

Banks laughed. 'That'll do nicely, too.' She took hold of his hand, and he felt her grip tightening as she climbed off the wall and stood up. 'Be careful now,' he said. 'The ground's quite treacherous.'

'Isn't it just,' she said, and moved towards him.

ALLAN GUTHRIE

DIRTY WORK

They wouldn't let him do it twice. Not even in Amsterdam. Ben hung up, slipped his phone into his pocket. Ah, well. He'd tried. Now he could focus on the job in hand. He'd done the hard bit.

It had taken the best part of two hours and he was sweating like tomorrow was execution day and he'd forgotten to place the order for his last meal. Who'd have thought digging a couple of holes would have been so exhausting?

Found some babywipes in the car. Gave his face a lick with one of them. Then he'd called Amsterdam while he was getting his breath back. So, back to work.

He put his gloves on, grabbed hold of the tongue and tugged. You wouldn't have any idea how hard it was to get the slippery fucker through the gap. Tight fit, and the damn thing wriggled in his hand like it was alive.

This was the sort of job Ben really didn't like. He was supposed to be selling guns, not doing this kind of shite. Could have farmed the job out, maybe. But he hadn't. Too risky. This was some-thing he had to do himself.

He let go of the tongue and dug his fingers through the hole in the corpse's throat. Prised the skin apart. Fumbled for the tongue again and this time forced it through. There. Ya wee beauty.

He yanked on it, made sure there was a good few inches poking through. Ought to be enough.

Sat back for a minute and took a breather.

Dirty work. Still, nothing new there.

Much as Ben would have loved to have gone home, showered, sank a couple of beers, watched TV with his cat on his lap and Janice by his side, he wasn't quite finished yet.

The body weighed a ton. He tried lifting it, but the muscles in his arms burned and his spine felt like it was about to snap. He stooped behind the body, stuck his hands under the armpits and dragged it a couple of inches before slumping. Took a deep breath and tried again. Landed on his arse hard enough to make him cry out.

'Jesus,' he said, 'why did you have to be such a fat fuck?'

It was true. The fat fuck didn't contradict him.

'Cat got your tongue?' Well, Ben could see clearly that that wasn't the case. He patted the corpse's plump knee. 'Sorry.'

Truth was, he felt pretty bad. Wouldn't have been so bad if it had been a bloke, but doing this to a woman was tough. Really fucking tough. All joking aside.

He had cut her throat post-mortem so there wasn't an awful lot of blood. Same reason he'd used a .22. Double-tap. Back of the head. Very little spatter. Still, enough blood to attract a couple of flies. He brushed them away.

He needed the money, you see. He wasn't doing this for fun. This was to make an impression. If the big lass was a cake, the Columbian necktie was the icing. But would her husband bite? Ben hoped to Christ he had a sweet tooth.

For Ben, this was the last resort. He'd already let some quack cut his big toe off for twenty grand. That's what he'd been phoning Amsterdam about. See if they'd let him do it again. Well, why not? Lots of medical students out there in Holland needed the practice.

What they did, see, was cut it off at the knuckle, then sewed it back on again straight away. And since it was now a couple of months later, and the toe was working OK – balance was a little off, right enough; and there was a bit of pain occasionally; and he'd never play football; and the scar was fairly unsightly – but all that aside, it had healed well enough for a second operation. Which meant another payment. But a repeat performance was out of the question, apparently.

It only occurred to him now that he needn't have mentioned he'd already had the operation.

That way, they could have done the other foot and no one need have been any the wiser.

Bollocks.

Records, though. They'd have had records. They'd have found out. Cancelled the op at the last minute. And then where would he be?

And if they'd found out about the first op, they'd have called off the second one. Having both big toes cut off and sewn back on screws up your balance too much, they'd told him. It's illegal. Even in Amsterdam.

Maybe he could try Brussels.

God, it was the hope that killed you.

Shit, it was better this way. Do this little number. Earn enough to keep the bastard off his back. For a while, at least.

The next payment was due next Thursday. Today was Friday. He had to get a move on.

Four months and counting. That's how long it had been.

The first call had come at three fifteen. He knew that because he'd looked at his watch. Once he'd put the light on. Three fifteen *A fucking M*.

'I know,' the caller had said.

At first Ben hadn't had an inkling what the caller meant. Ben's mouth tasted like a hamster had died in it, yet he'd been having a very pleasant dream about an old girlfriend. A strange combination of sensations guaranteed to disorientate the most focussed of individuals, which Ben, even when alert, wasn't. He said, 'Huh?'

'I know about Freddie.' The tosser had sniggered. Ben snapped awake, shook like hell, felt acid in his stomach and thought he was going to spew. He hung up. He was still shaking when the phone rang again a couple of minutes later.

He heard the same voice say, 'I know all about it.' The man chuckled. Scumbag jizzwad was laughing at him now.

Ben's initial thought was, how could this anonymous caller know about it? Wasn't possible. Nobody knew. It had to be a bluff. OK, so this guy knew about Freddie. But what else did he know?

Ben asked him.

The caller told him and Ben went cold from his stomach to his scrotum.

Fuck. Not only did he know, but the bastard claimed he also had photos.

Ben managed to drag the body over to a tree. Took an age, but he made it. All this exercise, he ought to sleep well tonight. Fetched some rope out of the car boot. Sat the body upright, back against the tree, wrapped the rope around her stomach and used a second piece to hold her head erect. Showed off her new tie to best effect.

Back to the car. Took the camera out of the glove compartment. 'Smile,' he said. She didn't. Just stuck her tongue out at him.

★　　★　　★

Thing about blackmail, you knew the payments were going to escalate. Started with a manageable amount, which of course Ben objected to paying, but considering the alternative, he didn't make too much of a song and dance about it. Pay the man, be done with it. And hope that was the end of it.

If those photos got out, Ben was fucked. The blackmailer was back within a couple of weeks and he was asking for a hell of a lot more.

So Ben decided to shoot him.

OK, it wasn't decided quite so matter-of-factly. Ben rarely killed anybody. In his whole life, he'd only killed four people. But the blackmailer had evidence that could destroy everything Ben held dear. Even if the fucker never demanded another penny, Ben couldn't live with the possibility that his life could be ruined at any second.

So, yeah, he was a little hesitant, sure. But once he'd made the decision it was pretty straight-forward. All he needed was a name. And a gun. Given that he sold guns for a living, the latter was no trouble. But fingering the blackmailer had been a little harder.

By the third payment, he was ready. Only five grand. Didn't seem like so much now. But at the time it had seemed outrageous. And Ben was getting angry. He hated being controlled.

The whole thing was getting out of hand and Ben decided to put an end to it. Regain control.

He called Joe-Bob. Yeah, a guy from Haddington

with a daft American name. Not that Joe-Bob liked it. In fact, he hated it. All stemmed from the fact that he abhorred Country and Western music, so some wit at university had . . . but that wasn't the point.

Rip the piss out of his name at your peril.

Joe-Bob was a fat bastard with a flat Mohican hair-cut, usually dyed red, but he was nobody's fool. Ben asked him to watch the drop, see who picked up the money bag and follow the fucker.

Well, Joe-Bob had done just that. Tailed the blackmailer all the way to a bar in the Grassmarket. Went inside, saw him disappear into a private back room. Provided Ben with a detailed description. Not somebody Ben recognised.

Ben persuaded Joe-Bob to hang around outside the pub every evening for a week or so in case the blackmailer returned. It drizzled permanently, only letting up during the daytime when he wasn't there. Come to think of it, one night it didn't rain. But it was so cold, Joe-Bob told him, it felt like somebody had wrapped cold cloths around his knees and tied them so tight they'd cut off his circulation.

Had a talent for melodrama, that boy.

Ben had been a little concerned Joe-Bob might get noticed. After all, he was distinctive looking. He'd bought Joe-Bob a hat as a disguise. A fedora. It suited him.

Got a call one night. 'He's here,' Joe-Bob said. It was around midnight by the time Ben joined

Joe-Bob on the pavement opposite the pub, and the blackmailer was still inside. One o'clock, he still hadn't left and Joe-Bob had been threatening to go home for the last fifteen minutes. He was soaked. Ben persuaded him to stay with the promise of a bottle of whisky of his choice. On top of what he was paying him already.

The blackmailer finally appeared around one thirty. Joe-Bob pointed him out, and said, 'Laphroaig, please.' Ben borrowed Joe-Bob's hat and followed the blackmailer.

The rain was great cover. Nobody pays anybody else any attention during a downpour and in any case the streets were almost deserted. Anybody who hadn't already left for home yet was probably going to wait a while longer, see if the weather let up.

There was no one at the bus stop. So Ben double-tapped him. Back of the head, just behind the ear. Quick tip of the fedora and Ben carried on walking with a spring in his step. Five minutes later, he jumped in a taxi.

He gave Joe-Bob the bottle of Laphroaig next day. Kept the hat, though.

The spring in Ben's step was short-lived. Couple of days on, his mobile rang.

'Very naughty,' the caller said. 'Going to have to get myself another messenger boy now. You'll pay for that. Twenty-five grand and a little lesson.' Jesus fuck. The blackmailer was still alive.

When Ben told Joe-Bob, Joe-Bob suggested

going to the police. Ben told him not to be a dickhead.

Which is just about the last thing Ben said to his friend before Joe-Bob was discovered eviscerated in Warriston Park cemetery.

Major hassle. The police detained Ben for six hours, which was the maximum they were allowed to hold anybody these days. Any longer, they had to make an arrest. Fortunately, on the evening of Joe-Bob's murder, Ben had been at the cinema with some associates from Manchester. And they'd all gone to a club afterwards. The police checked out his alibi and it held; they released him, but told him to watch his step.

Anyway, that's when he decided to get his toe cut off. One of the Manc lads had had the operation a couple of months back; said it was money for nowt.

If nothing else, the toe op would force Ben to tread carefully.

Ben placed the last shovelful of dirt on the grave and patted it down. He stamped across it, jumped up and down. Yeah, you could tell the earth had been recently dug up. But who was going to be looking?

He strolled back to his car. He had a long drive back home, which gave him plenty of time to think. He wished he could speak to Janice, but she was the last person he could talk to.

*　　*　　*

Janice's hair was still damp from her shower. Towel wrapped round her waist and tucked between her breasts. 'Good day?' she asked him.

He planted a kiss on her cheek. 'Tiring,' he said. ''Bout you?'

'So-so.' She untied the towel, dabbed at her chest and neck. Ran it over her shoulders. 'How tiring?'

Ben said, 'Not really that tiring at all,' and started unbuttoning his trousers.

First thing Saturday, he sent off the photo of the dead woman and a note that read: *fifty grand and no police or the boy gets the same.* Yeah, he only needed twenty-five but it wasn't going to stop, was it? Might as well take what he could.

On Tuesday, he called. Told Mr Paul Gardner when and where to deliver the money if he wanted to see his son alive again. Got the expected crap: 'I don't have that kind of money.'

'Don't fuck with me.'

'But, honestly—'

'You live in a million-pound home.'

'Mortgaged to the hilt. My money's all—'

'Be there. With the money. On your own. Or it's bye, bye, little Paul. Your call.'

Thought he handled that rather well. Couldn't raise fifty grand? Who was the rich fuck trying to kid?

* * *

Wednesday night and he was trying to relax. Course he was thinking about tomorrow, hoping everything was going to go to plan. He'd get the money. Use it to pay off the blackmailer. That would be it. Not a penny more. He'd stand firm, make sure the fucker understood.

But how could he do that? He'd get laughed at again.

Janice had fallen asleep. She was lying on her back, a tiny snore catching in her throat.

Sex was perfunctory these days. Ben wondered if that was a sign they should get married. She'd like that. She was always hassling him about it. Three years since he'd bought her that engagement ring. Worth a couple of grand, that. If he got desperate . . . No, he couldn't. There were limits.

He'd have liked to cuddle up to her and doze off. But there was too much on his mind.

How could he tell her?

Janice, something I've got to say.

The information the blackmailer was threatening to disclose was nothing like you'd imagine. No, Ben didn't paedo up some boy or shag his own brother or anything like that. He wasn't a fucking pervert.

It's about Freddie.

Damn it, he couldn't tell her. She'd leave him, go to the police. Even without the photos, the police would nail him. Somehow. Janice's word against his. They'd find something. The blackmailer would tell them. No reason not to.

It wasn't an accident.

The bedroom door burst open and Ben was hauled back to the present. The lights went on, Janice screamed and a masked gunman walked over to her and told her to shut up. Ben thought he recognised the voice.

The gunman swung his sawn-off shotgun at her.

I killed Freddie, Janice.

She kept screaming.

The gunman fired and Janice's head exploded. Bits of her splashed all over Ben. He wiped his face. Dabbed at his bare shoulder. He looked at the gunman.

The gunman shrugged. 'She was making a racket.'

'It *is* you.' The fucking blackmailer. 'You know about the boy?' The blackmailer jabbed him in the chin with the point of the barrel.

Jesus. Felt like the fucker had broken his jaw. He knew about the boy, all right. Must have been following Ben. Shit, Ben should have expected that.

Ben was drooling, or was it blood that was dribbling onto his chest? Was it his own or Janice's? The pain in his chin was excruciating. He wondered if Janice had felt anything. Happened so quickly, he doubted it. He stole another glance at her. Could feel his stomach bubbling.

Freddie was in the way, Janice. I couldn't get close to you whilst he was alive. You understand that?

He tried to speak. Wasn't so much the pain in his jaw stopping him as the fucking ridiculous sobbing that was making his shoulders wildly jerk up and down. Got the words out somehow. Punctuated each word with a sharp breath. 'I'll get you your money.'

'Gardner made me a much better offer.' The gunman levelled the shotgun at Ben's face.

Ben tried to picture the face behind the mask. This, after all, was the man who'd been blackmailing him. But it was hard to concentrate with a shotgun barrel in your face.

The blackmailer continued, 'After I told him I'd seen you in the woods burying a couple of members of his family.'

Ben was fucked. If Gardner knew the boy was dead, that was game over. Ben didn't know what to do, but he knew he had to do something. And quickly. He grabbed a pillow, flung it towards the gun and dived for the floor. Landed in a bruised heap, having achieved nothing.

The blackmailer stared at him, shook his head. After a minute, he turned, started to walk away.

'Where are you going?' Ben asked.

The blackmailer stopped. 'Got to go home. Catch up on my beauty sleep.'

'You're not . . . you're leaving?'

'You still owe me twenty-five grand.'

'And what's Gardner going to say?'

'Gardner's an arsehole. Gave me half the money up front. Asking to be ripped off. Anyway, if he wants you dead, he's going to have to cough up a lot more.'

'You didn't tell him my name?'

'Information is valuable, Ben. You think I'm the type who'd give it away? Now listen, at the moment, you're worth more to me alive than dead. But that could easily change. All it takes is for you to decide not to pay me. Or for Gardner to offer me more money than I can realistically get out of you. So don't let me down. OK?'

He turned, headed towards the door.

No, it wasn't OK. It was very fucking far from OK. The fucker had shot Janice. And for no reason. And because of that, Ben's main reason for handing over any more money to the scum-fuck had disappeared. Thought he was a right clever cunt, but he'd miscalculated. There were worse things than the threat of death. And now that Janice could never find out Ben had killed her husband, Ben felt liberated.

He scrambled to his feet and charged. The black-mailer turned, smacked him on the side of the head with his gun. A box of fireworks exploded in Ben's skull. He swayed, stumbled, and collapsed.

When he woke up in the morning, his head throbbed with a horrific intensity. He looked across at Janice and instantly threw up.

He stopped, eventually. Sat there for a while, not having a clue what he should do. Didn't seem any way out of this hell. Well, there was *one* way.

He fetched his gun. Flopped back onto the floor. Cocked the hammer. Pointed the muzzle at his head.

Didn't seem right.

Put the barrel in his mouth.

Better.

Come on, then. Squeeze.

No joy. Nah, he couldn't kill himself.

He dropped the gun onto the floor.

A shot rang out and something punched through his ribcage.

The gun rattled to a standstill.

He looked down. A red stain blossomed under his right nipple.

And it was hard to breathe.

If only he could make it to his feet. Stagger to the phone. Call an ambulance. Then he'd give himself a chance. But did he want a chance? Was there any point?

The way it had all worked out was pretty funny when you thought about it. But, fuck it, there was nothing worth surviving for.

He took a last look at Janice and closed his eyes.

CATHERINE AIRD

THE HOLLY AND THE POISON IVY

'So who's coming for Christmas dinner, then, Mum?' asked Joshua. 'Friends, foes or family?'

'Neighbours,' said his mother.

Both her children groaned. Her parents-in-law politely said nothing. Libby Hawkins smiled round the dining-table at them all. 'Besides, the family are here already – except Daddy, of course.' Her husband's business activities presently lay in a distant land whose national holidays – and Holy Days – did not fall in the month of December.

'Which neighbours?' demanded her son.

'The Viponds . . .' began Libby Hawkins.

'Oh, no,' protested Joshua. 'I can't stand him and his old jokes. I've heard them all a hundred times before. If not two hundred.'

'The Bentleys . . .' continued Libby serenely.

'He's so boring,' said her daughter, Clare, 'and I don't like her.'

'Mr Vipond does,' remarked Joshua.

'Joshua,' remonstrated his mother, 'you shouldn't say things like that.'

'Mrs Bentley's a man-eater,' insisted her son

135

unrepentantly. 'Even the milkman runs away from her and the postman won't knock. Ever. If he's got a parcel he just leaves it on the doorstep and scarpers.'

'What we've all got to remember,' said Libby Hawkins, 'is that she's not a nut-eater.' She turned to her mother-in-law. 'Melissa Bentley's got an allergy to nuts so we shan't be having chestnut stuffing in the turkey.'

'We didn't have any of those in my young days,' said the old lady.

'What? No chestnut stuffing, grandma?' said Joshua. 'What a shame.'

'No allergies,' said his grandmother briskly. 'Tell me, is Mr Vipond's devotion to Mrs Bentley reciprocated?'

'No,' said Libby Hawkins, aware that the elderly were less reticent than the young and even more difficult to divert.

Joshua snorted. 'She's got her claws into someone else, that's why . . .'

Libby shot her son a warning glance.

'Who else is coming?' asked Clare into the silence.

'All right,' sighed Libby. 'If you must know, the Hellaby-Lumbs.'

There were concerted moans from both her son and daughter.

'What have we done to deserve it?' asked Joshua histrionically, turning in appeal to his grandmother. 'I couldn't have led a better life if I'd tried, now could I, Granny?'

'That I wouldn't know, Joshua,' she said with gentle irony, 'would I?'

'Rumours would have reached you for sure if I hadn't . . .' he said gloomily. 'Bound to have done.'

'It's not what we've done to deserve it,' pointed out Libby Hawkins. 'It's what they're going to do for us. The Viponds have asked the whole family round for Boxing Day, and the Bentleys are having open house for the entire neighbourhood on Christmas Eve.'

'And the Hellaby-Lumbs?' asked Clare a little breathlessly.

'Don't tell her, Mummy,' interrupted Joshua. 'I bet it'll be the biggest bash of the lot. They're show-offs with attitude and too much money.'

'New Year's Eve,' said Libby mildly. 'With some musical group or other playing.'

'Which group?' asked Clare urgently. 'Oh, Mummy, which group?'

'I don't know, darling. You'll have to ask them yourself.'

Joshua Hawkins was silent for a while and then he murmured something to his grandmother which the rest of the family could not hear.

'It's rude to whisper,' said Clare.

'You, Joshua,' declared the old lady, suddenly sitting up very straight, 'have been reading too many murder stories. That's your trouble.'

'No, I haven't,' said Joshua Hawkins.

'Murder stories,' carried on his grandmother. 'You've always got your nose buried in one.'

'All I said, Granny, was that it would be quite fun to have a really old-fashioned Christmas this year. That's all.'

'And what I am saying,' insisted Arabella. Hawkins firmly, 'is that the way you found out what you are pleased to imagine an old-fashioned Christmas was really like has been by reading all those Golden Age detective stories.'

Joshua, as befitted the youth he was, considered this allegation carefully. 'Well,' he admitted, 'I suppose you could say I wouldn't have known much about butlers otherwise . . .'

'There you are, then.'

'Although,' admitted Joshua, 'I must say that I still don't understand exactly what it was that butlers did . . .'

'Damned if I ever knew myself,' remarked his grandfather from the other side of the dining-table.

'A cushy number, if you ask me.'

'Everything,' said Mrs Arabella Hawkins un-expectedly, her stern expression melting with sudden warmth. 'Butlers did everything.'

'I've always suspected that the Admirable Crichton wasn't all fiction . . .' murmured Libby Hawkins drily. The presence in the house of her two elderly parents-in-law – to say nothing of the absence of her husband – in what was arguably the busiest week of the whole year was not a great help when it came to making preparations for the festive season. But everyone was trying to make the best of it in their own way.

'If we were to have a really old-fashioned Christmas,' went on Joshua persuasively, 'I could be the butler. That would really be fun and I wouldn't have to sit down with everyone either . . .'

With wry detachment Libby Hawkins watched her son manoeuvring them all into compliance with his wishes. One fine day Joshua was going to make a great salesman – one fine day, that is, when he had finished his education and could get a job: any job at all. At the moment, though, she realised that he was just a very bored young man who was doing his best to inject a little interest into a family Christmas made duller by his father's absence abroad. And, of course, to avoid sitting in his place at the head of the table on the day itself.

Joshua was saying innocently 'The butler must have done something to earn his oats, Granddad . . .'

'He saw to the drink, of course,' said old Bertram Hawkins.

'In more ways than one, I expect,' grinned Joshua, adding with mock solemnity, 'Human nature doesn't change.'

'And the cigars . . . all that sort of thing,' Bertram Hawkins waved a hand.

'Ugh!' exclaimed Clare at once. 'This house is a 'no smoking zone'. We're not having cigars here, are we, Mummy?'

Libby nodded absently in agreement. Her daughter was a born proselytiser: where she would end up was anyone's guess at the moment. At least Clare herself wasn't smoking anything, – anything, that is, as far as she knew, added Libby mentally, her fingers crossed. That alone was something to be truly thankful for these days.

'And the silver,' Arabella Hawkins reminded them all. 'The butler always looked after the silver. He cleaned it and kept it in the safe in his pantry – you've heard about butlers' pantries and butlers' sinks, surely, haven't you, Joshua?'

Joshua, who had not thought about cleaning the silver, protested, 'That wasn't man's work, surely . . .'

'Sexist,' said Clare promptly.

'Libby, dear,' Mrs Hawkins leaned forward. 'What happened to that big old silver salver that we gave you?'

'It's in the art . . . it's upstairs,' Libby quickly amended her response. 'I'll bring it down and Joshua can give it a good polish.'

A polish of any sort was something the salver hadn't had in years but this was not the moment to say so.

'I'm sure that the maids would have laid the table anyway,' insisted Joshua. 'Clare can do that . . . and bring the food in here from the kitchen.'

'Oh, she can, can she?' responded that young woman spiritedly. 'Well, let me tell you, brother of mine, that . . .'

'But you'll have to be the maid,' said Joshua unanswerably, 'because there isn't anyone else.'

'There aren't as many maids about as there used to be,' remarked old Arabella Hawkins with deliberate ambiguity. She patted a stray wave of her white hair back into position. 'Not these days.'

'You can say that again, Granny,' retorted Joshua, with a wicked grin. 'Speaking for myself, I can only say that I haven't met many.'

'The butler would see to all the napery, too,' went on Arabella Hawkins, leaving everyone – but particularly Joshua – unsure whether he had known what she had meant.

Her mother-in-law's circle, decided Libby silently, had probably used coded speech where Joshua's generation dealt in *double entendre*. She sat back and relaxed while her son had it explained to him that 'napery' meant all the household table linen.

'Education isn't everything,' remarked Clare, who hadn't yet decided whether she wanted to go to College or not. 'Besides, we can't have a murder here at Christmas . . .'

'Why not?' asked Joshua – as she had known he would.

'Because,' said Clare, 'though you can be the butler and I can be the maid, we haven't got a library for the body to be found in, that's why.'

'We're not having a murder, darling,' murmured Libby. 'Just an old-fashioned Christmas.'

'I don't see not having a library as an insuperable obstacle . . .' began Joshua.

Libby decided against rising to this and said with

the skill born of long maternal practice in diversionary tactics, 'Don't forget that there's that lovely big white tablecloth which Granny gave us. I always keep it specially for Christmas . . .'

'That belonged to my grandmother,' said Arabella Hawkins complacently. 'You don't see real linen like that these days.'

Libby Hawkins made a mental note to see that the tablecloth was properly ironed in time, although exactly when she would do that, she wasn't sure. Her gaze drifted to the old-fashioned mirror hanging over the dining-room sideboard. That, too, had come from her parent-in-law's old house but it, at least, required nothing more than a gentle wipe before being garlanded with holly and ivy for the festive season.

'I do wish so many of the napkins hadn't disappeared over the years, Libby, dear,' her mother-in-law was saying. 'It was the laundry, you know.'

'Paper napkins will do just as well,' said Libby, thinking that it wouldn't be long before 'laundry' was nearly as an archaic word as 'butler'. 'They're so pretty these days.'

'Tell me,' enquired Arabella Hawkins, 'will the gentleman in whom you say Melissa Bentley has got her claws be with us at Christmas, too?'

'Yes. It's Mr Hellaby-Lumb, poor fish,' said Joshua.

'Ah,' remarked Arabella Hawkins. 'How interesting.'

'Anything else, Granny, that you can remember?'

asked Clare. 'About Christmas in the old days, I mean.'

A reminiscent look came over Arabella Hawkins' lined face. 'Lots of lovely things to eat but best of all were the Elvas plums . . .'

Libby made a mental note to lay in a supply of crystallised fruit.

'. . . But what I really remember about the Christmases when I was young was how lovely the dinner table looked.'

She gave a sweet smile. 'And, Joshua . . .'

'Yes, Granny?'

'That was the butler's job.'

Clare made a face at him.

'What made it so beautiful?' asked Libby swiftly.

'The epergne,' said the old lady.

'All right, Granny,' said Joshua. 'I surrender. What's an epergne?'

'A table centre with lots of little dishes hanging from it with pretty things to eat in them – bon-bons and chocolates . . .'

Libby mentally added sugared almonds to her shopping list. Melissa Bentley needn't eat them.

'And,' continued her mother-in-law, well back in her own childhood now, 'the epergne would have been decorated all over with trailing ivy. That looked really lovely against the white cloth.'

Libby relaxed. There was ivy in the garden and she and Clare could do something pretty with it round the old silver candelabrum, another gift that had also been relegated to the artic. It really wasn't any wonder that silver had gone so out of fashion – cleaning that, too, would keep Joshua busy.

'And when I was a lad,' contributed Bertram Hawkins, 'they used something called smilax on the table centre instead.'

He grinned. 'Got you there, haven't I, Joshua? We didn't have any murders but I bet you don't know what smilax is.'

'Sounds like a patent medicine, Grandpa.'

'A climbing species of asparagus that people used to used for decoration.' He sat back in his chair. 'And no, you didn't eat it.'

In the end the smilax was about the only feature that was missing from the table on Christmas Day. Libby had enhanced the effect of the candelabrum and its red candles by placing it on the large silver salver retrieved from the back of the attic and polished back into brightness. She had draped the substitute epergne with ivy and Clare had contrived to hang a little dish of sweetmeats from each branch. Her mother-in-law, pleased, pronounced it as good an epergne as she had seen in years.

Joshua, bustling about with a corkscrew, had paused to admire it, too. 'I like the mirror effect of the salver . . .'

'Stop slacking, Narcissus,' commanded Clare, 'and give me a hand with these side-plates instead of admiring your own reflection.'

'I don't have a reflection,' said Joshua. 'I'm a vampire . . .'

By evening all was ready. Joshua answered the front door with aplomb, announced the guests with considerable *empressement* and dispensed the drinks before withdrawing to collapse, helpless with laughter, behind the kitchen door.

'Don't!' pleaded Clare. 'I'm sure I'm going to giggle when I go in. I can't help it.'

'Mr Hellaby-Lumb liked it when I called him "sir",' said Joshua.

'I'll bet.'

He grinned. 'But I could tell that Mrs Bentley didn't care one little bit for the way I called her "madam".'

'Joshua, you are awful.'

'Mr Vipond can't take his eyes off her but she's trying to get her claws into Mr Hellaby-Lumb, the poor fish . . .'

'Well,' said Clare with the unconscious realism of the young, 'he is the one with the money.'

'Money isn't everything . . .'

'Want to bet?' she said, starting off in the direction of the dining-room with the soup. 'Just light the candles, will you, and then you can tell everyone that dinner is served . . .'

Libby Hawkins picked up her soup spoon and relaxed. Joshua and Clare were clearly enjoying acting in their new roles and the guests had entered into the Christmas spirit with evident relish.

'Are they open to offers of work?' asked Gordon Hellaby-Lumb jovially as they reached the coffee stage. 'They're as good as those professionals we've got lined up for New Year's Eve, aren't they, my dear?'

Mrs Hellaby-Lumb gave a remote smile, her eyes not leaving Melissa Bentley. That lady had devoted her evening to chatting up Mr Hellaby-Lumb. And Mr Vipond had spent all his time making sheep's eyes at Mrs Bentley – to her obvious enjoyment and in spite of the equally apparent misgivings of Mrs Vipond.

The boring Mr Bentley, sitting between Mrs Vipond and Mrs Hellaby-Lumb, had been dull but courteously attentive to both whilst studiously appearing not to notice his wife's outrageous flirting with Gordon Hellaby-Lumb and her occasional titillating encouragement of Paul Vipond. Melissa Bentley was sitting between her two admirers, almost invisible from her husband, and was clearly enjoying herself mightly behind the shelter of the epergne. At the head of the table Bertram Hawkins was taking pleasure from watching his grandchildren milking what fun they could from acting as butler and parlour-maid. What Arabella Hawkins was thinking was anyone's guess. Her shrewd old eyes were darting about, watching everyone, and missing nothing.

This was just as well. Her observations were to prove very helpful when she came to describe the evening again and again to Detective Inspector Sloan, Head of the tiny Criminal Investigation Department of the Berebury Police Force. This was after the sudden death of Melissa Bentley from an acute anaphylactic reaction to nuts.

'She drank some coffee, Inspector,' said Arabella Hawkins, 'just a sip, I should say . . . then she started to complain that her mouth and throat were burning . . .'

The detective inspector nodded.

'And almsot immediately after that her hands and face started to swell. This was before she collapsed, of course. She was dead before the ambulance arrived.' Arabella Hawkins did not sound too disturbed at this. It was Libby and the children who were too distraught to be comforted.

They still had to be questioned, though.

'If,' said Detective Inspector Sloan patiently to Joshua, 'we might go through everything once more . . .'

'Like I said,' repeated Joshua for the fourth or fifth time, 'Clare made the coffee in the kitchen and brought it through to the dining-room.'

'And?'

'And she stood the pot over there.' He waved a hand in the direction of the sideboard under the big mirror. 'The coffee cups were there already. And there wasn't anything in them then,' he added defiantly.

'What were you doing at the time?' Detective Inspector Sloan wasn't completely *au fait* himself with the arcane duties of Joshua's temporary office but he did not say so. 'Were you still butlering?'

'Putting the nuts and crystallised fruit on the

table . . .' Joshua said dully. 'With the dates and the figs.'

'Then?'

'Clare poured out the coffee and I passed the cups down the table to everyone.'

'You didn't hand them round yourself?'

'No. I just took them from Clare and put them on the table.'

He looked at the policeman and said belligerently, 'I know that's not the right thing to do but Clare and I were only doing this for a lark. We hadn't ever done it before.'

'What about the cream?' asked Sloan, pointing to a jug.

'I passed it down after the coffee, with the sugar.' Joshua scowled. 'And, no, I didn't put anything in the cups except coffee.'

'Quite so.' Detective Inspector Sloan didn't for one moment suppose that he had. As the policeman saw it, any motive for handing a fatal dose of nuts to Melissa Bentley lay between Mrs Vipond and Mrs Hellaby-Lumb, with her husband, Paul Bentley, also well in the running. The man might well be as dull as everyone said he was, but even so to Sloan's more experienced eye he didn't have the look of a *mari complaisant*: more one of a vengeful man suppressing great anger. 'Then what?'

'Mr Vipond accidentally put some cream in a coffee that Mrs Bentley wanted black.'

'And?' Detective Inspector Sloan didn't think

that old aphorism about always killing the thing you loved applied to Mr Vipond but he couldn't be overlooked.

'So Mrs Bentley passed the cup back across the table – round that candlestick thing to her husband who does take cream in his coffee and someone else passed a black coffee back for her instead through – or, rather, round – the centrepiece.' He gulped. 'I think that must have been the one that Mrs Bentley had – the one that had the nut in it.'

So did Detective Inspector Sloan. The finger-print people weren't prepared to commit themselves. The elegant little eggshell handles of the hastily cleared coffee cups had been singularly unrevealing in this respect. 'Who handed it to her?'

Joshua suddenly looked defenceless. 'I don't know for sure. It was difficult to see across the table from where I was standing what with all that ivy trailing round and anyway I was still pouring the coffee. All I saw for sure when I looked down from my side of the table was a hand with a cup in it reflected in the silver salver coming out from under all the ivy.'

'Man's or woman's?'

'Woman's.' That, at least, he was sure about.

'Right or left?'

He paused for thought. 'Left from where I saw it reflected on the salver – that means it would have been her right, doesn't it?'

The Inspector didn't answer this. 'Wedding ring?' he asked instead.

'I couldn't see that because there was a cup in her hand.'

Clare had only seen things through the mirror above the sideboard. She stood in front of it now and tried to explain. 'I heard them talking about Mrs Bentley having cream in her coffee when she didn't like it.' She gave a little shiver. 'It reminded me of Cecily Cardew putting sugar in Gwendolen Fairfax's tea just because she didn't want it in *The Importance of Being Earnest*, Inspector.'

'Really, miss?' In his book there were even more important things than being earnest. There was being right in the important matter of murder. 'Now, suppose you tell me exactly what you saw in your mirror . . .' Sloan went and stood beside Clare, both of them facing the sideboard and the great mirror above it.

Mrs Vipond, Mr Bentley and Mrs Hellaby-Lumb, all sitting on the side of the table opposite Melissa Bentley, had been uniformly vague about what they had and hadn't seen. In fact, they had reminded Detective Inspector Sloan of nothing so much as the three monkeys who saw no evil, heard no evil and spoke no evil. And weren't going to, either. In one way or another Melissa Bentley's behaviour had been a threat to all three.

'I just saw a hand passing over a cup of coffee which was going across the table, Inspector,' said Clare, still very shaken and tearful. 'I had my back to the table, getting the cups ready for Joshua, like we are now, and I was rather in the way of the reflection of the person themselves so I didn't see who it was.' Mr Vipond and Mr Hellaby-Lumb on the other side of the table had declared that they had not noticed anything at all, being busy with passing more cups round. The adult Hawkins's had similarly noticed nothing.

'Left or right hand?' he asked Clare patiently.

Clare raised her own hand in front of the mirror. 'My right, so her left,' she said promptly, 'because it would a mirror-image, wouldn't it?'

Detective Inspector Sloan left her standing in front of the mirror while he went back to the table and sat where Mrs Hellaby-Lumb had been sitting. He advanced his own right hand across the table.

'No, Inspector,' said Clare. Your other hand.'

Obligingly, he put out his left hand.

'That's right. That's the one I saw.'

He turned to Joshua and asked him to stand where he had been earlier, looking down at the reflection in the salver. Sloan put out his own hand again.

'Tell me again which hand you saw come round from the other side of the table in the salver . . .'

'A left hand,' he said promptly. 'Her right, I suppose.'

Detective Inspector Sloan shook his head.

'We can't both be right,' wailed Clare, dismayed.

He smiled benignly. 'Oh, yes, you can.'

'Someone's going to get away with murder,'

muttered Joshua, who suddenly discovered that he minded about this.

'No, they aren't,' said the Inspector. 'Two witnesses should be enough for any prosecution . . .'

'But what about us?' stammered Joshua. 'We don't agree.'

'We saw different hands,' said Clare starting to cry again.

'The lawyers will make mincemeat of either Clare or me,' said Joshua, feeling suddenly less grown-up than he liked.

His sister shivered. 'Of both of us, I expect.'

Detective Inspector Sloan explained himself. 'If a mirror is parallel to an image it reverses it from left to right . . .'

'That's right,' agreed Clare eagerly. 'Like the mirror on the wall . . .'

The policeman nodded. 'But when the mirror is at ninety degrees to the image . . .'

'As the salver was,' agreed Joshua, greatly puzzled. 'It was flat on the table . . .'

'And you saw the image while you were standing up . . .'

'True, but . . .'

'When it reverses the image top to bottom instead of right to left,' finished Detective Inspector Sloan. 'You both saw the same hand over the coffee cup – Mrs Hellaby-Lumb's left one. Mrs Vipond would only have been able to get her right one into that position by leaning across Mr Bentley.'

Clare swallowed as her natural realism reasserted itself. 'I suppose you could say Mrs Hellaby-Lumb had the most to lose . . .'

'She had means, motive and opportunity,' said Joshua, recovering some of his aplomb. 'And you have two witnesses.'

Turning politely to the police inspector, he resumed his butler mode and asked 'Will that be all, sir?'

'Yes, thank you, Hawkins,' said Detective Inspector Sloan, entering into the spirit of things. 'For the time being, anyway.'

PAUL CHARLES

IN THE MIDNIGHT HOUR

The door slammed shut behind him.

It wasn't exactly that the slamming created a particularly loud bang. It was more that it was a bang of great finality. A very definite closure as it were.

'Rory,' the slammer of the door hissed, sneering through the corner of his mouth, 'so what have you been up to this time? For goodness sake man, don't you realise the Sabbath is only a matter of a few minutes old.'

'Ah, now Inspector Starrett,' Rory Sullivan began, his confidence draining the more Starrett's bloodshot eyes bore down on him, 'I ah, I . . . well, I suppose I'm what you'd call a victim of circumstance.'

'A victim of circumstance, is it?' Starrett laughed, displaying two rows of snow-white molars, which created a very non-patriotic combination of colours with his eyes and jumper, 'I'd say it was more a case of light fingers not being capable of heavy work.'

'Ah,' Sullivan began, openly dejected.

'You know what, Rory, do you know what's really troubling me?'

'What's that Inspector?'

'I'll tell you, Rory, Even after all these years in the Gardai I'm still bewildered why some people choose the crooked path, the path of deceit, rather than the God-fearing, work for a living type. I mean, take you for instance. It isn't as though we can blame your family. Rory tell me this, I need to understand this, why you do it?'

Rory Sullivan clicked his teeth. He was twenty-eight years old, the middle of three brothers. His major problem, as far as he was concerned, was that he was born and raised in Ramelton – a village in Donegal, Ireland's most picturesque county – and not in Santa Fe, New Mexico, in the United States of America.

To Rory Sullivan even the line that summed up the States, 'The land of the free and the home of the brave' was seductive, and compelling. He had been hooked on Americana from the age of eleven.

Like a lot of youths growing up in Ireland in the late Sixties, Rory was fascinated by the whole American culture. He immersed himself completely and utterly in all things American: movies; television shows; Voice of America radio; comics; magazines; vinyl records; Superman; the Lone Ranger and Tonto; *Wagon Train*; Cadillac cars; Harley-Davidson motorbikes; the Beach Boys; the Drifters; cigarette lighters and bowie knives.

He even had a pristine one-dollar bill, carefully folded away in an envelope, which he kept under his mattress. From when he was old enough to count, he automatically converted the local currency directly into dollars – it varied from three to four American dollars to the Irish pound, but the fluctuation always ensured that Rory was ahead in his maths class, particularly when it came to long division.

As a teenager he modelled himself on the new wave of American actors, changing his short back and sides hairstyle, with curls on top, for a Tony Curtis ducktail. Unfortunately the end result, for Rory, was more Karl Malden than James Dean.

Rory completed his American look with an extra-white T-shirt (his mother didn't mind spending the extra few pence on Persil, 'the results are obvious,' she'd say to anyone who'd listen), grey-black Levi jeans, a cheap leather jacket – black with white piping, and permanently off-white (more Daz than Persil) tennis shoes although few if any who wore them ever got to see a tennis court, let alone play on one.

He was always careful not to smile when he was cutting his James Dean pose. Only his green eyes and apple-red flushed checks betrayed the fact that he was Irish and a wannabe American.

'Well?' Starrett asked after thirty-three un-interrupted clicks of the wall-clock.

'Listen, what can I tell you,' Rory said expansively, 'really, what can I tell you? I see myself more as a William H. Bonney character than a real criminal. Like Billy, I've never knowingly taken from someone who couldn't afford it. I've never touched the poor.'

'And you've always proved to be very ingenious in your raids,' Starrett sighed, 'but my point would be that if you used even a small fraction of that guile and cunning on something more worthwhile and honest we'd all be a lot better off.'

'Yeah,' Rory conceded, then following a few more ticks of the second hand of the clock, 'but if I went straight I'd never be able to save enough money to fly Cherry and myself to New Mexico?'

'What? So that you can follow every other Irish immigrant and spend the rest of your life being homesick for dear old mother Ireland? You know, you really should wake up and smell the Monbretia and all the other flowers which grace this spectacular countryside of ours.'

'Ah, not Cherry and me Inspector, in our case the other man's grass is definitely greener.'

'Not in New Mexico it's not, sure it's too darned hot there for anything but the flies.'

Rory just smiled.

'And tell me,' Starrett continued, sure to wipe away Rory's smile, 'while we're talking about Cherry, would that be the same Cheryl Mary Teresa Kavanagh who has just sworn a statement charging you with stealing property belonging to her?'

Starrett sighed and picked up the file he'd brought into the badly lit questioning room, which was situated in the basement of Ramelton's Garda

Station. He opened the file wide in front of him as if he knew he was going to need to view all of the information contained therein.

'That wasn't theft, Inspector. Sure didn't I get the very same radio for her as a present? I just needed to borrow it to raise twenty dollars to bankroll my next job.'

Starrett needed the file sooner than he thought:

'By any chance would that be the same radio, a Roberts US Valve Special, serial number 23091949 which we found in the back of Edmund Davies' car half an hour ago?'

'Yes . . .' Rory replied with an implied, 'So?'

'And would that be the same Roberts radio that was originally stolen from Bryson's Electricians in Letterkenny three months ago and mentioned here in their insurance manifest?' Starrett tapped a piece of paper in the file several times with his index finger. The finger was permanently semi-bent as a result of an accident and was always very disconcerting when used to emphasis something. The detective was fifty-four but his finger looked like the finger of a ninety-year old man. It always looked like it might just break off from the rest of his hand.

'Ah,' Rory replied, this time with nothing implied.

'You see Rory, as I was saying, if you'd just put as much of your energy into going straight as you do into being a highwayman, there would have been a good chance you might have reached your beloved America in the next five or six years, whereas now it's looking like you might be going down for at least that amount of time.'

'Ah but . . .' Rory cut in, 'I can't be put down for . . .'

'Armed robbery is a serious offence, Rory.'

'Armed robbery!' Rory screamed in a pitch perfect Little Richard refrain. 'I've never done an armed robbery in my life.'

'Yes,' Starrett said, and again consulted his file, it was an unnecessary but highly effective gesture, 'and a Mrs Mina Bates has also filed a complaint against you. Apparently you threatened her with a knife in the early hours of this morning.'

'Oh, it wasn't anything like that at all,' Rory replied noticeably relieved.

'OK Rory, could you tell me exactly what it was like then?' Starrett inquired, for the record, leaning back in his metallic chair and putting his fine black-shoed feet up on the desk, stretching his arms and clasping his hands behind, and in support of, his head.

'OK, you see Cherry, well she said . . .'

'Rory,' Starret began, closing his eyes, 'we'll all be finished here a whole lot sooner if you start at the beginning.'

'OK,' Rory replied and leaned in over the desk earnestly. He was so close to Starrett he could smell the mixture of leather and polish from his shoes. If he'd leaned in a little closer he'd have noticed that they were so well polished he would have been able to see his own reflection in the toe-caps. 'Cherry said that was it, we were finished if I didn't come up with the money to buy our tickets to America, like I promised her I would. She gave me one last chance. Now, as luck would have it, it just so happened that I did have a job in mind, over the previous couple of months in fact and I just needed a small job to bankroll it.'

'Bankroll it Rory? What's that all about?'

'Well I needed a getaway car . . .'

'Edmund Davies?' Starrett said without opening his eyes.

'Well, you caught Eddie and me together so you know he was involved. Anyway, Eddie wouldn't agree to doing the job with me unless I paid him for the use of his car up front.'

'Ah Jez Rory, you don't mean to tell me that your accomplice wanted his money in advance?'

'Well, only the car payment part, he needed that in advance, to get it ready he said, and then I was going to give him a cut as well.'

'Ah Rory son, you've surely been watching the wrong movies. Come on, will you, I'm missing my sleep, let's get back to your story.'

'OK, so I borrowed Cherry's radio to bankroll the job, but I couldn't get anyone to buy it. Eddie wasn't much help either and he downright refused to accept it as payment for his car for the job. Anyway, as you know, I've done Widow Bates' rectory before and she's always good for a bit of cash.'

'Yeah,' Starrett sighed, opening his eyes and looking in the file again. 'I believe you got fifty quid last time.'

'More like about one hundred dollars, I never take more than a hundred dollars from private citizens. Anyway, I break in Saturday morning, in the early hours, to pick up the cash. She always hides it in the same place: in the biscuit tin, which is in the cupboard above the sink in the kitchen. It's always packed with crisp notes, but, like I told you, I never take more than a ton. So I'm in the kitchen, it's five o'clock in the morning and I'm feeling a bit peckish. Cherry, God bless her soul, never has any food in our house, so I think, what's the harm of helping myself to some of Widow Bates' food? I mean she's a widow, her cupboards are always packed to bursting, how much food does one woman need?'

'Come now Rory, it's her money, she can spend it on what she wants.'

'Right, sorry, of course, so anyway, I stick the old rasher-wagon on the gas ring. I'm assuming Widow Bates won't be up for three more hours and because our Cherry is always trying to catch up on her beauty sleep, I've learnt to cook quietly . . .'

'It wasn't the noise of your cooking that woke up Mina, it was the smell of the bacon frying in the pan, that's what was your undoing Rory,' Starrett offered, unable to resist a smile.

161

'Yeah, so she sneaked down into the kitchen and caught me . . . but to claim it was armed robbery, well that's just a downright lie.'

'She claims you waved a knife at her at she walked into her own kitchen,' Starrett said.

'Not guilty your honour,' Rory said becoming animated and leaning up from resting on his elbow on the table. 'She walks in; I've got the bread knife in my hand preparing bread for toast. I pointed the knife to the bread and asked her if she wanted some. Of course I was referring to the bread and not the knife.'

'I sure hope that the judge also believes you.'

'Phew . . .' Rory tutted, '. . . with my luck?'

'What exactly did Mrs Bates say to you as you pointed to the bread?'

'Well, she said, "As you've already got the pan fired up Mr Sullivan the least you can do is stick in a few slices of bacon and a couple of eggs for me."'

'And so you, the thief, and Widow Bates, the victim, sat down to break bread and to enjoy breakfast together?'

'Pretty much.'

'Un-fecking-believable, Rory,' Starrett laughed, 'Hardly Al Capone, mate.'

'Al Capone wasn't the toughest of the American gangsters you know,' Rory said with a bit of a whine, 'that honour goes to a Donegal man, Vincent Coll, have you ever heard about him Inspector? He didn't suffer fools gladly.'

'Oh, I've heard all about Mad Dog, Rory,' Starrett said smiling, 'talking about famous people, what was it the *Donegal Chronicle* chap wrote about you after your last job?'

'Ah, he said, "I've seen organised crime in Ireland's future and it's Rory Sullivan."' Rory said, recalling the quote. To give him his proper due he'd didn't recite the quote with any degree of pride.

'Well, all I can say Rory, is that I hope he's right, so that the Gardai of Donegal can sleep easier at night. Talking about sleep let's get to the last chapter in your recent escapade, the bank robbery, tell me about that?'

When the Gardai patrol car picked Rory up, caught in the act as it were, they left him in the back of the car while they viewed the scene of the crime, the Bank of Erin. The bank building directly overlooked the River Leannan. The two officers discovered nothing, absolutely zero. There were no broken windows, no rammed doors, no sign of explosives, no signs of tunnelling on the inside.

Starrett had to admit that tunnelling had been his first thought. How else had Rory Sullivan managed to get in and out of the Bank of Erin without leaving any obvious tell-tale signs. The River Leannan bridge literally ran at right angles up to the front oak door of the bank, which of course meant, to Starrett's way of thinking that the final arch of the bridge, closest to the Bank acted as a natural tunnel which had, as one side, the foundations to the one hundred and thirty year old ivy covered, Georgian, two storey building. Starrett had always considered this to be a vulnerable point in the bank's structure. The bank's manager, the affable Max McDowd, would always cut him off with, 'I'll tell you what, Inspectar,' the 'tar' being the local lazy slant on the word, spoken especially lazy following a few pints, 'if someone wants to try and get in that way, I'll not only provide them with the dynamite, but I'll let them take what they find in the vaults.'

Starrett could never work out if McDowd meant that the bank was impenetrable or that he'd already emptied the vaults himself. Before the conversation went any further, McDowd would add something like: 'Never fear man. I tell you what, let's stop wasting our time onmy bank's security and pay a visit to the Bridge Bar for some liquid refreshment and craic.'

Starrett wasn't convinced about the strength of the bank but on the other hand he was rather partial to a pint or three of the Bridge Bar's finest black and cream. So, for now, nothing more would be mentioned about it.

That was of course until Sullivan's daring and intriguing raid.

Sullivan *had* been caught red-handed but *off* the premises. Starrett even visited the scene of the crime himself and his investigation, including a welly-assisted visit under the bridge, produced absolutely nothing, not even a dickey bird in fact.

Starrett examined the area immediately around the locks of the door for tell-tale scrapings of someone trying to pick the locks. Stranger things had happened, particularly involving Rory Sullivan. But the grand door's two Chubb locks and single triple-roll-bar lock were as good as new. Starrett wasn't too preoccupied about the lack of evidence. He knew full well that once Sullivan felt his back against the wall he would be happy to sing sweetly so everyone could stand back and enjoy his handiwork.

Ever since he had started his illicit career, he'd been gaining a bit of a reputation for finding extraordinary means with which to perpetrate his crimes. He'd spend hours working out elaborate ways for his foolproof, he hoped, escapades. Mostly though he'd stumble and fall at the last fence. Just like the time Sullivan carried out the robbery of Bryson's Electricians. He hid away in the lavatory towards the end of shopping hours and then when the shop closed down, he nipped into the stock room and helped himself before returning to the sanctuary of the toilet. His only problem on that occasion was that Bryson's had one of the most luxurious and comfortable mensroom in Letterkenny so he fell into a deep contented sleep only to be discovered by one of the staff members the following morning. He had the last laugh though. They repossessed their visible goods and let him off with a flea in his ear, but they didn't bother to search deep enough into his shoulder bag where, if they had been more diligent, they'd have found, safely tucked beneath the flask of coffee, and his stash of life-saving Cadbury's milk chocolate bars and banana sandwiches, several other small items *and* the aforementioned Roberts radio; the same Roberts radio that ended up with Cherry, Ramelton's only Doris Day look-alike.

'Look Rory,' Starrett sighed, betraying his impatience, not to mention the thought of his half-finished pint of Guinness still standing on the bar in his corner of the Bridge Bar, 'thanks to Cherry, we've got you on the radio and thanks to Widow Bates we've got you on breaking and entering at the rectory. Listen, I might even be persuaded to see if Mina could suffer a slight attack of amnesia over the knife incident. But there's more, we've got Edmund Davies two doors down and he's singing like a bird about the Bank of Erin job, so why don't you just come clean about it?'

Rory Sullivan rose from his chair and put his hands in his back pockets, Bette Davies style, and walked around the room. Starrett ignored him, for fear of disturbing Rory's thought process.

'Can I plead the fifth, Inspector?' Rory enquired.

'Rory, old son, wrong fecking movie, we're talking more *Lavender Hill Mob* here.'

Forty-five ticks of the second hand later (Starrett counted each and every one of them), Rory said 'It's all about doing your recce, isn't it Inspector?'

'I'll take your word for it Rory, but what I want to know is, how you got in and out of the bank without causing any disturbance?' Starrett asked, now genuinely in awe.

'Easy, com' 'ere I'll tell you. Your regular drinking buddy, McDowd, never drinks with you on a Saturday night does he?'

'Actually, that's right, how did you know that?'

'Recce, Inspector, reconnaissance, that's what successful crime is all about,' Rory boasted, clearly confident as he sat down at the table again. 'And I'll tell you why he never drinks with you on a Saturday night . . .'

'Go on, I'm listening?'

'Well isn't Saturday night the night all married men go out for a drink.'

'Yeah, and?'

'And what happens when married men go out drinking on a Saturday night?'

'I don't know Rory, you tell me,' Starrett said and then posted a late, 'they get drunk?'

'Sometimes, but not all of the times,' Rory said, singsong style, 'but what they do all-of-the-time is that they leave their married wives at home by themselves, don't they?'

This woke up Starrett with a jolt. 'You mean McDowd has been . . .'

'Well, I believe the way he'd put it would be, "distributing a bit of joy around the village."'

'Be jeepers,' Starrett said, grinning from ear to ear, 'and with whom?'

'Well, when you don't drink with your regular drinking buddy on a Saturday night, who do you usually end up drinking with on an average of fifty Saturday nights of the year?'

'Shit, Gary Brittan, you don't mean McDowd and Patsy Brittan. Fecking hell, Gary'll kill him. Kill him dead. The silly . . .'

Starrett's mind raced forward through several scenaros all of them ending with him undertaking massive paperwork. Most of the little scenes he visualised involved the spilling of blood, and one unsettling little scenario even had some of his own blood splattered around several walls.

Somehow he found his way back to the original track. 'But I still don't understand how you . . .'

'OK, I'll spell it out for you. The Brittans never, ever, lock their back door do they? Gary's always boasting that no one is ever going to break into his house and heaven help the first one who does. Well McDowd didn't exactly have to break into the house. Patsy welcomed him with open arms. He always leaves his jacket hanging on the inside of the back door. He dallies for a few minutes in the scullery with Patsy, they enjoy a drink or two and then they go off to find somewhere to recline I imagine. I simply slipped into the scullery, borrowed his keys, scooted down the road and opened the bank door. It's a noisy old door so I used the midnight chimes of the church clock to drown out the loud creaking and then I nipped inside and helped myself.'

'Ah Rory, how'd you ever think you'd get away with it?'

'Well I would have gotten away with it; the only thing I didn't calculate was how heavy the jar of money was. I nearly had a hernia trying to carry it to Eddie's car.'

'Why did you go for the auld jar anyway?'

'Well, I'd worked out how to get into the bank sure enough, but I didn't have time to figure out how to get into the vaults. Anyway I didn't really need to. There's the big jar of money by the door, it's called, the Staff's Pension Plan pot or something, and sure don't some ejits still go and put some of their hard-earned cash in the big bruiser. Some people just need to give a public display of their generous nature and so they'll throw money at anyone who's collecting. Including the not so charitable bank staff. Then one day I happened to overhear one of the bank tellers say to a colleague that there must be over two grand in the jar. And that was more than I needed to set me and Cherry up in America.'

'Ah Rory, you've gone and gotten yourself into in fine mess.'

'Aye, well, you caught me fair and square and you'll tell the judge I came clean with you, won't you?' Rory said and then stopped.

Starrett figured that he'd something else to say so he just continued to look at the criminal, nodding his head back and forth trying to encourage the final words out of him.

Eventually Rory Sullivan spoke. 'Hey,' he said fighting back emotion, 'I suppose you better tell Cherry not to bother waiting around for me.'

But that wasn't that.

Inspector Starrett proved that the midnight hour is not as much the end of one day as it is the beginning of the next. Some could call his action good-natured; others would call it taking evasive action to avoid a civil riot about the streets of Ramelton.

Starrett proceeded to take a statement from Rory Sullivan. Yes, you could say that he even coaxed Sullivan to using particular words for the statement.

There were none more surprised than Rory when twenty minutes later he signed a statement saying in effect that he, Rory Sullivan, was on his way home from the Bridge Bar when he saw something suspicious occurring around the door of the Bank of Erin. He spotted someone coming out carrying something that appeared very heavy and he shouted across to the stranger. The stranger bolted, dropping the jar and a set of keys to the ground. Surprisingly the glass didn't shatter into a million smithereens. Rory went over, took the keys and, with great difficulty, lifted the jar. He was in the process of returning the jar to the Bank when the squad car came upon him. Clearly the strain of lifting the weight confused his bearings, so that it appeared he was actually moving away from the bank rather than towards it at the time he was apprehended. Obviously the Gardai officers *mistakenly* thought Rory was the culprit. But, the statement claimed, he just hadn't had time to return the jar to the bank and lock the door.

Inspector Starrett not only stated, for the record, that he unconditionally accepted Rory's statement, but he also cajoled the Bank of Erin and McDowd, the bank manager, into giving Rory a reward of two grand for saving the bank further loss. Starrett didn't recognise the dollar currency, so he ensured Sullivan was paid his bounty in Irish pounds. Which was how, four weeks later, Rory Sullivan and Cheryl Mary Teresa Kavanagh where sitting on board a Pan Am flight from Shannon Airport to New York City with four thousand dollars to spare.

On Starrett's recommendation, they immediately continued to New Jersey and met up with a colleague of his who made sure Sullivan enrolled as a New Jersey State Trooper. Two years passed and Rory graduated with honours. Many years and scars later, he joined the exclusive Colonel's Row when he became their Superintendent, proving for once and for all that he could use his brain to ensure his fame and fortune on the *right* side of the law.

To this day he still has his first American dollar. It's now framed and has pride of place amongst the awards, diplomas and celebrity photographs busily littered on the wall behind his desk.

Oh yeah, Starrett was happy as well. With Rory out of the way he found he'd a lot more time on his hands to hang out at his favourite retreat, the Bridge Bar.

MARTIN EDWARDS

TEST DRIVE

People are like cars. Since Patrick told me this, I can't get it out of my mind. That's one of his gifts. He comes out with something that makes no sense at first, but the moment he explains, you start to see the world through new eyes. Patrick's eyes. He said people are like cars that day in the showroom, the first time we'd met for years. A throwaway line, but when my eyebrows lifted, he jerked a thumb towards the forecourt. Towards the executive saloons and SUVs gleaming in the sunlight, a line of vehicles as immaculate as soldiers on parade.

'You think I'm joking? Come on, Terry, you work with cars all day, every day, you must see I'm right.' He flicked a speck from the cuff of his jacket. Armani, of course. 'Take a look at that muscular roadster. A mean machine, if ever I saw one. When that beast growls, you'd better watch out.'

I laughed. Same old Patrick. People always laughed when he was around. He never needed encouragement and now he was in full flow.

'And the model with lissom lines over there?

Chic and elegant, but beware. You can't put your trust in her.'

'Like Olivia Lumb,' I said, joining in. Out of the blue, our old friendship was being rekindled. 'Remember warning me off that night at the Bali, telling me I'd do better with Sarah-Jane? I wonder whatever happened to Olivia.'

Something changed in Patrick's expression, as if suddenly his skin had been stretched too tight over his cheekbones. But he kept smiling. Even as a teenager, I'd envied the whiteness of his teeth but now they shone with all the brilliance that cosmetic dentistry can bestow. When he spoke, his voice hadn't lost a degree of warmth.

'Matter of fact, Terry, I married her.'

'Oh, right.'

My face burned for a few moments, but what had I said? Olivia was beautiful, he'd fallen on his feet. As usual. Years ago, his nickname was Lucky Patrick, everyone called him that, even those who hated him. And a few kids did hate him, the sour and bitter ones who were jealous that he only had to snap his fingers and any girl would come running. Olivia Lumb, eh? After Patrick himself told me that she was bad news, the night of the leavers' disco?

Frankly, I'd always thought she was out of my league, but that night a couple of drinks emboldened me. When I confided in Patrick that I meant to ask her for a dance, he warned me she was heartless and selfish. Not that she cared so well even for herself. She went on eating binges and then made herself sick. She'd scratched at her wrists with her brother's pen-knife, she'd swallowed her mum's sleeping pills and been rushed into hospital to have her stomach pumped. She dosed up with Prozac because she couldn't cope, she was the ultimate mixed-up kid.

Afterwards, I spent the evening in a corner, talking non-stop and cracking jokes to cheer up Sarah-Jane, whose crush on Patrick he'd encouraged, then failed to reciprocate. Six weeks later I proposed and she said yes. I owed so much to Patrick; his words of warning, and his playing hard-to-get with Sarah-Jane had changed my life.

I mustered a man-to-man grin. 'Lucky Patrick, eh?'

'Yes,' Patrick said. 'Lucky me.'

'She was the most gorgeous girl in the class,' I said quickly. 'Obviously I never had a chance. You did me a favour, it avoided any embarrassment. So you finished up together? Well, congratulations.'

'Know something, Terry? You really haven't changed.'

'You don't think so?' I took it as a compliment, but with Patrick you could never be quite sure. Even at seventeen, at eighteen, his wit used to sting.

'Course not,' he assured me. 'A snappy mover, always smart and reliable, even if your steering is a bit erratic, lets you down every now and then.'

I wasn't offended. No point in taking umbrage with Patrick. You could never win an argument, he shifted his ground with the speed of a Ferrari. Besides, he was right. Occasionally I do try too hard, I suppose. I go over the top when I'm trying to close a difficult sale. I take corners too fast when I'm trying out a new sports car. I'm one endorsement away from losing my licence, I know I ought to take more care.

'It's great to see you again,' I said.

I meant it, and not only because he fancied buying our top-of-the-range executive saloon. The sale would guarantee enough commission to earn the award for representative of the month and win a weekend break for two in Rome, no expense spared. Just the pick-me-up Sarah-Jane needed. More even than that, I'd missed Patrick. We'd hung around together at sixth form college. Both of us were bored with the academic stuff, neither of us wanted to doss around at uni for another three years, simply to help the government massage the employment figures. We yearned to get out into the real world and start earning serious money. I learned a lot from Patrick, he was like a smart older brother, although there were only six months between us. He talked about going into sales and that's where I got the idea for my own career. But I didn't need telling that he'd climbed the greasy pole much faster. The Swiss watch and the cream, crisply tailored suit spoke louder than any words.

Fixing on his Ray-Ban Aviators, he nodded at the forecourt. 'Let's have a closer look, shall we?'

'You'll love her.'

We strolled into the sun, side by side, just like old times. Showing Patrick the features, and as he put the car through its paces on the test drive, I felt confidence surging through me, revving up my engine. This was what I did, it wasn't just selling cars, it was selling dreams. I knew the brochure by heart, the phrases came spinning out as if I'd just thought of them.

The style is very emotive . . . good looks based on clear reasoning . . . touch the sports mode console button for a yet more spirited ride . . . sensuous curves of the door panels and dashboard . . . suspension, chassis and engine all operate in perfect harmony . . . the precise synergy . . . the 15-speaker premium system wraps your senses in rich, true to life, beautiful surround sound with concert hall acoustics . . . intelligent thermal control seat heating . . . ultrasonic sensors for the science of perfect parking . . . real-time enabled DVD-based satellite navigation . . . twin tail pipe baffles lend a sporting accent . . . potent, passionate, state-of-the-art . . . blending priceless power with complete control . . . not so much the finest car in its class as a definitive lifestyle statement.

They are the poets of the twenty-first century in my opinion, these men (or maybe women?) who script the luxury car brochures. When I borrow their words, for

177

a few minutes I feel like an actor, declaiming Shakespeare on the stage. And guess what Shakespeare would be writing if he was alive today? Not stodgy plays about tempests or Julius Caesar, that's for sure.

'So what do you think?' I asked as we pulled back on to the forecourt. 'Isn't it simply the smoothest ride you've ever known?'

'Yeah, yeah.' Patrick's long fingers grazed the leather upholstery. For some strange reason, a picture jostled into my head, an image of him stroking Olivia's pale face while he murmured to her. 'Lovely mover. So what sort of deal are we talking for cash upfront?'

I clasped his arm. 'For you, I'm sure we can sort out something very special.'

He smiled at me in a hungry way. Like a fat man contemplating an unwrapped chocolate bar.

'You've made a good salesman, Terry, one of the best. I can picture you with other customers, teasing them like an angler with a fish on the line.'

His words cheered me as we discussed figures. I knew Patrick was a skilled negotiator and I did my best to show him how much I too had learned. Working in tandem with bernard, my sales director, like a comic and a sad-faced straight man, I utilised every – I nearly said, 'trick in the book' – *stratagem* to avoid taking too much of a bite out of our profit margin. It wasn't exactly a success, because half an hour later we were signing up to the biggest discount I'd ever agreed. The commission was much less than I'd anticipated, but even Bernard was no match for Patrick. I could see why my old friend was no longer in sales. He'd made enough to set up his own business. Financial services. While Bernard was making a nervous call to seek head office authorisation, Patrick whispered that he could give me a fantastic opportunity with tax-efficient shelters for my investments. He'd be happy to design a personal balanced-risk strategy for me, as a sort of thank-you for my candour as well as the flexibility on the price of his car.

As we said goodbye, I joked that he'd cost Sarah-Jane and me a weekend in Rome. He smiled and asked after her.

'Lovely girl, you did well there. That cascading red hair, I remember it well. Lot of firepower under the bonnet, eh?'

His cheeky wink wasn't in the least embarrassing. Far from it: his approval of my wife sent a shiver of pleasure down my spine. For years I'd shrunk from the reflection that he'd spurned her advances in the months leading up to the leavers' disco. I hated thinking of her – or of myself, for that matter – as second best. She hadn't hidden her bitterness; that was why we hadn't kept in touch with Patrick. A reluctant sacrifice, but what choice did I have? Besides, she and I were enough for each other.

I contented myself with a smirk of satisfaction. 'Let's just say I don't have any complaints.'

'I bet you don't, you sly dog. How is she?'

'Fine, absolutely fine. Well . . .'

Honesty compelled me not to leave it there. I told him about the miscarriage and his face became grave. How sad, he said, and then he told me that Olivia didn't want children yet, she wasn't ready and that was fine by him. The fact he was taking me into his confidence at all was flattering; so was the way he talked about Sarah-Jane. It was as though her wellbeing meant more to him than I had ever realised.

'Remember me to her, now, don't forget. Tell her Lucky Patrick was asking after her.'

'I'll do that,' I said, glowing. This man was a success, he had money, status, a beautiful wife, but he hadn't lost his generosity of spirit. How much I'd missed his friendship. 'Let me give you a ring when the paperwork's sorted.'

'Thanks.' He gripped my hand. 'It's been good, Terry. I heard you'd done well, but I didn't know quite how well. We ought to keep in touch.'

'Too right.' I must have sounded as eager as a teenager, but it didn't matter. He and I went back a long way. 'Maybe we could get together again sometime.'

'The four of us? Fantastic idea, it'll be just like old times.'

It wasn't precisely what I had in mind. Olivia and Sarah-Jane as well? Not like old times at all, strictly speaking. But it was just a figure of speech, I knew what he meant. Time's a great healer.

✦   ✦   ✦

'I don't think so,' Sarah-Jane said. 'I really don't think so.'

She was perched on a kitchen stool, wearing a grubby housecoat. I'd always liked the way she took care of herself, it's important to have pride in your appearance. But since the miscarriage, she'd become moody and irritable and didn't seem to care about anything. The dishwasher had broken down and she hadn't bothered to call out the repairman, let alone tackle the mountain of unwashed crockery in the sink.

'You mooned after him at one time,' I reminded her.

'That was then,' she said. 'Anyway, I finished up with you, didn't I?'

'Don't make it sound like a prison sentence,' I joked, wanting to lift her spirits. 'Listen, it's just one evening, all right? We're not talking a dinner party, you don't have to entertain them. We'll meet in a bar, so we're not under any obligation to ask them back here sometime. You don't have to see him again.'

'But you'll keep seeing him.'

'What's wrong with that? He's smart, he's intelligent. Most of all, he's a friend.'

She cast her eyes to the heavens. 'There's just no arguing with you, is there? OK, OK, you win.' A long sigh. 'Salesmen Reunited, huh?'

I reached for her, tried to undo the top button of the housecoat, but she flapped me away, as if swatting a fly.

'I told you last night, I need some personal space.'

Of course, I didn't push my luck. During the past couple of months she'd cried so easily. Once, in a temper, she'd slapped my face over something and nothing. I needed to give her time, just like it said in the problem pages of the magazines she devoured. She read a lot about life-coaching and unlocking her personal potential. The column-writers promised to give her the key to happiness, but she was still looking for the right door to open. Fair enough, I could do 'patient and caring'. Besides, she'd agreed to see Patrick again. I could show my old friend exactly what he'd missed.

Sarah-Jane may have had mixed feelings about meeting up with Patrick and Olivia, but when it came to the crunch, she didn't let me down. For the first time in an age, we were hitting the town and she summoned up the enthusiasm to put on her make-up and wear the slinky new dress I'd bought by way of encouragement. We couldn't mourn forever, that was my philosophy. We had to move on.

The evening went even better than I'd dared to hope. Patrick was on his very best form and funny anecdotes streamed from him like spray from a fountain. In front of the girls, he congratulated me on my shrewd negotiating techniques. I thought I had the gift of the blarney, he said, but

Terry knows his cars inside out, you know he can torque for England.

I hadn't seen Sarah-Jane laugh like that in a long time. As for Olivia, she'd always been silent and mysterious and nothing had changed. She spoke in enigmatic monosyllables and paid no more attention to me than when we were both eighteen. I stole a glance at her wrist and saw that it was scarred. The marks were red and recent, not the legacy of a long-ago experiment in self-harm. Hurriedly, I averted my gaze. Her own eyes locked on Patrick all night, though it didn't seem to make him feel uncomfortable. It was as if he expected nothing less.

Sarah-Jane did her best to make conversation. 'I'm longing for the day when the doctor signs me off and I can get back to work.'

'Terry tells me you work for an estate agency,' Patrick said. 'I keep trying to persuade Olivia to do a bit of secretarial work to help me out in the business since my last PA left. But it doesn't suit.'

Olivia finished her pina colada and gave a faraway smile. 'I look after the house.'

'I expect it's a mansion,' I said cheerily.

'Seven bedrooms, five reception, a cellar and a granny annexe,' Patrick said. 'Not that we've got a granny, obviously.' He mentioned the address; I knew the house, although I'd never seen it. A long curving drive wandered away between massive rhododendron bushes on its journey to the front door.

Olivia's flowing dark hair was even silkier than I remembered, though there still wasn't a spot of colour in her delicate cheeks. I couldn't help recalling how I'd worshipped her from the back of the class when I should have been listening to the teacher's words of wisdom on some writer whose name I forget. He used to say that all animals are equal, but some are more equal than others. It's the only snippet from those lessons that has stuck in my mind. Of course, it's true we don't live in a fair and just world, no sense in moping about it, you just have to do the best that you can for yourself. Beauty is like money, it isn't divided out to us all in neat proportions. How many women can match the elegance of Olivia Lumb? But I told myself I was more fortunate than Patrick. Looks matter, but a man wants more from his wife.

As Patrick might have said, Olivia was as svelte as the sportiest coupe in the dealership, but never mind. In the early years of our marriage, Sarah-Jane's handling had been tenacious, her performance superb. Of course, nothing lasts forever. It's as true of people as it is of cars. I'd hung my hopes on our starting a family, and losing the baby had devastated both of us. And then, in the course of a single evening at the bar, I saw Sarah-Jane coming back to life, like Sleeping Beauty awoken from a deep slumber. I had Patrick to thank for giving my wife back to me.

★   ★   ★

For both of us, making friends with Patrick again turned out to be a sort of elixir. He gave me plenty of inside advice on the markets. Tips that made so much sense I didn't hesitate in shifting the money my parents had left me from the building society account into the shelters he recommended. As he pointed out, even keeping cash under the floorboards was far from risk-free. After all, if you were missing out on high dividends and extra performance, you were taking an investment decision, and not a smart one.

As for Sarah-Jane, her eyes regained their sparkle, her cheeks their fresh glow. When I teased her that she hadn't even wanted to set eyes on Patrick after these years, she had to accept I'd been proved right. She was even happy for us to host a barbecue on our new patio, so that we could reciprocate after a dinner party at Patrick's lovely home. Olivia didn't cook the meal, her household management seemed to consist of hiring posh outside caterers. It didn't matter. I sat next to another of Patrick's clients and spent an enjoyable evening extolling the virtues of the 475 while Patrick entertained Sarah-Jane with tales of double-dealing in the murky world of financial services. People talk about dishonest car salesmen, and fair enough, but the money men are a hundred times worse if Patrick's gleeful anecdotes about his business competitors were to be believed.

We asked Bernard and his wife along to the barbecue and it wasn't until we'd guzzled the last hot dog that I found myself together with Olivia. As usual, she'd said little or nothing. I'd drunk a lot of strong red wine, Tesco's finest, and probably I talked too long about how difficult it had been to lay the patio flags in just the right way. She kept looking over my shoulder towards Patrick, who was sharing a joke with Sarah-Jane and our guests. Her lack of attention was worse than irritating, it was downright rude. I found myself wanting to get under her skin, to provoke her into some sort of response. Any response.

'I ought to make a confession,' I said, wiping a smear of tomato ketchup off my cheek with a paper napkin. 'Ease my conscience, you know? This has been preying on my mind for years.'

'Oh yes?' She raised a languid eyebrow.

'Yes,' I said firmly. 'It's about you and me.'

She contrived the faintest of frowns, but a frond of Virginia creeper, trailing from the pergola, seemed to cause her more concern. She flicked it out of her face and murmured, 'You and me?'

I covered my mouth to conceal a hiccup, but I'm not sure she even noticed. 'Well, I don't know whether you ever realised, when we were in the sixth form together I mean, but I had a thing about you. Quite a serious thing.'

'Oh,' she said. That was all.

I'd hoped to intrigue her. Over-optimistic, obviously. Never mind, I'd started, so I would finish. 'You're a very attractive woman, Olivia. Patrick's a lucky fellow.'

'You think so?'

I leaned towards her, stumbling for a moment, but quickly regaining my balance. 'Yes, I do think so. He thinks people are like cars. In my book, you're a high-performance model.'

She peered into my eyes, as if seeing them for the first time. 'Your wife's prettier than I remembered. I might have known.'

That was all she said. *I might have known?* I stared back at her, puzzled, but before I could ask her what she meant, a strong arm wrapped itself around my shoulder and Patrick's voice was in my ear.

'Now then, Terry. You'll be making me jealous, monopolising my lovely wife all the time.'

I could smell the alcohol on his breath, as well as a pungent after-shave. And I could hear Sarah-Jane's tinkling laughter as he spoke again.

'Always did have an eye for a pretty lady, didn't you?'

The next time we got together, for a meal at an Indian restaurant a stone's throw from the showroom, Patrick offered Sarah-Jane a job as his PA. I'm not sure how it came about. One moment they were talking idly about her plans to return to work the following week, the next Patrick was waxing lyrical about how someone with her administrative skills could play a vital role in his business. He needed a right hand woman to rely on, he said, and who better than an old friend?

I glanced at Olivia. She was sitting very still, saying nothing, just twisting her napkin into tight little knots, as if it was a make-believe garrotte. Her gaze was fixed on her husband, as usual, as if the rest of us did not exist.

I assumed that Sarah-Jane would turn him down flat. In the estate agency, she was deputy to the branch manager and stood in for him when he was on holiday. There was a decent pension scheme, too. But to my amazement, she positively basked in his admiration and said she'd love to accept. It would be a challenge, she said merrily, to keep Patrick on the straight and narrow. Before I could say a word, Patrick was summoning the waiter and demanding champagne. One look at my wife's face convinced me it was a done deal. Even though nothing had been said about salary, let alone sick pay or holiday entitlements.

At least I need not have worried on those counts. Within a couple of days, Patrick hand-delivered her letter of appointment. The terms were generous; in fact, her basic rate was a tad higher than mine. When I pointed this out, Patrick was firm.

'I'm sure she's worth it, Terry. And to be honest, I'm a demanding boss. I work long hours and spend a lot of time travelling. I'll need Sarah-Jane by my side. She'll be my right hand, so I'm prepared to pay a premium.'

I shot my wife a glance. 'I don't think . . .'

'It'll be fine,' she said, patting me on the hand. 'A new environment, a fresh start. I can't wait.'

'But don't you think . . . I mean, after having so long at home . . . ?'

'I'm ready,' she said. 'I've gathered my strength. You're sweet to me, darling, but I don't expect to be wrapped in cotton wool for the rest of my life.'

'Don't worry,' Patrick said to me. 'I'll take good care of her.'

I can't put my finger on one single incident that caused me to believe that Patrick and Sarah-Jane were having an affair. My brain didn't suddenly crash into gear. The suspicion grew over time. Like when you begin to hear a faint knocking each time your well-loved car rounds a corner at speed. At first you don't take any notice, after a while you can't ignore the noise altogether, but you persuade yourself that it's nothing, really, that if you don't panic, sooner or later it will go away of its own accord. But it never goes away, of course, not ever.

Little things, insignificant in themselves, began to add up. She started to wear raunchy underwear again, just as she had done in those exciting days when we first got together. To begin with, I was thrilled. It was a sign she was putting the miscarriage behind her. But when I turned to her in bed at night, she continued to push me away. She was tired, she explained, the new job was taking so much out of her. It seemed fair enough, but when I suggested that it was unreasonable for Patrick to propose that she accompanied him for a week-long trip to Edinburgh, to meet people from a life

189

company he did business with, she brushed my protests aside. The long hours came with the territory, she said. Patrick had given her a wonderful opportunity. She could not, would not let him down.

Even when she was at home, she was never off the mobile, talking to him in muffled tones while I busied myself in another room. Client business was highly confidential, she reminded me when I ventured a mild complaint. I suggested several times that the four of us might go out for another meal together, but it was never convenient. Olivia wasn't well, apparently. Although Sarah-Jane was discreet, I gathered that her old rival was seeing a psychiatrist regularly. I said that maybe Patrick would want to spend more time with his own wife, but Sarah-Jane said I didn't understand. There was a reason why my old friend buried himself in his work. He didn't need the money, it was all about having a safety valve. A means of escape from the pressures of being married to a neurotic cow.

One night Sarah-Jane announced that she would have to up at the crack of dawn the next morning to catch the early flight to Paris. Patrick thought the European market was full of opportunities and they were going to spend forty-eight hours there. Putting out feelers, making contacts.

'Are you taking the camera?'

She wrinkled her nose. 'Won't have time for that. You don't realise, Terry, just what it's like. This is high-powered stuff, but it's hard work. Long meetings in offices, talking business over lunch and dinner. One hotel is much like another, it's scarcely a tourist trip.'

'Your mobile always seems to be busy or switched off when I call.'

'Exactly. It's non-stop, I can tell you. I really don't want to be disturbed. And don't fret about the phone bill, by the way. Patrick pays for everything, of course he does.'

An hour later, her mobile rang again. At one time I'd liked the 'I Will Survive' ringtone, all of a sudden I hated it. While she retreated to the kitchen to take the call, closing the door behind her, I did something rather dishonourable. I crept up the stairs in my stockinged feet and opened up the suitcase she'd been packing. There were new shoes I didn't recognise, clothes with designer labels that I'd never seen before. Along with furry handcuffs, a velvet blindfold and a whip.

When at last she came off the phone, I didn't say a word about what I'd discovered. Only for a few seconds had I contemplated a confrontation. But I couldn't face it. Suppose I challenged her and she admitted everything? Said that she loved Patrick and that, compared to him, I was nothing?

How could I deny it? Lucky Patrick, he won every time.

All through their absence in Paris, I felt numb. At the showroom, I was going through the motions, scarcely caring when a customer reckoned he could beat my price by going to the dealership on the other side of town. One lunchtime, when Bernard passed me the latest copy of *What Car?* I left it unopened on the table while I nibbled at a chicken tikka sandwich and stared moodily through the glass at the drizzle spattering the windscreens of the saloons on the forecourt. Bernard asked if I was all right and my reply was a non-committal grunt.

Of course I wasn't all right, my wife and best friend were betraying me. Worse, they were treating me like a fool. At once I saw that really, it had always been like this. Patrick used people and discarded them like he used and discarded his cars.

And I meant to do something about it.

I still hadn't decided what to do when Patrick dropped Sarah-Jane off at home that evening. I'd seen his car pulling up outside the gate and I'd wandered down the path, to greet them. Good old Terry, I thought to myself as I forced a good-natured wave. Always reliable.

'Good trip?'

'Fine,' Sarah-Jane said. I don't think I'd ever seen her red hair so lustrous, her skin so delicate. 'Hard work, obviously.'

'No peace for the wicked,' Patrick confirmed with his customary grin. 'I don't know what I'd do without my trusty PA . . .'

'Taking things down for you?' I interrupted, with as much jocularity as I could muster.

'Absolutely.'

He roared with laughter, but out of the corner of my eye, I saw Sarah-Jane start. When she thought I wasn't looking, she shot Patrick a cautionary glance, but he wasn't fazed. The worm – I *knew* he thought this – was incapable of turning.

In bed that night, for the first time in an age, she reached for me. I sighed and said I was tired and turned away. Even though I still wanted her so much, I would not touch her again until I knew she was mine forever.

The truth dawned on me a couple of days later. I couldn't sort this on my own. I needed help, and only one person could provide it. But I'd need all my sales skills. Before I lost my nerve, I picked up the phone and rang the number of Patrick's house. I held for a full minute before someone answered.

'Hello?'

'Olivia? It's me. Terry. We need to talk.'

'What about?' Her voice was faint. I could tell she was at a low ebb.

'I think you know.'

There was a long pause before she said, 'So you finally worked it out.'

'I suppose you think I'm an idiot, a poor naïve idiot?'

I could picture her shrugging. 'Well . . .'

'Like I said, we ought to talk.'

'What for? You seriously imagine I'm going to cry on your shoulder? Or let you cry on mine?'

'I want you to come here, to the showroom.' I wasn't going to be swayed by her scorn. Suddenly, I had never felt so masterful. 'We have to do something.'

Another pause. 'Do something?'

'I'll see you at reception at three o'clock. Pretend you're a customer. I'll take you on a test drive and we can decide.'

Looking out through the glass windows as Olivia arrived in her Fiat runabout, Bernard recognised her and shot me a sharp glance. I smiled and said, 'I finally persuaded Patrick to cough up for his wife's new car. She was ready for a change.'

He raised his eyebrows. 'Oh yes? Well, take care, young man. She's a loose cannon, that one.'

'The two of us go back years,' I said. 'I can handle her. No worries.'

Five minutes later, Olivia was at the wheel of a new fiery orange Supermini. Lovely little motor, alloy wheels, sill extensions and a tiny spoiler above the tailgate, plus bags of equipment for the money. From the styling, you would never guess it was designed in Korea. But this afternoon, I wasn't interested in selling a car.

'Sarah-Jane isn't the first, is she?' I asked, as we paused at a red light.

'So you finally realised?'

'This is different from the others, isn't it?'

'What makes you think that?' Her voice was empty of emotion. I didn't have a clue what was going on in her head.

'Because I know Sarah-Jane. She lost him once, she won't let him slip away again. It's only now that I see the truth. She's been grieving for him for years. He was what she wanted, not me.'

She kept her eyes on the road. 'Perhaps you're right. Perhaps this is different.'

'You've picked up hints?'

'The others never lasted this long. I always knew he would come back to me in the end. This time . . .'

We moved on to the dual carriageway, picking up speed as we moved out of town.

'What can we do about it?' I asked. 'How can we stop them?'

'Is that what you want, to stop them?'

'Of course. Does that surprise you?'

'He could always twist you around his little finger, Terry. I thought – you were willing to put up with it. As long as you thought he was making money on your investments, as long as he kept flattering you, made you feel like a big man.'

It wasn't the longest speech, but then, I don't think I'd ever heard her put more than three sentences together at one time before.

'I don't care about the money,' I said hotly.

'That's just as well, because there won't be as

much for you as you'd like to think. The business is going down the tube.'

'What?'

Her knuckles were white against the steering wheel. 'He's always been lazy and now he doesn't have time for anyone or anything but your wife. The creditors are pressing, Terry. Better watch out, or they'll take your money as well as his.'

I didn't speak again for a couple of minutes, I just gazed out of the window, watching the pylons in the fields, their arms out-stretched as if denying guilt. Until then, I suppose I'd had pangs of conscience. I'm not a naturally violent man. In principle, I think it's right to turn the other cheek. But there are limits, and I had raced past mine.

'You can stop him,' I said eventually. 'That's why I needed to talk to you, Olivia. Not to weep and wail. I just want an end to it.'

Ideas were shifting inside my head, even as I sat beside her. I hadn't been thinking straight. I'd thought: *what if she kills herself?* It wasn't nice, but looking at it another way, you might say it was only a question of time before Olivia stopped crying for help and finally went all the way. Imagining the headlines gave me grim satisfaction. *Faithless financier finds wife dead. Betrayed woman could not take any more.* It would finish everything between Sarah-Jane and Patrick. Their relationship would be tainted for all time. I knew enough of him to be sure he would want to get out of it, make a new beginning with someone else. Someone else's wife, most likely.

But maybe there was a different solution, leaving less to chance. Bernard's words lodged in my brain. He was no fool, he had Olivia's number. She *was* a loose cannon, they didn't come any looser. What if she was fired at Patrick himself?

Signs were scattered along the grass verge warning of police speed enforcement, pictures of so-called safety cameras and a board bragging about how many poor old motorists had been caught exceeding the limit in the past six months. None of it seemed to register with Olivia. The yellow camera wasn't hidden from view, there was no panda car lurking in the bushes, she had every chance to slow down before we reached the white lines on the road, but far from easing off the accelerator, she put her foot down. We leapt past the camera and it flashed twice in anger. I couldn't help wincing, but at the same time I felt blood rushing to my head. This was a sort of liberation. I was manoeuvring Olivia as if she was a car to be squeezed into a tight parking space. And Patrick's luck was about to run dry.

'He deserves to suffer,' she said.

'Yes.'

She tossed me a glance. It was gone in a moment, but for the first time since I'd known her, I thought she was actually *seeing* me. But I still couldn't guess what she thought about what she saw.

'Olivia loves the special edition,' I told Bernard. 'I offered her the chance to take it home, try it out for twenty-four hours before she signs on the dotted line. The insurance is fine, she's not a time-waster, trust me.'

He gave me the sort of look you give delinquents on street corners, but said nothing. No way could he guess the thoughts jockeying inside my head. My voice was as calm as a priest's, yielding no hint of the excitement churning in my guts.

I had made a sale, the biggest of my career.

Olivia had told Patrick she'd be out shopping all day. She was sure he'd have seized the chance, taken Sarah-Jane home so that the two of them could romp in the comfort of the kingsize bed. She was going to drive straight home and catch them out.

What weapon would she choose? From our visit to their lovely house, I remembered the array of knives kept in a wooden block on the breakfast bar. And there was a cast-iron doorstop, a croquet mallet, the possibilities were endless.

Pictures floated through my mind as I shuffled through price lists for gadgets and accessories. Patrick's damaged face peeping from out of the covering sheet in the mortuary. Solemn policemen, shaking their heads. Sarah-Jane, pale and contrite, kissing my cheek. Whispering the question: could I ever forgive her?

Of course I could. I'm not a cruel or bitter man. I'd promise her that we would work at the marriage. Pick up the pieces.

Patrick was right about one thing, I decided. People *are* like cars. They just need the right driver.

My mobile rang. I keyed *Answer* and heard Olivia. Breathless, triumphant.

'So easy, Terry, it was so easy. They were on the drive outside the porch. Kissing, they only had eyes for each other.'

'You – did it?'

She laughed, a high, hysterical peal. 'It's like nothing else. The feeling as your wheels go over someone. Crushing out the life – *squish, squish*. The screams urge you on. I felt so empowered, so much in control. But I reversed over the body, just to make sure.'

'So . . .'

I heard her gasp and then another voice on the line. A voice I never wanted to hear again. Frantic, horrified.

'Terry, you put her up to this, you bastard. You jealous, murdering bastard.'

It was Patrick, lucky Patrick.

My mind stalled, useless as an old banger. I couldn't take this in, couldn't comprehend what Olivia had done. If Patrick was alive – what had happened to Sarah-Jane?

ADRIAN MCKINTY

THE ONLY EASY DAY WAS YESTERDAY

D ust rose in vortices over the mosque, mingling with the prayers coming from the loudspeaker on the mud brick minaret; but unlike the invocations of surrender, the spirals reached not as far as heaven, nor even as high as the muezzin's tower, instead becoming quickly absorbed into the low orange sky made up of the fine sand of the *khamseen*.

The Americans covered their faces and, following the guide, were soon on the very edge of the desert.

Fused shades of yellow and green blurred into desiccated creams and greys. The landscape empty now but for a few rocks and smaller stones and over the hard ground a thin layer of migrating sand. No sign of man or beast and to the west and south only emptiness that stretched for another thousand miles and more.

The cold *khamseen* wind had been blowing since they got here and some of the Americans grumbled that they were underdressed. Who knew Egypt could be like this, even in February?

Mitchell had a scarf over his mouth and a wool hat on his head. *He* knew.

Taking up the rear he joined a semicircle around the guide who had been talking the whole time. Because of the howling wind, no one had really heard a word. Now that he had stopped in the lee of the step pyramid they could hear properly.

'. . . the pyramids of Sakkhara are of course very different than those of the more well known examples on the Gizan plateau. Older, with none of the precision architecture we associate with Giza. But even so if you look north it is still very striking. This is the best picture we are going to get today. A real Kodak moment.'

Some of the party took photographs of the step pyramids among the wasteland.

Mitchell did not.

He had seen the pyramids before.

He hobbled over to the guide, a thin, moustachioed man with a white shirt and a hooded anorak.

'I'm not feeling well,' Mitchell said.

'Is it the same as yesterday?' the guide asked without concern.

'Yeah.'

'Do you wish to go back to the bus?' the guide wondered and discreetly looked the elderly American up and down. Mitchell could tell what he was thinking. He had seen the contempt on his face at every glance in the minibus mirror. A contempt hidden sometimes by obsequiousness.

None of the Americans were in what you would call good shape. They were fat, many obese and all – in the Egyptian's eyes – loud and vulgar. They weren't even particularly interested in what he had been telling them. Few of them thought of this as a 'trip of a lifetime' to be savoured at every second. These were retired and quite wealthy people who had the money to enjoy many of these trips. Egypt was just one more country and experience to be knocked off.

But Mitchell seemed an unlikely candidate to have taken ill so early on the tour. He was one of the youngest in the group. He was only about sixty-two or sixty-three and while he couldn't be described as lithe he certainly wasn't as portly as the others. He was six foot tall, perhaps two hundred pounds. He still had most of his grey hair and if the guide had been more astute he would have seen the alert cold-ness in Mitchell's blue grey eyes, and maybe he wouldn't have been so blasé about him.

In any case, definitely the fittest and youngest looking of the lot of them.

The guide shook his head.

It was always the ones you least expected.

That ninety-year-old crone from Alabama would probably be perky all the way to Luxor.

'I'm too sick for the bus,' Mitchell said.

'What do you want me to do?' the guide asked on the verge of impertinence.

'Nothing. I'll get a taxi back to the hotel,' Mitchell said.

The guide nodded.

'It should be no more than ten Egyptian pounds. Fix the price before you leave,' the guide said.

Mitchell nodded.

'Thank you,' he said.

Mitchell walked to the car park through the long line of hawkers and hangers on crying out for *baksheesh*. The children were the worst. He distributed a few coins and made it through the rank of underpowered Fiats that were the workhorses of Cairo's taxi fleet.

The ride took him on a slight mystery tour through the southern suburbs and Mitchell didn't even bother to argue when the driver demanded an extortionate twenty Egyptian pounds.

When he walked into the reception of the Marriot, Sandy, the pencil thin, brassy, blonde, Saga Tours rep was waiting for him.

'Mr Mitchell, I was sorry to hear that you had taken ill again. Do you want me to get you a doctor?' she asked.

'Nah. I know what it is. Doc said I shouldn't have come. Prostate.'

Sandy's botox-tight forty-something face tried and failed to frown.

'Your prostate? Are you sure? Perhaps we should send out for a doctor,' she suggested.

Mitchell shook his head.

'I'm sure. I knew it might be a problem. Doc advised me against coming out.'

Sandy nodded and made a mental note. Lying

about a pre-existing medical condition would certainly violate any rebate.

'I'm going to call it quits. Seen what I came to see anyway,' Mitchell said.

Sandy's head bobbed up and down like an apple on a stick.

'If you are going to need treatment it might be better to fly back to Europe rather than risk infection in a Cairo hospital,' she said helpfully.

'That's what I was thinking. If you book me on a flight to London tonight I would be most appreciative. Don't worry about the rest of the tour. It can go on without me. Like I say, I've seen the pyramids and that's enough,' Mitchell said.

Sandy nodded. Perhaps that would be best. Certainly one less old codger to worry about.

'I'll try and find you a flight,' she said breezily.

A little too breezily. Mitchell didn't want there to be any delay. He took out his wallet.

'There's an eight p.m. flight to London tonight. First Class please, here's my card,' he said giving her his American Express Platinum Club, which he figured would be the one she'd be most impressed by.

She nodded and went off to make the arrangements. When she was gone he ignored the elevator and took the stairs four flights to his room.

When he got in, he had a shower, towelled off, and was about to call Margaret when there was a knock at the door.

He pulled on a robe and opened the door.

The hotel manager, an older Egyptian man about his own age. Elegant guy, dressed in a three piece.

'Mr Mitchell, I regret to hear of your illness, is there anything I can do for you?'

Mitchell shook his head.

'Everything has been very satisfactory, you guys have been great . . . Look I don't want to be rude but I really have to call my doctor in Virginia.'

The manager nodded.

'I hope the remainder of your stay will be a pleasant one,' the manager said kindly.

Mitchell nodded and when the man had gone muttered 'I wouldn't bet on it,' under his breath.

He had a shave, dressed and called Margaret.

'Hi,' he said.

'Frank, how are you?' she replied.

'Good. How are you?'

'I'm fine Frank, we're all fine.'

There was a pause and he wondered if it was wise to spill the beans – but there was no two ways about it, he knew that he had to tell her in case anything went wrong.

'Listen Margaret, I'm going to try for it tonight,' he said simply.

'Oh my God,' Margaret replied and took an intake of breath. There was a pause. He knew she was putting her hand over the receiver and taking a series of deep breaths. He gave her a minute to come back on.

'Frank?'

'Yes?'

'This is the only time I'm going to ask it,' she said slowly.

'What?'

Another pause.

'You do know what you're doing, don't you Frank?'

'I know,' Mitchell said.

'And you'll be careful?'

'Don't worry about me honey. I'll be fine.'

'Oh Frank I—'

'Listen honey,' he interrupted, before the tears came, 'I better go. I love you sweetie, I love you very much and don't worry about a thing.'

An hour later he picked up his airline ticket at the reception desk and had his luggage checked in at the hotel's Sky Cap service.

He was wearing a long black sweater, blue jeans and carrying a small backpack. The backpack was stuffed full of clothes and supplies but the only thing in it that belonged to him was a black ski mask.

He went outside the hotel and hailed a cab.

A blue Fiat that was being held together by rust and prayers.

'Speak English?' he asked.

The driver nodded, as they all did, whether they spoke English or not.

He got inside and gave the driver a piece of paper.

'Can you read it?' he asked in Arabic.

'Of course,' the driver replied.

They set off.

Mitchell had read that hundreds of taxi drivers were seriously injured, many killed, every year in road accidents in Cairo. There were virtually no traffic laws, few traffic police and the rule of the road was: give way to the bigger and more aggressive vehicle, or else. This driver was no different and he nearly got into several collisions before Mitchell had to tell him to slow down.

'American?' the driver asked.

'Yeah.'

'But Americans are always in a hurry.'

'Not me. Safety is my priority,' Mitchell said.

'Our lives are in the will of Allah. *Inshallah* we will be safe.'

'Yeah, doubtless, but keep your eyes on the road anyway pal,' Mitchell said. The man turned and gave him a betel-stained grin.

'I am good driver. For some it is hard to see with dust, the *khamseen*, but not me.'

'That a fact?'

'Yes. Drive good, save, one day I drive cab in Chicago, like my cousin.'

'Great.'

The driver grimaced at Mitchell's unenthusiastic response to his life plan but said nothing.

They drove over the Nile, into the eastern suburbs, well off the tourist trail.

'You are Jewish?' the driver asked after a while.

Mitchell shook his head.

'You Americans help Israel. Let me tell you my friend, the day of reckoning comes for the Zionist Entity. We will destroy it soon.'

Mitchell nodded.

'Yeah, you should invade Israel, it's worked so well the last three times you've tried it.'

The driver had competent English but it wasn't good enough to get sarcasm. He launched into an explanation of the failures of the past and why the next time would all be different.

Mitchell ceased to listen.

One of his qualities.

'Stop right here,' he said suddenly at a busy intersection.

The driver slammed on the brakes.

Mitchell opened the cab door.

'Wait here,' he said and went into what (from all the pots and pans hanging outside) appeared to be a hardware store.

He bought a heavy, steel-headed, claw hammer with a rubber grip. German made. Perfect.

He tried to give the shopkeeper ten Egyptian pounds but the man insisted that he had overpaid him and handed him six pounds in change.

'*Shukran*,' Mitchell said and ran back to the cab.

It took them thirty minutes to get to the address. A rundown neighbourhood filled with shoddily built five storey apartment buildings. Garbage all over the road, slabs of concrete peeling from the tenement walls. There were no cards here, just posters of Mubarak, stray dogs and the occasional motorcycle loaded with three or even four people.

He took out a twenty dollar bill and gave it to the taxi driver.

'Listen to me buddy, we seem to have a pretty good relationship going here, I want you to do me a favour, I want you to wait here for me for about ten minutes, do you understand?'

The driver nodded.

'And when I come back you're going to take me to the airport and I'm going to give you these,' he said showing the man five more twenties.

'Yes sir,' the driver said eagerly.

He would wait, probably a month's wages for him, Mitchell thought.

Mitchell got out of the cab and looked about.

They were really right on the edge of the city here. To the south lost in the gloom there was an old mosque and rows of shanty houses made of cinder blocks and salvaged wood. Then the desert, except that once again there were no undulating dunes of golden sand, just a stony bleak, lifeless and inhospitable plain.

And that biting wind that was beginning to churn up the sand so that it was hard to see fifty yards. Let it blow, Mitchell thought, just so long as the flights aren't delayed.

He walked across the empty street, found the building, put on the ski mask and knocked on the door. He kept the hammer down by his side. He was afraid now. But fear was good, fear kept you on your toes. You needed it. Especially if you were an old geezer retired from this kind of thing for several years.

He knocked again. Footsteps, then a man of about twenty-five answered the door.

He had a moustache and a gold chain drooping over a dirty red 'Ferrari' T-shirt. Mitchell recognised him from the photograph. Aziz's younger brother, Mohammed.

'*Marha-ba*,' Mohammed said before he saw the ski mask.

Mitchell hit him once in the forehead with the hammer. The blow smashed Mohammed's skull and penetrated through the cranium into the frontal lobe. Mitchell removed the hammer with a jerk and Mohammed tottered backwards slowly enough for Mitchell to grab him and ease him to the floor. Blood was pouring from his skull and frothing at his lips. Mitchell watched his legs twitch for a moment and then stop.

He was still breathing but it would be touch and go whether he lived or not.

Jesus. Well now I'm pot committed, Mitchell thought.

He stood and walked down a long corridor. Cracked tiles, flaking plaster and a naked twenty-watt light bulb above his head. Some kind of animal droppings on the floor.

A door to the left that was slightly ajar.

He looked in.

Two men watching a soccer game on TV.

210

Mitchell ignored them, eased the door closed and walked into the first courtyard.

An odd sight.

Dozens of rabbits running about – nibbling at a pile of lettuce leaves and rotting fruit. In any other circumstance it might have been comic.

He avoided the bunnies and looked for the yellow wooden door to the women's quarters.

He saw it behind a pail of filthy water.

He walked over to the door and pushed it open.

Another smaller courtyard beyond.

The sun peaking out of the orange sky. More rabbits, an emaciated dog tied to a stick, washing hanging on a line.

A woman in a *burka* frozen over a basket, staring at him, open mouthed.

Mitchell put his fingers to his lips, walked across the courtyard and pushed on a second yellow door.

Two more women in full *burkas*.

One of them screamed. Mitchell pushed them out of the way and turned left into a small bedroom. A mattress on the floor, rabbit droppings and, there, in the corner, a crib much too small for a near one year old.

The baby was crying and lying on a filthy sheet. She was skinny, pale and they had pierced her ears. She had a diaper on but the diaper was soaked through. Mitchell picked her up in his left arm and held her like a football.

He walked out of the room. One of the two

women began yelling and the other tried to prevent him from leaving. Mitchell kicked her in the stomach and she stumbled backwards into a table breaking it. Her companion screamed. Mitchell ran into the inner courtyard, slipped, almost fell, righted himself.

The woman bent over the washing watched him impassively.

He pushed on the first heavy yellow door and ran into the outer courtyard.

A boy of about eleven was standing in front of him shouting something. Mitchell kicked him in the chest and the boy crumpled to the floor.

The kid was out and wouldn't be a problem but by now the TV watching men had appeared from the corridor in front of him blocking the exit to the street. Both were carrying knives.

The men were saying something to him in a hate-filled language of curses and venom. Good, their rage would make them make mistakes. The baby beside him started to cry again.

'*Allahu Akhbar*,' one of the men yelled and ran at him with a large curved meat knife. Mitchell stepped to one side to lower his profile and protect the baby. In the same move he avoided a clumsy knife thrust and hit the man in the arm with the hammer. Before the man could even cry out Mitchell had turned the hammer backwards and smashed him in the head with the two stainless steel claws. They hooked into the man's face with a sickening thud. Mitchell pulled hard and the man's nose and half his cheek came off in a spout of blood and cartilage. Mitchell elbowed him to the ground.

The other man screamed and ran at him, moving so fast that his knife – a small dagger – managed to avoid Mitchell's block and embed itself in his right shoulder. It was a good attack but you don't stab with that kind of knife, Mitchell thought, as he kicked the man in the left kneecap and brought the hammer down twice on the poor bastard's head.

Avoiding treading on the rabbits, he walked across the courtyard, stepped around Mohammed in the corridor, ignored the sounds of screaming behind him and ran into the busy street. There was a bus outside with a noisy diesel engine that would help for a bit, but not too long. Soon neighbours, cops, tourist police, the whole gamut would be showing up, yelling for blood.

He looked for the taxi driver and half expected him to have bolted. His contingency plan was to hijack a private car, but no, that wouldn't be necessary for there he was. With a wince of pain he took the knife out of his shoulder and put it in his pocket.

The driver looked aghast at the hammer and the baby and opened his mouth to protest. Mitchell hooked the hammer under his arm, opened the taxi door, got in the back, set the baby down on the seat and passed the man five twenty dollar bills.

'Airport,' Mitchell said.

'What is going on here?'

Mitchell grabbed the driver around the neck with his left hand and brought the knife to the driver's throat. He tickled the man's carotid artery with the blade.

'Airport now pal. A hundred dollars or this knife in your goddamn neck, your call.'

'I go,' the driver said.

Mitchell released him and the driver set off.

'Any funny business and I'll kill ya, understand?' Mitchell said.

The driver nodded. Mitchell watched him for a minute and then reached in his backpack and pulled out a pacifier, a packet of Huggies and baby wipes. He took off the soiled diaper, wiped the baby girl, applied some rash cream, a Huggy and put her in a sleep suit. He gave her a bottle of formula and a pacifier. Halfway to the airport she stopped crying and in another few minutes she had fallen asleep. She had dark eyes and dark hair and was woefully thin. Maybe twenty pounds at the most. Of course she was still very beautiful.

Mitchell took off the black sweater and looked at the knife wound in his arm. Not bad. He removed his T-shirt and examined it closely. A puncture about an inch deep in the fleshy part of his shoulder, right above the tattooed letters USMC.

He wrapped the wound in gauze which he tightened off with duct tape. He poured water on the black sweater and rinsed the blood out. He put the sweater back on. It didn't look good but there was a leather jacket in his bag at the airport that he'd put on in the lounge bathroom.

'We are at the airport,' the driver said nervously.

'Departures, and take it easy, if you do anything I don't like we can let Allah decide if you live with a knife in your neck.'

They pulled into a parking space at Departures.

Mitchell gave the driver the five twenties and then held out one of two hundred dollar bills.

'You did good. Just remember this, if I'm stopped by the police before I can get on my flight, I'm going to tell them who my accomplice was, the person who helped me get away.'

'I did nothing,' the driver protested.

'Who they gonna believe?'

The driver thought about it and nodded.

'So let me ask you a question, chief, who was your passenger today?' Mitchell said brandishing the Benjamin.

The driver looked at the bill hungrily, took it between his thumb and forefinger and placed it in his shirt pocket.

'An English woman that I drove to the pyramids,' the driver said.

Mitchell gave him the other hundred dollar bill and got out of the cab.

He walked to the First Class lounge, had a cup of coffee, ignored the snooty looks, changed the baby again, gave her a kiss, put on his leather jacket, checked his luggage and then went through security. He showed his own passport and the baby's passport. There was a minor fuss when the inspector couldn't find the baby's entry stamp.

'What was your business in Egypt, Mr Mitchell?'

'I was on a Saga Tour with my wife but the baby got a little unwell, it was a bad idea to bring her, so I'm taking her back to the States and my wife's going on to Luxor.'

'No stamp for the child. Perhaps they stamped your wife's passport twice?' the inspector suggested helpfully.

'Yeah that's it, I think they did that, is there a fine we should pay or something?' Mitchell asked and finessed the situation with another hundred dollar bill.

He got through security and bought a newspaper.

There was another minor problem at the gate.

The British Airways flight attendant said that his ticket didn't include a passenger. Mitchell said that he didn't think he needed a ticket for the baby since she was sitting in his lap. The flight attendant shook her head and it really might have been a problem if he hadn't been flying First Class. Instead, after some grumbling she cut him another ticket for the baby and let him through.

Mitchell waited until they had left Egyptian airspace before making the call.

'Hello,' he said.

'Frank,' Margaret said and burst into tears.

216

'Take it easy,' he said.

'Are you hurt?' she asked.

'Scratch. Nothing serious,' he said.

'Thank God.'

She didn't ask if he got the baby – she could tell that from that first syllable.

'Don't do anything stupid like calling the media, or worse, the State Department,' Mitchell said.

'We won't Frank. We know better.'

'Good. OK, she needs to feed, better go. See you in London.'

'Love you Frank.'

'Love you too,' he said and hung up.

The wound in his shoulder started acting up. The bleeding began again and he had to take a trip to the bathroom to wash the puncture and change the gauze. He took the girl with him in a Baby Bjorn and set her down on the changing platform. He threw away the bloody bandage and put on a new dressing. He took another good look at the dagger's best efforts. Might affect the golf swing, but he'd live.

He put the baby back in the Bjorn and found his seat again.

He stared out the window.

The rough stuff was over but maybe the hard part was still to come. There would be lawyers, there would be questions, there might even be an attempt to extradite him, or kidnap the baby away from his daughter again. He remembered something the instructors had told him at Seal Beach,

San Diego, thirty-three years ago: 'the only easy day was yesterday', and for the hundredth time since hearing that it made him feel a little better.

Over Sicily the baby woke and was inconsolable until he fed her a piece of mashed banana and sang the Streets of Laredo three times.

The plane flew over the darkening Mediterranean.

Stars appeared in the eastern sky.

The stewardess went past smelling of jasmine and oranges.

He closed his eyes.

And yes, of course, there would be hardships, there would be hassles, but whatever was coming, they would deal with it as a family this time, united and together.

'We can take it,' he said to himself and then, after what had been a long, long day, with his only granddaughter safe and resting peacefully on his chest, he allowed himself the slightest of smiles and fell into a brief, but untroubled sleep.

CHRIS SIMMS

BABA'S BITES

Lamb rogan josh. My favourite curry and, once you've got the basic spices, one of the easiest to make. Brown off your lamb cubes and put to one side. Add a generous glug of oil to a wide pan, put the heat on medium high and throw in some cardamom pods, bay leaves, cloves, peppercorns, cinnamon, onions, ginger and garlic. Stir for thirty seconds. Add cumin, coriander, paprika and salt. Stir for another thirty seconds. Add the lamb, some yoghurt and a cup of water. Simmer for as long as you can resist.

I thought I had the curry sussed, until that night in Baba's Bites. Meat cooked until the strands barely hung together, yoghurt and spices perfectly balanced and some other ingredient that brought the dish springing to life. I thought of all the previous times I'd eaten it and knew I'd been stumbling around in the dark.

'Kaz,' I said, hunched over the shallow polystyrene tray, prodding towards the riot of flavours with a plastic fork, 'this is delicious. New cook or something?'

Kaz's brother usually prepared the curries, but

I'd only had to smell this one to know it was in a different league. Kaz smiled as he sprinkled his homemade chilli sauce over a doner kebab and held it out to the customer who stood swaying on my side of the little takeaway's counter.

'No, no mate. I mean loads of chilli sauce,' the young bloke drunkenly said, trying to speak slowly and clearly for the benefit of what he thought were foreign ears. In a larger version of the action I'd just made with my fork, the customer jerked his hand up and down to demonstrate that he wanted the kebab to be drowned. The smile didn't leave Kaz's face as he soaked the open pitta bread with gouts of fiery liquid.

'Cheers mate,' said the customer, grabbing the paper wrapped package and staggering out the door, leaving a trail of crimson drops behind him.

Kaz looked over at me and, with an accent that combined the nasal twang of Manchester with the thicker tones of the Middle East, said, 'Yeah mate. It's good then?'

My mouth was too full for any spoken reply. Holding up a thumb, I nodded vigorously. Kaz looked pleased as he turned back to the huge hunk of processed meat slowly revolving on the oil soaked spike. Flourishing a long knife, he began carving away at its outer layer.

Once I'd swallowed my mouthful I said, 'So what's your brother doing then?'

'Oh, he's pursuing a new business interest. He won't be around so much from now on.'

The curry was too good for me to continue talking so, before tucking into it once more, I quickly said, 'Well, compliments to the chef.'

I'd dropped out of my chemical engineering degree halfway through my second year. There was no way I could imagine a career in it. Life, I decided, was too short to spend doing something you didn't enjoy. I sat down and tried to imagine a job that I would enjoy. Twenty-one years old, with a series of mind-numbing McJobs behind me and I was struggling. But during my gap year I went to Thailand (original choice, I know). Though I was far too much of a traveller to ever step inside Koh Samui's flashy tourist hotels full of mere holidaymakers, I watched the tour reps at work. I reckoned I could handle a life working in some of the most beautiful places on earth. Work it out for yourself: Manchester versus the Maldives. Britain versus Barbados. So a degree in Travel and Tourism it was.

Which left me with a new set of course fees rolled into almost two years of student debt. I got a night job in the bakers just down the road from my digs. 'Mr Wing's Chinese Bakers'. There can't be many of those in Britain. But you wouldn't believe the amount of stuff he churns out. During the day it's things like doughy rolls filled with sweet and sour pork, kung po chicken or special seafood mix or batches of little buns sprinkled with sesame seeds and filled with chestnut puree or honey paste. At five o'clock the day shift goes home, the front of shop shuts and the night shift appears round the back. While the rest of the country is slumped in front of the box, or enjoying themselves in pubs and restaurants, the output changes to speciality, or ethnic breads as they're classed on the supermarket shelves. Pittas, naans, raithas, chapattis, lavache, ciabatta – all that stuff. The monstrous silver ovens never get the chance to cool down. Staff scurry around them, transporting away the steady flow of produce like worker ants carrying off the stream of eggs laid by their queen.

My co-workers chat happily away in languages from India, Asia or Africa, but hardly any speak English. It's obvious most haven't got to Britain by legal means either. The cash changes hands just before dawn and, unlike my rate of pay, theirs reflects the twilight world they operate in. The minimum wage doesn't even come into it. It's probably because I'm an official British citizen with a clean driving licence that I got the job of doing drop offs. And, seeing as working next to a furnace half the night wasn't my idea of fun, that was fine by me. I deliver to city centre takeaway joints that need more stock or the Indian restaurants on Manchester's curry mile that prefer to serve freshly baked produce. They all know Mr Wing's never shuts. The phone rings and I'm off in the little van with their order.

Baba's Bites called on my very first night. As soon as I wandered in with the tray of naans and pittas, Kaz spotted me for someone who was prepared to do a deal. And this is how it works: Kaz rings with an order, I pick what he wants from the racks of stuff in the storage room and swipe an extra tray or two. In return he gives me a free curry.

Baba's Bites – it's your typical late night, city centre takeaway place. A few stools and a narrow counter running along the plate glass window at the front. Overflowing bin by the door. Rear of the shop partitioned off by a counter with a glass case on top. Underneath the warm panels of glass are stainless steel dishes full of curry, lumps of sheek kebab on skewers, mounds of onion bhajis, savaloy sausages and pakoras. Above the counter is a huge back-lit menu. A panel of photos showing juicy morsels which generally bear no resemblance to what gets handed over. Along the back wall is the inevitable kebab turning in one corner, a couple of hot trays for the meat he skims off, a chip fryer, a hot plate for flipping burgers, a microwave for pizzas, a glass fronted fridge full of cans and a small sink (never used). In the other corner is the tiny hatchway through to the kitchen. Although you can hear the clatter of pans in the kitchen, you can't actually see into it – a hanging screen of multi-coloured plastic strips ensures that. Kaz shouts through and a short while later whoever is doing the cooking presses a buzzer. Kaz then reaches in and picks up the next batch of burgers, sheek kebabs or boiled rice. When I arrive Kaz always scoops me a portion of lamb rogan josh, then passes it through the hatch for the extra coriander and sliced tomatoes that I like to be added.

Where Kaz was lucky – and why Baba's Bites does so well while countless other similar places just scrape by – is that less than a year ago a massive late-night bar and club opened opposite. Now he's assured of a steady flow of revellers being drawn across the road to the glow of his shop like moths to a flame. Unlike the melting pot of ethnic foods on sale, the clientele are mostly white, mostly male, usually in their twenties. Eyes bright, they burst raucously through the door, vying with each other at the counter, sometimes loudly critical at what's on offer, sometimes reverently appreciative like kids in a sweet shop. Who knows which way alcohol will tip them. As they wait for their orders they discuss all manner of topics. The standard of women in the club they'd just left, how United or City are doing, the lack of black cabs. Sometimes it's stuff from the news – the state of the country's immigration system, scrounging asylum seekers, the flood of immigrants ruining the country. Even when they start to bitterly discuss pakis or ragheads, Kaz's smile remains unchanged as he plays the dutiful patron, quietly carrying out their commands. Serving them food from the very countries they curse.

To the left of Baba's Bites is a Slow Boat Chinese takeaway, on the other side a 24-hour Spar complete with bouncers to stop shoplifters escaping. After that is a dive of a pub. The rest of the row of shops on his stretch of the street consists of daytime businesses – dry cleaners, a newsagent's and places like that. At the other end is a fish and chip shop which, for some reason, always shuts at around eight o'clock. The shutters are drawn down and padlocked long before I ever show up. Above the chip shop is a massage parlour. You'd miss it from the street, but in the alleyway round the back a discreet sign above the permanently open door leading up the stairs reads, 'Far Eastern Massage. Open 24 hours.' I only know this because, when I arrive with a delivery for Kaz, I have to carry it up the alleyway to his shop's rear door.

As you'd probably guess from the swell of my belly, I'm not too fussed about my food. As long as there's enough of it. But I'm sure plenty of people happily gorging themselves at the front would spit it out in disgust if they could see the state of things round the back. The alleyway is narrow and it stinks. While the food places are open for business, the extractor fans sound like a collection of giant vacuum cleaners left permanently on. The grills pump out warm, grease-laden fumes that mingle with the sickly sweet aroma of rotting food. The alleyway is littered with trays of all shapes and sizes dumped from the back doors of the shops. Most usually contain the remains of food: broken eggshells, mangled halves of oranges or overripe tomatoes with skins that are split and weeping. Discarded twenty-five litre drums of economy cooking oil sit piled next to empty beer barrels and crates of bottles from the pub. Industrial size wheelie bins seem permanently stuffed to the top, the lids unable to ever close properly. Crowding round them are broods of bulging bin bags, haphazardly piled on to one another. Water, pooled in the pitted surface of the alley is either a foul smelling milky colour or tinged with a surface of glistening oil.

Kaz's door is like all the others – heavily metal plated. He's spray painted a large red 29 on it and I kick it twice to let whoever's in the kitchen know I've dropped off. I'm always back in the light cast by the lamps on the main road before the bolts go back and the cardboard trays vanish, dragged inside by, I presume, one of the kitchen assistants.

I found the note in about my eighth curry prepared by the new cook. Because I always have lamb rogan josh with extra coriander and freshly sliced tomatoes, she must have worked out it was the same customer asking for it each time. In fact, I was fairly certain that I was Kaz's only regular customer – the rest just stumble in because it's the first place they find serving food after coming out of the club. Most of them probably couldn't even remember what they'd eaten by the next day. I was halfway through my usual, watching with amusement as three lads attempted to cross the road. After about ten o'clock on a weekend it seemed pedestrians, vehicles and the watching police silently agree that daytime rules don't apply. Made impatient by booze, people would lurch out into the path of cars that instantly slow down or stop to allow them to cross. Similarly cab drivers pull up whenever they like or make U turns anywhere they fancy. The whole thing is a mélée yet, apart from the occasional slanging match, it seems to work.

The three lads had made it through the door and were debating about whether to go for doner kebabs or quarter pounders when I bit on the strange object. At first I thought it was gristle – but it was too hard for that. An exploratory poke with my tongue revealed that it was something folded up. With a forefinger and thumb I extracted it from my mouth, sucking the remains of curry sauce from it as I did so. I held it up and saw that it was greaseproof paper, tightly folded. Carefully I opened it out and there, in the middle of the small square, were the words, 'Help me. I am prisoner here.'

I stared with puzzlement at the paper. Placing it carefully to one side, I decided to show it to Kaz once he'd finished serving the group at the counter. The first two had taken their burgers and wandered out onto the street. The third one waited at the counter, a twenty pound note dangling from his hand. But as he was handed his order, the customer whipped the money from Kaz's reach and spun around to run for the door.

From the corner of my eye, I saw his two mates sprint away up the street. Until then I'd only ever seen Kaz from the chest up. He was of a thickset build and I didn't think particularly agile. But he vaulted across that counter in a flash. The lad had bumped against the door frame and lost a second as a result. Kaz sprang across the shop, grabbed him by the collar and dragged him back to the counter in one movement. With his other hand he reached behind it and produced a baseball bat. He shoved it hard up against the customer's mouth, the wooden tip audibly catching on his teeth. A smear of blood appeared on his lips.

'Pay me,' Kaz demanded, aggression lowering his voice to a growl. All traces of the amiable kebab shop owner with a limited understanding of English had vanished and I looked at the muscles bunched in his shoulders and arms, knowing that he meant it. The prospect of imminent violence hung menacingly in the air and I felt a surge of queasiness in my stomach. Thankfully the customer quickly produced the note from the breast pocket of his Ben Sherman shirt. Kaz snatched it, walked him back to the doorway and said, 'Night then.'

The lad walked shakily off up the street and Kaz returned to behind the counter. He looked at me and said, 'Why do people have to be like that? I work hard all night, give him what he wanted and he tries to rob me.' He shook his head regretfully. 'It's a bad world Richard, a bad world out there.'

His eyes turned to the street and he gazed with sadness at the procession of people flowing past. Then, with a smile and shrug of his shoulders, he picked up a ladle and began stirring the curries.

I couldn't believe how quickly he readopted his previous persona. It was like having a friendly dog snarl at you one moment, then wag its tail the next. Finding it hard to keep the same easy familiarity in my voice, I said, 'You're right there.' I looked at the piece of paper and, having witnessed this new side to him, decided against letting him see it.

Two nights later I was making a delivery at Baba's Bites again, but this time I had slipped my own note into the tray of naan breads. It read, 'Who are you? Why are you a prisoner?'

Not knowing if I would ever get a reply, I banged on the back door and then went round to the front and stepped inside. 'Same as usual?' asked Kaz, already spooning rogan josh on to a pile of rice.

'Yeah, cheers,' I replied and sat down on my favourite stool in the corner. He handed the tray through the hatch and a few minutes later it was returned with a garnish of coriander and tomato. Shielding the food from him with one forearm I sifted through the curry with my fork. A thrill of excitement shot through me when I found the little wedge of paper. Quickly I wrapped it in a serviette and slipped it into my pocket.

And so began a correspondence that would change my outlook on life forever. Over the next two weeks we exchanged a series of notes. Mine written on lined sheets, hers scrawled in a microscopic hand on lengths of greaseproof paper. She'd write them at night, sacrificing valuable sleep to describe to me her plight. Her name was Meera and she was a seventeen-year-old Hindu girl from the war-torn region of Kashmir sandwiched uncomfortably between India and Pakistan. Her father and both brothers had died in the crossfire between militants and government troops. That left her as the eldest of four remaining daughters. After a long and tearful talk, she had persuaded her mother that the only way to prevent the family from becoming destitute was for her to leave the war-ravaged region and look for work. So they had paid almost all their savings to a man who promised to find Meera a well paid job as a cook in an Indian restaurant in London. Abandoning her dream of a university place in Jammu to read law, she had climbed into the back of a lorry with seventeen other people and begun the slow trek overland to Britain. The group was occasionally allowed to emerged at night for a few minutes. Twice they transferred to other lorries – the one taking them on the final leg of the journey was the newest. They sat at its end, crammed in on all sides by crates of tulips. Eventually they were all dropped off at a house, herded inside and the men and women separated. They were told they were in Britain, but certain arrangements still had to be made. After two days locked in a room with only a bucket for a toilet, some bottles of water and a few loaves of bread, a different man kicked open the door. Meera was dragged out by her hair and told the cost of her passage to England had gone up. Her passport was taken off her and she was told that, to repay her debt, she could work in a brothel or a kitchen. Of course she opted for the kitchen and was bundled into the back of a van and driven to Baba's Bites. When she asked me which city she was in, tears sprang to my eyes.

She arrived late at night and was led up the stinking alley, marched through the back door and chained to the sink pipes. She had enough slack to get around the kitchen and reach the toilet and sink in a tiny room at the back. She slept on a camp bed in the corner and hadn't seen daylight since arriving; the nearest she got to that was when the back door was opened up to take in deliveries. But she was made to hide in the toilet when that happened. After cooking from lunchtime to the early hours, she would clean the kitchen. Once Kaz had bolted the back door, he left by the front of the shop, padlocking the metal shutters behind him. Then he went round to the alley way and bolted the back-door from the outside too. Once he was gone she was able to grab a few hours sleep before he or his brother returned late-morning. Then she would be preparing food – including my curries – until the shop raised its shutters once again at lunchtime.

In one of my first ever replies to her I offered to go straight to the police. But she wouldn't let me. If any officials were involved, she reasoned, deportation would inevitably follow. She needed to remain in Britain, working in a job that paid her cash to send home to her family. All she wanted to do was escape from Kaz's kitchen. She told me that the pipe she was chained to was old and flimsy; she was confident that she could bend or even break it. What she needed me to do was slide the bolts back on the outside of the back door, she would do the same to the ones on the inside of the door, and then she would be free. She didn't want any more help than that.

The situation she was in made me feel sick – and outraged at Kaz. I agreed to help her and we arranged that the next time Kaz rang, I was to put a note in the tray of breads confirming that tonight was the night. A previous note she sent me had stressed the importance of successfully getting her out; she was terrified of what Kaz would do if she tried to escape and failed. I wished she had room on the piece of paper to elaborate, but I reasoned we would soon have plenty of opportunity to talk face to face.

Friday night and I was sitting in the office, fan directed straight at my face, trying to learn the main aspects of insurance law relating to groups travelling abroad. (One of the less glamorous modules of my course.) At 10:43 the phone's ring put a welcome end to my study.

Pushing the door shut, I picked up the receiver and said, 'Mr Wing's Bakery.'

'Rick? It's Kaz here.'

By keeping to our established patter, I was able to hide the revulsion in my voice, 'Kaz, how's business mate?'

'Busy, my friend. Very busy. I need six dozen more pittas, two dozen naans and one dozen peshwari naans.'

'No problem. Any extras?'

'Just naans my friend. All you can get.'

'Coming right up. I'll be there in half an hour.'

Twenty-six minutes later I pulled up outside Baba's Bites. The place was heaving. A couple were sitting on the pavement outside, he finishing off a burger while she rested her head on her knees and moaned about how pissed she was. In the doorway four boisterous lads were struggling over a pizza, each one trying to grab the quarter with the most pepperoni on. I rapped on the window and once Kaz caught sight of me, I pointed to the trays of bread balanced on my other arm then set off round to the back door. As I picked my way between the debris in the alley I saw shadows moving in the glow of light shining from the massage parlour doorway. Keeping in the shadows, I watched as two men emerged into the alley. Both smiling, they turned round to shake hands with the man who had escorted them to the bottom of the stairs and I realised with a shock that it was Kaz's brother. He patted each man on the shoulder and, as they disappeared round the corner, he headed back up the stairs. So that was the new business interest.

I banged twice on the door and as I leaned down to place the trays on the step, noticed for the first time the bolt drawn back its base. Looking up I saw another at the top. They hadn't been there a few weeks ago and, knowing the reason for their sudden appearance, anger surged through me – if a fire broke out at night Meera stood no chance of escape.

In Baba's Bites I stood silently in the far corner and waited for the skinny man sitting on my stool to finish his curry. I knew my presence by his shoulder was unsettling him, but I didn't back off. I even wanted him to say something; a confrontation might dissipate the ugly knot of aggression lodged in my chest. Alternatively it might aggravate it further: either way I didn't care. Hurriedly the man wiped up the remains of his curry sauce with a piece of naan bread and popped it into his mouth. Glancing at me from the corner of his eye, he left the shop. I sat down and scowled out the window at the people blundering past, all of their spirits lifted by the arrival of the weekend. I watched and wondered if any had the slightest concern for the army of anonymous workers slaving to keep them served with a plentiful supply of cheap takeaways and taxis. Sitting there I began to think about other parts of the economy that were kept running by illegal immigrants. The people who deliver our pizzas, clean our offices, pick our fruit and vegetables, iron our shirts and wash our soiled sheets. No one on the street outside looked as if they could care less. A minute later Kaz called me over and handed me my curry. Hardly able to meet his eyes, I took it with a brief smile and reclaimed my seat.

Looking at the bright red curry I guessed that I'd put on a good half a stone over the past fortnight. It was as delicious as usual; Meera had explained in one note that it was Kashmiri rogan josh I was eating: she used fennel, cloves and a pungent resin called asafetida. As I finished it off I saw the tiny scrap of greaseproof paper. Surreptitiously I unfolded it and saw she had just been able to scrawl the words, 'Please do not fail me.'

Raising my voice unnecessarily, I said goodnight to Kaz, hoping Meera was able to hear me in the back kitchen. The bakery night shift finished just after 4 a.m. and immediately I drove back to Baba's Bites.

Most of the clubs had shut around an hour before and now just a smattering of mini cabs roamed the streets searching for their last fare of the night. The shutters at Baba's Bites were drawn down and padlocked, the bin outside overflowing with the remains of that night's sales. Polystyrene trays were thrown into the doorways of the neighbouring shops, chips dotted the pavement like pale fat slugs. I pulled up at the corner and quietly made my way up the alley. The council bin lorry came round every Sunday and Thursday – which meant the refuse had been cleared from the alley only last night. However Fridays were probably the week's busiest night and already the alleyway was piled with bags of rubbish, boxes and packaging hurled from the back doors of the shops. At the other end light shone from the massage parlour's open door. It spilled across the narrow passageway, helping me pick my way forward. Up ahead an enormous rat heard my approach. We looked at each other for a few seconds then, to my relief, it casually crept back into the overflow of a nearby drain. At the back door of Baba's Bites I put my ear up against the cool metal surface and listened. But there was nothing to hear. Tentatively I knocked twice. Instantly a knock was returned. She must have broken free of the pipe and was sitting on the other side of the door listening for my arrival.

Urgently I whispered, 'Meera, is that you?' Instantly I felt stupid: it could hardly have been anyone else.

Her voice was light and sonorous: and would have been beautiful to hear if it wasn't packed with so much fear. 'Yes Richard, it's me. I have broken the pipe, the kitchen is flooded.'

Looking down I saw water seeping out from the bottom of the door. Metal began to clunk and rattle as she started undoing the bolts on her side of the door. I stepped back to slide open the ones on my side – and to my dismay saw they were secured with two heavy-duty padlocks. I shut my eyes and silently swore. I didn't think Kaz would bother padlocking a door that was bolted shut from both the inside and out. But now it seemed an obvious precaution, especially considering the prisoner he kept inside. Meera's trembling voice sounded through the thick barrier separating us. 'I have done it. Can you open the door?'

'Meera,' I whispered. 'He's padlocked the bolts. I can't unlock them.'

'You must,' she cried, now panic-stricken. 'I must leave here!'

I needed a hacksaw; and nowhere would be open until morning. By then our chance would be gone. Even if Kaz turned up late, I couldn't stand there in broad daylight breaking into the back of a shop. 'I'm so sorry Meera, I need a hacksaw. I'll get one later and come back the same time tomorrow.'

'No!' she pleaded. 'I cannot be here when he comes. He will know what I have done.'

I looked at the tamper-proof screws protecting the door hinges: there was no way I could free her. I slapped the palm of my hand against the wall in frustration. 'I'm sorry Meera. I promise to come back.'

She began to sob, 'He beat me for burning the rice. He said he will send me somewhere far worse than here if I do wrong again. Help me Richard.'

Desperately I whispered back, 'I will, tomorrow.'

I heard her slump against the door and start to cry. At the other end of the alley male voices were audible coming down the stairs of the massage parlour. Pressing my hands against the door, I could only whisper, 'I'll come back tomorrow night,' before quickly walking back out on to the street.

As soon as B&Q opened I was searching the place for hacksaws. An elderly assistant saw me scanning the aisles and took me to the correct section. 'It's a big padlock. The hasp is about a centimetre thick,' I told him.

'Well,' he said, rubbing his chin with one hand. 'This will get through it in about five minutes.'

'Great,' I said, taking the saw from his hands and hurrying to the tills.

After that I went to the supermarket and bought a load of food, including a pile of fresh fruit and vegetables. I had already decided to insist that Meera stay at my place until she was sorted out with a job. I was confident I could get a place for her in Mr Wing's bakery, even if it would be for a pittance. Now, given what she had said about Kaz beating her, I wasn't sure what sort of a state she might be in when I finally got that door open. I had formed an image of her face – long dark hair, fragile features and large brown eyes. Picturing her now covered in bruises, I added bottles of ibuprofen and paracetamol to my trolley.

The rest of the day was spent dozing fitfully on my sofa. I kept waking up, my mind dwelling on what he'd do to her. He wouldn't hurt her too badly, I reasoned. After all, he needed her to cook. But I'd seen the flash of his temper and an uneasy feeling sat heavy in my mind. Flicking on the telly,

I caught the lunchtime news. The presenter was describing how a major ring in peddling African children into the British sex trade had been broken up by the police. The implications of Kaz's brother's new business interest suddenly hit me like a slap in the face. Kaz himself had said she would end up somewhere far worse if she did anything wrong again. An image of a grimy bed in the Far Eastern Massage Parlour forced its way into my mind. Meera chained to it, a queue of punters at the door, pulses racing at the prospect of a new girl in her teens. I tried to push the thought away.

In Mr Wing's that night I sat staring at the Chinese calendar on the wall of his office. It was the Year of the Monkey, judging by the number of little primates adorning the pages. The relief I felt when the phone finally rang was instantly diminished when I heard Kaz's voice. Sounding unsettled, he asked for double quantities of just about everything. He hadn't time to make it to the cash 'n' carry, he explained. At least I now could make a delivery and then sit at the counter and observe him. Try and gauge by his behaviour just what he might have done to her.

So, after dumping the trays at the back door and kicking it twice, I marched round to the front of the shop. As soon as I stepped inside it was obvious something was wrong. For a start there was no lump of doner kebab turning on its vertical skewer in the corner. The fridge of canned drinks was almost empty – just cream soda and cans of shandy remained. People were waiting restlessly for their orders while Kaz hurried around behind the counter looking totally stressed out.

'Forget the chicken,' said one customer. 'I haven't got all night. How much are those things?' He pointed down at the skewers of sheek kebabs lined up under the counter.

'£2.50 each, including pitta bread and salad. How many?' asked Kaz, acknowledging me with a quick wave and passing a portion of lamb rogan josh through the hatch.

'Two,' the young man snapped, rapping a pound coin impatiently against the counter.

I took my corner seat and after a longer wait than usual, my curry arrived. 'You alright?' I asked as Kaz handed it to me over the counter.

'Yeah, staff problems that's all,' he replied distractedly. As I took the polystyrene tray I noticed a long scratch running across the back of his hand. Pretending I hadn't seen it, I took my curry and sat back down. With the first forkful I knew it hadn't been cooked by Meera. The sauce was watery, my extra garnish of coriander was missing, the lamb was burnt and the rice had been left in the pan until the grains were bloated and soft. As soon as it entered my mouth it turned into something that resembled semolina. I struggled through it, wondering what this meant. Was Meera beaten so badly that she couldn't cook? Or had she already been bundled up the alley and into the massage parlour?

Binning the container, I waited a few moments to try and ask Kaz where his usual cook was, but the shop had grown too busy again. Drunken men milled around at the counter, confused by the lack of doner kebab and settling reluctantly for the poorly prepared alternatives. Not wanting to arouse Kaz's suspicions by lingering for too long, I slipped back out and returned to Mr Wing's.

As soon as the bakery shut, I said my goodnights and hurried along the street to my car. Checking that the hacksaw was still safely stashed on the back seat, I set off straight back to Kaz's. In the alleyway I picked my way through the debris, nose wrinkling at the fruity smell being given off by a tray of rotten bananas.

Now, at the door, I knock on it twice and wait for a reply. Nothing. 'Meera?' I whisper loudly. 'Can you hear me?' On the other side of the door is only silence. Dark thoughts crowd my brain. Have they gagged her? Can she no longer speak because her mouth is so badly swollen? I raise up the hacksaw but, just as I start to saw, I realise that without her to unlock the inner bolts, the door will be impossible to open. Voices at the other end of the alley cause me to crouch behind a pile of bin bags. Four men emerge from the massage parlour. They step out into the alley, laughing and patting each other's backs. One mimes a whipping motion as if he's urging a horse to the finish line and they all roar with laughter again. Holding up hands to slap each other's palms, they head back on to the street and disappear round the corner.

The image of Meera chained to the bed, legs spread, reappears in my mind and I throw the hacksaw angrily down. Looking at the entrance to the massage parlour, I consider barging my way up the stairs and demanding to see her. Two more men appear at the corner and disappear into the open doorway. Angrily I pull out my mobile phone and dial 999. Once connected to the operator I ask for the police. I'm put through to a tired sounding man and I explain that I have reason to believe there is an illegal female immigrant being held against her will in the Far Eastern Massage Parlour, just off Cross Street in central Manchester. The person asks how I know this for certain and when I reply that I don't, he says they'll try and arrange for a patrol car to call the next day.

'But you need to send someone now. She's probably up there being raped this very moment,' I almost shout.

The person at the other end of the line barely attempts to mask their boredom, assuring me that my report has been logged and will be dealt with at the earliest opportunity. But, he adds, with it being Saturday night, that may well be some time.

Furiously I yell, 'Now! You must send someone now!' and kick out at the nearest bin bag. The thin plastic splits and among the scraps of shredded cabbage, tomato and cucumber that tumble out, is a human hand. Long feminine fingers, bone and gristle visible at the neatly severed wrist. I think of the rows and rows of sheek kebabs Kaz was so eager to sell and the lumps of crudely butchered meat in the curry I'd eaten earlier. As the vomit erupts from my mouth all I can hear is the officer saying, 'Sir, are you all right? Can you hear me sir? Sir?'

ROBERT BARNARD

WAITING FOR NEMESIS

The Walthamstow locals were unanimous when Harriet Blackstone died. Standing in the doorways of Gladstone Road (the renamed O'Connor Street), watching the police horse and cart clip-clopping away to the morgue, they looked at each other, and either said it or left it unsaid but understood: 'She asked for it.'

It was in truth, only what they had been saying about Mrs Blackstone for years. When they saw her cleaning her attic-floor windows on long ladders borrowed from Mr Dean the builder (what had she got on *him*? they asked themselves), when they saw her sharpening her kitchen knives at the front door, saw her buying arsenic (for the rats) and cyanide (for the wasps) at the chemist's or the general stores, they always looked on these habits as hubristic, without ever using the word. 'She's asking for it,' they had said, shaking their heads. Now there was the satisfaction of seeing their prophecies come true, as well as a more general satisfaction. That night they had a street party, with Eccles cakes and muffins, and bottles left over from the Diamond Jubilee. Everyone came except Harriet's daughter Sylvia, and she seemed regretful at missing the fun.

'Don't get many chances of a good knees-up,' said Mr Rowlands at number twenty. 'Won't be decent when the old Queen goes.'

'Not decent at all,' said Mrs Whitchurch, his neighbour. 'Mind you, after that there'll be the Coronation . . .'

And the thought of the first coronation for sixty-odd years gave an added zest to the evening.

Harriet Blackstone had married beneath her, after some years of trying for someone above or on a level with her. Her father had run a failing ironmonger's in Deptford, and her husband had peddled insurance in the poorer areas of cockney London. 'Poor blighter,' everyone said about him when she made him the happiest of men. Nine years later he had gone to his well-deserved rest, having fathered a sickly but determined little girl. The neighbours suggested 'For this relief much thanks' as an appropriate inscription for his grave-stone, but the one Harriet had erected merely said 'Sacred to the memory of' and left room for two more names. Harriet did not intend Sylvia to marry. She was needed for the heavy work.

'All men are good for nothing,' she told her daughter, but Sylvia had heard about one of two things that they were good for, and began marking out potential husbands from an early age. They represented not only satisfactions of an earthly kind, but escape as well. So when the jollifications were going on down in the street below, Sylvia watched them from behind the curtains of her cramped little two-up-two-down, wishing she could go down and have a dance and a glass of something nice. She sighed, but she felt that it would not do, and soon she went back to bed with her plasterer husband, and had a giggle and a good time with him.

Relations with her mother had, in fact, been resumed two months before. The marriage had been marked by Mrs Blackstone only by curtains drawn as for a funeral, but some weeks later she had sprained her ankle while unblocking a drain, and had sent one of the neighbouring boys with a note to her daughter, rewarding him with a ha'penny (half the going rate). The note had simply said, 'Sprained ankle. Come.' When Sylvia came round she had finished unblocking the drain, peeled a few potatoes, cut a few slices of cold meat, and then left. All this had been done to a continual ground bass of complaint and criticism not one whit lessened by the fact that her daughter was doing her a favour.

'I could forgive treachery,' Mrs Blackstone said at one point, 'I could forgive the disobedience and the loose morals – because what had been going on *before* the wedding I shudder to think – but what I *cannot* forgive is my daughter taking her sheets to the Communal Wash House to be boiled. The shame of that will be with me to my dying day.'

Sylvia had said nothing and left. But she went back at least once a day during the next week, and now and then thereafter when the ankle was recovered. 'Blood is thicker than water,' she said when the neighbours commented. Behind her back they nodded sagely.

'Who else is there to leave the house to?' they asked each other. When such remarks were repeated to Charlie Paxman, Sylvia's husband, he licked the foam off his lips and said:

'Silly old buzzard will probably leave it to the Primitive Methodists.' So far, at any rate, she had not. All the neighbourhood would have known if she had taken the momentous leap step of going to a solicitor's.

Harriet was indeed a regular worshipper at the Ebenezer Chapel in Trafalgar Street, where the rigorous and belligerent tone of the services matched her own martial spirit. She was no Sunday Christian, but had brought her values into every corner of everyday life. She had a withering glance that could have felled a bay tree, and she used it against young people holding hands, sometimes followed by 'Shame on you' or some variant of it. Children playing ball in the street were sent scurrying for cover by her shrill objections, and any woman whose clothes were visibly dirty would be assailed by words such as 'slattern' or 'slut'. Cleanliness and teetotalism were up there beside godliness in her scale of values: Boys emerging from the Gentleman's convenience in Trafalgar

Street would be asked to show her that they'd washed their hands, and the smell of beer on the breath of a passing labourer would elicit the outraged cry of 'Drunken beast!'

'Give it a rest, old woman,' said one of her victims. 'Just because your tipple is vinegar doesn't mean the rest of us can't enjoy a pint or two of summat nicer.'

But the object of her particular wrath in the months before her death was the house on the corner of Trafalgar Street and Gladstone Road, one whose entrance she could see from all the front windows of her own house. After the death of Mr Wisbeach, the house had been sold (his son lived in Wimbledon, and had no conscience about what happened to the neighbourhood he grew up in). It soon became clear to Harriet Blackstone that the new owners were unusual. There were several women apparently living there, but no man. To be precise, the house contained no man, but from time to time it did contain men. Several members of the frail sex came and went, often regularly, but none of them lived there. Harriet soon began to suspect that some of the women were also only there on an occasional basis. The explanation for this irregularity eventually occurred to her.

'The place is no less than a brothel!' she said to the Ebenezer's minister.

'I should prefer the phrase "House of Pleasure",' he said. There was no inconsistency in his rebuke. 'Pleasure' was always, for him, a dirty word.

Steady and prolonged observation of the house only strengthened Harriet's conviction. One fine afternoon she marched around to the Walthamstow police station and demanded to see the inspector in charge, refusing to say what she wanted to talk to him about. Such was her force of personality that she got her way, though normally the constable on the duty desk would have shielded his boss from the force of any public indignation.

Inspector Cochrane took his feet off the desk (he wore size thirteen boots, which had for a long time hindered his promotion, as being more suitable for a walker of the beat rather than one undertaking a more thoughtful role, but eventually merit had won out). He welcomed Mrs Blackstone and heard her detailed account of the occupants of number three, Gladstone Road, and the male visitors that had been seen going there. He took no action to cut her short, merely lighting a cigarette and enduring the vicious glances she cast at it. When at last she drew to a close, he tipped the ash off the end of it and got a word in himself.

'Right,' he began. 'Now, it may surprise you to know that you're not the first to come to us over this little matter. I feel people might have done better to talk to the inhabitants of number three, so they got their facts right first, but new residents always take time to be accepted, don't they? Anyway, we've made enquiries, and the family who bought the house from Mr Wisbeach are called

O'Hare. Their grandfather came over from Ireland to work on the Manchester to Leeds railway, and their father came south to work on building the station at Liverpool Street and on the lines going out from it. He died last year. It's a big family, and the men in it are either married or working here and there around the country.'

'One of the regular visitors bears a distinct resemblance to the constable who directs the traffic at one end of Walthamstow High Street,' said Harriet waspishly.

'PC O'Hare. Quite,' said Inspector Cochrane. 'Some of the men of the family visit regularly, some less often if they live further away – just as you'd expect. The mother, widow of the man who worked on Liverpool Street station, is not too badly off, and one of the daughters works for a dressmaker in Clerkenwell. I'm not sure I should be telling you their business, but I feel I should save time. So there you are. Problem solved.'

Harriet Blackstone, after a few moments' meditation, cast him one of her bay-tree-withering looks.

'You're telling me I've been wasting my time,' she said.

'I've said nothing of the sort.'

'Well, let's wait and see: It's Time as will tell,' she said, and she marched out of his office and the police station without so much as a goodbye.

As ill luck would have it, it was later that afternoon, when Harriet was still in a foul mood, that

Charlie Paxman made his first visit to his new mother-in-law's home. He had seen Sylvia going in when he was arriving back early from a job, and he had knocked at the front door to tell her he was off to the Wolf and Whistle for a pint.

'Bring him in. Let's have a look at him!' shouted Harriet in the kitchen to her daughter at the front door. Charlie went through sheepishly and she surveyed his white-spattered and overalled form from top to toe.

'Well, you're never going to set the Thames on fire,' she said.

'Such was never my ambition,' said Charlie genially. 'And I doubt if Mr Gladstone 'imself could 'ave achieved it.'

Mrs Blackstone continued sharpening her carving knife on her whetstone, her way of relieving her frustration, and continued the attack. 'Don't you take the name of that godly man in vain,' she said (never having heard of the great man's determined work among the fallen women of the Westminster area). 'He was worth a hundred of you. I suppose you're off to the pub?'

'Just called in to tell Sylv I'm off to do a little job in Trafalgar Street,' said Charlie, winking at his wife. 'You're doing a fine job on that knife, Ma. I could use that in my job, a fine sharp one like that. Just take care you don't whetstone the 'ole thing away, though.'

'When I want advice from a sot like you, I'll ask

251

for it,' said Harriet. 'Get off to your beer palace and your drunken mates.'

'Yes, I could do with a good sharp knife like that,' said Charlie meditatively as he left the house.

'Don't know what you've got against drink,' said Sylvia, greatly daring. 'I like the odd Guinness myself these days. Or a port and lemon.' And she put down what she was doing and followed her husband.

Three days later, when she was putting out cyanide against the insects and hoping it would also tempt any stray dog in the neighbourhood that penetrated her backyard to have a lick, Harriet had a set-to with Jim Parsons in the next house. Jim had worked on the roads, and was no invalided out with a pittance of a pension.

'That stuff smells like a charnel house,' he shouted. 'I wonder you don't drop dead on the spot, just putting it out.'

'You wouldn't understand the first thing about hygiene,' she shouted.

'No, I wouldn't. But I tell you, if one of my pigeons dies, there'll be another death follows on.'

Jim Parson loved his birds more than he had ever loved mortal, and his love of them made Mrs Blackstone wish she could wipe out the entire loft of them, and make a feathered carpet of Parson's backyard.

The end, when it came, was sudden. It was an early morning death, so most of the activity in Gladstone Road was centred on the back kitchens.

Paul Dean, the builder, had left his long ladder outside the Blackstone residence at half past six (he was not being blackmailed by Harriet, and merely did it for a quiet life). Since it was the second Thursday in the month, everyone in the street knew it was Mrs Blackstone's day for cleaning her windows. Being convinced that everyone had a duty to do the difficult things first – as they should eat their vegetables before their meat, if any – Harriet always began with the attic windows. She climbed the stepladder, as always soon after seven o'clock. Her long skirts did not make things easy, but she was used to that problem, and she coped with that and with the bucket she was carrying. The police ascertained later that the glass in the right-hand side of the double window had been cleaned, and she had just begun on the left-hand side, abutting Jim Parsons' house, when she fell. She dropped her bucket immediately, and managed to grasp the guttering along the top of Jim Parsons' house. The iron was much eroded by the pigeon droppings, of which the gutter itself was nearly full, and the whole section broke off with her weight. She fell to her death on the pavement below, hitting her head on Parsons' front step. She lay face up, the face half-covered with pigeon dirt. The doctor at the other end of Trafalgar Street was called out from his breakfast, and he pronounced her dead.

'Any fool could have seen *that*,' said Charlie Paxman, who nevertheless stood guard in the street and moved people on when they were inclined to gossip or crow.

The police investigation was brief, not to say cursory. The foolishness of a woman in long and bulky skirts cleaning regularly the windows of a room that was never used, at a level too high for the dirt to be seen from the road, was evident to all the (male) members of the force who looked into the matter. The details of the accident hardly seemed of any moment, and in any case were irretrievable. A man on his way to an early start at a factory in Ilford had walked along Gladstone Road on his way to the omnibus in Trafalgar Street. He had seen Harriet Blackstone up her ladder but had seen nothing untoward about her activity, which he'd seen her at regularly over the years. He had seen a boy running down a side lane in the direction of Gladstone Road at a great tilt, and said he had the look of Dick Gregory, who had lived in the area up until six months before. After he turned the corner into Trafalgar Street he had heard a crash, but his omnibus was approaching his stop, so he had no time to investigate even if he'd thought it important. In fact he hadn't thought twice about it. No one had heard anything of Dick Gregory since his family had moved away, and were not to hear anything of him again for six or seven years, at which time he joined the police force and was frequently to be seen trying doors and reprimanding children and vagrants along a regular beat, splendid in his hard helmet, with his truncheon swinging from his belt. At the time the police paid very little attention to the workman who brought up his name. All boys look pretty alike, they said.

On the night of her death, when the jollifications had died down in the street and her daughter was sleeping in the arms of her lawful husband, there was quite a lot of activity in number three, the house that had engaged so much of Harriet's attention in the last week of her life. In one of the front bedrooms a man and a woman were preparing for bed, he undressing with enthusiasm, she with a practiced routine. They were laughing over the events of the day. The woman, in bed first, lay back against the pillow, looked at his boots beside the bed, and giggled. 'Funny, all the times you've been, and I don't even know your name. I always think of you as size thirteens.'

'Come to that, I don't know yours,' said the man.

'Call me Collette. Collette O'Hare.'

'O'Hare, of course. And you can call me Prince Albert.'

And then, with the sort of thoroughness and dedication for which that prince was famous, he got down to the job.

EDWARD MARSTON

THE COMICAL REVENGE

'**W**here on earth have you been?' asked
Henry Redmayne, petulantly. 'You
must have received my letter hours ago.'

'I came as soon as I could,' said Christopher.

'Well, it was not soon enough. Heavens, I'm your
brother!'

'I was busy, Henry. My client wanted to be
shown over the house.'

'And does the demand of a client take prece-
dence over a heartfelt plea from your only sibling?
I declare, Christopher, that your memory is
wondrously short. But for me,' said Henry, striking
a pose, 'you would have no clients.'

'You did help me to launch my career, it's true,
and I'm eternally grateful.'

'Then why not show your gratitude by
responding to my summons?'

'I've done so.'

'Hours too late.'

Arms folded, Henry turned his back to show his
displeasure. Christopher was far too accustomed
to his brother's irritable behavior to let it upset
him. Over the years, he had endured Henry's bad

256

temper, his capriciousness and his blatant selfishness, with a weary affection. They were in the drawing room of Henry's house in Bedford Street and Christopher was waiting patiently for his brother's ire to cool. A gifted young man, he was one of the many architects helping to rebuild London after the ravages of the Great Fire, and he had achieved marked success in his short career. He never forgot that it was Henry who, by introducing him to a friend, provided him with his first client.

Christopher always dressed smartly but his brother wore nothing that was not flamboyant. As he swung round to confront his visitor, Henry was wearing a pair of red velvet petticoat breeches, edged with ribbon and hanging from his hips, a blue and gold doublet over a billowing linen shirt and a pair of shoes whose silver buckles positively gleamed. To hide his thinning hair, he had on a full periwig but it did not disguise the clear signs of dissipation in his face. With his handsome features, his healthy complexion and his long hair with its reddish tinge, Christopher looked as if twenty long years separated them and not merely a short few.

Henry put a hand to his chest. 'I face a terrible dilemma,' he announced.

'There is no novelty in that,' said Christopher with a tolerant smile.

'Do not mock me. I speak in earnest.'

'What is it this time – gambling debts?'

'No.'

'A stern warning from Father?'

'The old gentleman has not written for a month, thank God.'

'Then there must be some vexing problem at your place of work.'

'The Navy Office is an agreeable sinecure.'

'That leaves one possibility,' decided Christopher. 'There's a woman in the case. You've put yourself in a compromising position yet again.' He heaved a sigh. 'Will you never learn, Henry?'

'Stop sounding like Father,' retorted the other. 'It's bad enough to have one clergyman in the family. Read me no sermons, Christopher. Every supposition you make is entirely wrong. Do me the courtesy of listening to me and you'll hear why I'm in such a dire predicament.'

'Very well,' said Christopher, sitting down. 'I am all ears.'

'Last night, I went to the theatre with a friend to watch the Duke's Company. The play was called The Comical Revenge.'

'I remember it well. I saw it some years ago when it was first performed. George Etherege has a wicked eye and sparkling wit. The Comical Revenge is almost as good as his new play, She Would If She Could.'

Henry stamped a foot. 'Damnation! Who is telling this story – you or me?'

'I'll say no more.'

'Thank you. Now, where was I?'

'Going to the theatre with a friend.'

'Will you please be quiet, Christopher!' His younger brother put a hand to his lips to signal that he would remain silent. 'Let me try again,' said Henry, measuring his words before he spoke them. 'What I tell you is in the strictest confidence and must be divulged to nobody. Do you understand?' Christopher nodded obediently. 'The friend whom I accompanied last night was Sir Beresford Tyte, an odd fellow in some ways but generous to a fault. He has saved me time and again with a providential loan. Now, however,' he went on, grimacing, 'Sir Beresford wants repayment.'

'I knew that it was a gambling debt!'

'But it's not – at least, not entirely. Sir Beresford had an unfortunate encounter at the playhouse. We chanced to meet the egregious Lord Plumer there. Sir Beresford – and here I must remind you how crucial discretion is – has become closely acquainted with that divine creature, Ariana, my Lady Plumer. It seems that her husband finally learned of the attachment,' said Henry, rolling his eyes. 'There was a frightful scene. My friend denied ever having seen the wife, as any decent man would have done, but my Lord Plumer insisted on revenge. He challenged Sir Beresford to a duel.'

'That was very rash,' observed Christopher. 'Sir Beresford must be thirty years younger than him. He's bound to triumph.'

'Sadly, he is not.'

'Why?'

'Because he will not be crossing swords with that old cuckold, that's why. He has a substitute,' said Henry, ruefully. 'I've been engaged to fight in his stead.'

Christopher was astonished. 'You?'

'Yes,' confessed the other, taking a seat opposite him. 'My friend and I are of the same height and build. If I wear that black periwig of his and don his apparel – years out of fashion, though it be – I can pass for Sir Beresford Tyte easily enough.'

'But why should you have to?'

'To settle my debt to him.'

'On such demanding terms.'

'I owe the fellow hundreds of pounds.'

'Let me help you to pay it off.'

'If only it were that easy, Christopher,' said his brother, woefully, 'but it is not, I fear. After the play, we adjourned to a certain house to take our pleasure with the ladies of the establishment. A modicum of drink was consumed.'

'In short, you became hopelessly drunk and gave him your word.'

'As a matter of honour, I have to keep it. Yes,' he added, seeing his brother's look of disapproval, 'honour is at stake here. When the idea was first put to me, I found it rather appealing. Just think of it, Christopher. Five minutes of swordplay and I wipe out debts that took me years to build up. I'd be free of obligation.'

'Sir Beresford is the man with the obligation. It is he who was challenged last night. If honor has any meaning,' insisted Christopher, 'he should face his mistress's husband with a sword in his hand. Is he too cowardly to do so?'

'No, he's too fearful of losing Ariana's love. It's one thing to put horns on the head of my Lord Plumer. To thrust a rapier through his heart is a different matter.'

'So he expects you to kill the old man in his place?'

'He'd prefer me to wound and disable him.'

'That's a monstrous imposition to place upon a friend.'

'It did not seem so at the time,' said Henry. 'I am no mean swordsman and have no fear that the old goat will get the better of me. If I drew blood from him, I foolishly assumed, he'd turn tail and quit the field. Duty done, debt discharged.' He ran a worried hand across his chin. 'Then I learned a little more about my Lord Plumer.'

'I think I can guess what you are going to tell me,' said Christopher. 'If this lady is the young and beautiful wife of a much older man, she will have more than one suitor after her. Sir Beresford Tyte may just be the latest.'

'You've hit the mark, brother.'

'My Lord Plumer will have challenged others to a duel before now. Why does he do so when he has little chance of prevailing with a sword in his hand?'

'Because his bullies have cudgels in theirs, Christopher.'

'Ah, I see. He is determined to win at all costs.'

'The last man whom he accused of a liaison with his wife was found battered almost to death. The one before that had his nose slit.' Henry shivered. 'I prefer my nose as it is, thank you. It's one of my best features. And I've no wish to be cudgeled until every bone in my body is broken.' He spread his arms in despair. 'What am I to do?'

'Let your friend suffer the consequences of his dalliance,' said Christopher. 'Sir Beresford must have known the risk that he was running. Husbands do not like it when their wives are led astray. This is a mess of his own making.'

'But I'm the one who has to get out of it somehow. Whatever I do, I'll not go back to Sir Beresford. He's counting on me.'

'To take punishment on his behalf. That's an unjust contract to enforce.'

'Teach me a way to escape from it, Christopher. I need your counsel.'

'Why? You always ignore it. I've been telling you for years to shed the company of rakes like Sir Beresford Tyte, but you'll not hear of it. You see the result of it now.'

Henry put up his hands defensively. 'Not another homily – please.'

Christopher bit back what he was going to say. His brother was in great distress but censure would not help him. Only positive action could rescue Henry Redmayne. The difficulty lay in extracting him from a desperate situation while keeping his honor intact. Christopher pondered. Henry reached out to touch him.

'Will you protect me, Christopher?' he asked. 'Will you act as my second?'

'That will not suffice.'

'Do not betray me in my hour of need.'

'I'd never do that,' said Christopher, smiling as an idea suddenly popped into his head. 'Where is this duel to take place?'

'At a time and spot of our own choosing.'

'Then the problem is solved.'

'How?'

'All will become clear in time, Henry. Talk to Sir Beresford,' he instructed. 'Let him send word that the duel will take place at seven o'clock on Sunday morning.'

'Sunday?' Henry was surprised. 'A sword fight on the Lord's Day?'

'There's a reason behind it.'

'And where will Sir Beresford – or his deputy – meet his challenger?'

'At the new house that I've designed,' said Christopher. 'It's only half-built but the garden has been walled. It's very private. Sunday is the one time when none of the builders or gardeners will be there.'

'But I hoped you'd find a way to get me out of this duel.'

'Trust me, Henry. I'm doing just that.'

* * *

The house was in Baynard's Castle ward, a district that had suffered badly during the Great Fire and lost its parish churches as well as a large number of other properties. Christopher Redmayne had designed one of the many new houses to fill the vacant gaps. Tall, stately and with an impressive façade, the building had a garden that ran down to the river where, in due course, it would have its own landing stage. Trees, bushes and flowers had already been planted but most of the garden was given over to a series of rectangular lawns. It was on the biggest of these swards that the duel was to take place.

Christopher did not recognize his brother when they met. Henry had not only put on apparel belonging to Sir Beresford Tyte, he was wearing the man's periwig and had adopted his friend's posture and gait. It was a convincing disguise. Christopher used a key to let them into the house. They went through it into the garden. Henry was tense and uncharacteristically reticent. His brother led him into the shadow of some bushes. They did not have long to wait. Within minutes, the garden gate opened and Roger, Lord Plumer, entered with two brawny companions.

'I thought you said I would not have to fight,' complained Henry.

'Take up your position,' said Christopher. 'That is all.'

'And then?'

Henry's question went unanswered because his

adversary was bearing down on them. Lord Plumer was a short, fat, waddling man in his late fifties with a neat grey beard. Identifying Henry as his opponent, he got close enough to sneer at him.

'So you had the courage to turn up, did you?' he said with disdain. 'I'll make you rue that decision, Sir Beresford. You tried to steal my wife's affections away from me, you libertine. By the time I've finished with you, my friend, you'll not be able to consort with any lady. Make yourself ready, sir!'

'Not so fast, my lord,' said Christopher, stepping forward. 'If a duel is to take place, it must abide strictly by the rules.'

'A plague on any rules!' snorted the other, drawing his sword. 'Defend yourself, Sir Beresford. I'm coming to relieve you of your manhood.'

And without further warning, he charged forward, brandishing his rapier. Henry barely had time to unsheathe his weapon in order to defend himself. Parrying the first thrust, he backed away. Christopher kept one eye on the two seconds as they tried to move in behind his brother to distract him. It was clear that, if their master faltered, they were to rescue him and overpower Henry. As a precaution, Christopher kept a hand on the hilt of his own sword but he did not have to draw it. Salvation appeared in exactly the way that he had planned.

'Hold, sirs!' yelled Bale. 'You are breaking the law!'

Two constables had just burst in through the gate. Jonathan Bale, the first of them, was a big, powerful man with an authoritative voice. There was disgust in his face as he strode across the lawn.

'Shame on you both!' he cried. 'Is this how you celebrate the Day of Rest? Would you defy God by fighting on the Sabbath?'

Relieved by the interruption, and recognizing Bale as his brother's close friend, Henry backed away. He had been rescued. In turning up in place of another man, he felt that honour has been satisfied. Tossing a smile of thanks to Christopher, he sheathed his sword. But his opponent was not so ready to abandon the duel. One of his seconds pulled a pistol from his belt and handed it to his master. Lord Plumer took aim. Before Henry realized what was happening, there was a loud report and something stung him on the temple. With blood streaming down his face, he collapsed to the ground.

Shocked by what he had witnessed, Bale ran towards the injured man. The other constable, meanwhile, tried to arrest Roger, Lord Plumer, but he was brushed aside by the two seconds. They ran to the gate with their master and got away in their carriage.

Christopher paid no attention to their escape. His only concern was the fate of his brother. Bending solicitously beside him, he cased the wig off so that he could examine the wound properly. Bale looked anxiously over his friend's shoulder at the fallen man.

'You did not tell me that it was your brother, Mr Redmayne,' he said.

Christopher did not mince his words. As he stood outside his brother's bedchamber, he let Sir Beresford Tyte know exactly what he thought of the man's behavior.

'What you did was unforgivable,' he said with controlled passion. 'It was cruel, ungentlemanly and tinged with cowardice. Thanks to you, my brother might easily have been killed.'

'I did not mean this to happen,' said the other.

'Then you should have met your own obligations, and not shuffled them off on to Henry. You exposed him to unnecessary danger.'

'I thought he would simply wound my Lord Plumer and put him to flight.'

'While you were hiding at home. Really, Sir Beresford, I thought better of you.'

Sir Beresford Tyte had the grace to look shamefaced. He was a tall, thin man in his late twenties with an air of prosperity about him. Unlike Henry, his life of debauchery had left no visible signs on him. He was undeniably handsome and Christopher could see why the lady in question had been attracted to him.

'How is Henry?' asked Tyte with obvious concern.

'We shall know when the doctor has finished examining him.'

'I was horrified when I heard the news.'

'Had you fought the duel yourself, my brother would not have been shot.'

'No,' rejoined Tyte, 'but I might have been. How was I to know that that old fool would have a pistol at hand?' He tried to mollify Christopher with a smile. 'Do not be too harsh on me, Christopher. Your brother has profited from this venture. All his debts have been paid off in this action.'

'That is no consolation to him – or to me.'

'I'll be revenged on my lord Plumer for this!'

'And who will you get to do that on your behalf?' asked Christopher, sharply.

Tyte looked embarrassed. The next moment, the door opened and the doctor, an elderly man with a pronounced stoop, came out of the bedchamber. They turned to him.

'Well?' asked Tyte.

'He's a fortunate man,' said the doctor. 'The bullet only grazed his temple. It drew blood and will leave a scar, but there's no lasting damage. The patient, however, is still badly shocked by the experience. I've given him a sleeping draught.'

'May I not speak to him?'

'You may try, Sir Beresford, but do not expect a conversation with him.'

Tyte nodded and went quickly into the bedchamber to apologise to his friend. Reassured by the diagnosis, Christopher led the doctor downstairs and showed him out of the house. He then went across to Jonathan Bale who had been waiting in the hall. The constable was trying not to look at a painting on the wall of naked women in a Roman orgy. Christopher repeated what the doctor had told them.

'I'm relieved to hear it,' said Bale, seriously. 'I could never bring myself to approve of your brother's way of life,' he added, glancing at the painting that troubled him so much, 'but I do not wish him any ill. He was the victim of attempted murder and the culprit must answer for it.'

'He will do, Jonathan,' promised Christopher.

'Tell me his name and I'll obtain a warrant for his arrest.'

'That would not achieve anything, alas. The gentleman is far too well connected to fear the process of law. His brother is a judge and he has a dozen politicians in his pocket. Besides,' he went on, 'Henry would not want this matter to go to court or he will be charged with taking part in a duel.'

'Why did he do so in disguise, Mr Redmayne?'

'I will tell you when this whole business has blown over.'

Christopher was very fond of the constable but he knew that his friend's Puritan conscience would be aroused if he heard the full facts of the case. Infidelity and large gambling debts lay behind the affair. Both were anathema to

269

Jonathan Bale. At a later date, Christopher resolved, he would give his friend an edited account of events.

'I'll not let this crime go unpunished,' warned Bale.

'Nor will it be, Jonathan. I am already devising a reprisal.'

'I hope that you do not intend to challenge the fellow to a duel.'

Christopher grinned. 'I'd never do that,' he said. 'Duelling is illegal. You'd have to arrest me and I'd hate to put you in a position to do that.'

'Thank you,' said Bale with a rare smile. 'My wife would never forgive me, if I arrested you. Sarah would not let me hear the end of it.' He became solemn. 'As long as an attempt to kill your brother does not go unanswered.'

'It will have the most appropriate answer of all, Jonathan.'

'And what is that?'

'A comical revenge.'

Convinced that he had killed his wife's lover, Roger, Lord Plumer, returned to his house in high spirits. He found his wife, Ariana, alone in the drawing room. She looked up with disappointment when he entered.

'Yes,' he said, knowingly. 'You may well be surprised to see your husband when you were hoping that Sir Beresford Tyte would call on you.'

'I awaited only your return,' she said, retaining her composure.

'That is how it will be from now on, Ariana. Whether we are in London or on our estate in the country, you'll keep to the house and await my return.'

'Would you make a prisoner of me, sir?'

'I thought I'd done that when I married you. But I see that I'll need to put more formal constraints upon you. Do not stir abroad without my permission.'

'This is intolerable!' she complained.

'It is what befits a Lady Plumer.'

'I'll not be kept behind bars like that.'

'You were allowed far too much licence, Ariana. Those days are gone.'

His wife rose from her chair and crossed to the window. Still in her twenties, she was a shapely woman of medium height with a quiet loveliness that was now vitiated by a deep frown. Having married her husband for his title and his wealth, she had soon regretted her decision. It was not long before she was seeking interest and affection from outside the bonds of matrimony. Without such diversions, her life would be unbearable. The future suddenly looked bleak.

'Forget him, Ariana,' said her husband, moving to stand behind her. 'You'll never see Sir Beresford again – unless you attend his funeral, that is.'

She spun round in alarm. 'His funeral?' she gasped.

271

'Yes, my wayward darling. I killed him in a duel this very morning.'

The sleeping draught administered by the doctor was quick to take effect. No sooner had Sir Beresford Tyte told his friend how deeply he regretted what had happened than Henry Redmayne drifted off. When he woke up again a few hours later, he found Tyte still at his bedside. Christopher was also there.

'How do you feel now?' asked his brother, softly.

'In agony,' replied Henry, determined to get maximum sympathy from the situation even though he was in no pain. 'My stomach churns, my heart is about to burst and my head stings as though someone inserted a dagger in my ear. The wonder is that I'm still alive after that ordeal.'

'I blame myself for that,' admitted Tyte.

'So you should,' said Christopher.

'Tell me how I can make amends and I'll do it.'

'A loan of fifty pounds would be an admirable gesture,' suggested Henry.

'Take it as a gift,' insisted Tyte. 'You've earned it, my friend.'

'I've an idea how it might usefully be spent,' said Christopher. 'An attempt was made on your life this morning, Henry. A sly and cowardly attempt. The culprit must pay for that. Jonathan Bale wanted to arrest him but the deception would then be exposed in open court.'

'We must not have that, Christopher!'

'Dear Lord, no!' agreed Tyte. 'If it were known that I let Henry deputise for me, my reputation would be ruined.'

'It's already been seriously compromised, Sir Beresford,' said Christopher, 'but enough of that. Let us turn to my Lord Plumer. Though he is swift to denounce anyone who dallies with his wife, I hear that he is not above straying away from the marital couch.'

'Indeed not!' declared Henry, sitting up in bed. 'For all his wrinkles, he's a rampant satyr at times. His mistress is one Betty Malahide, a comely creature and worthy of far better than him.'

'The lady is aware of that,' said Tyte. 'From what I hear, Betty Malahide tired of him and brought an end to the liaison. That made him choleric. It also forced him to spend more time at home where he found evidence that Ariana and I were more than passing acquaintances. Had he still been involved with his mistress,' he went on with rancour, 'then I would still be enjoying favours from his wife.'

'And I would not have had to face a madman with a pistol,' said Henry.

Christopher was curious. 'Do either of you know this Betty Malahide?'

'We both do, Christopher, and I would sue to know her better.'

'If she discarded my lord Plumer, she will have only bitter memories of him. Do you think she would help us to wreak our revenge on him?'

'At a price,' said Tyte. 'Betty will do anything for a price.'

'Then the fifty pounds you offered Henry will be a sound investment.'

'But I need the money,' wailed his brother.

'You need satisfaction,' said Christopher, 'and the only way you can get that is by humiliating my Lord Plumer to the point where he has to quit London.'

'Yes,' said Tyte. 'I'll subscribe to any plan that does that. I want him well and truly out of the way. While he's in the city, he remains a danger to me.'

'Return home, Sir Beresford. Give out that you've been injured and are lying at death's door. That will content my Lord Plumer and put him off guard.'

'What of Betty Malahide?' wondered Henry.

'You must introduce me to her,' said Christopher. 'I have a proposition that might appeal to the lady.'

Lord Plumer was at his favorite coffee house when the letter was delivered to him. It was a request from his erstwhile mistress and he responded with alacrity. Excusing himself from his friends, he went out to his carriage and told his coachman where to take him. He was certain that Betty Malahide had repented of her decision to end her relationship with him, and was going to beg him to return to her bed. That put him in a position to exact

274

conditions from her. He whiled away the journey by musing on what those conditions might be.

Admitted to her house, he was immediately conducted upstairs and that confirmed his belief that she wished to be reconciled with him. As he tapped on the door of her bedchamber, he expected a welcoming call to enter the room where he had enjoyed so much pleasure in the past. All that he heard, however, was a frightened voice.

'Is that you, my lord?' asked Betty Malahide. 'Do please come in.'

As he opened the door, a second surprise awaited him. Hoping to find her contrite and anxious to atone for the unkind way she had spurned him, he instead discovered that his mistress was not even alone. Betty Malahide, a buxom woman with a swarthy hue that he found irresistible, was perched on the edge of the bed. A plump man in black attire seemed to be examining her. Pulling her gown around her with embarrassment, she shot the newcomer a glance of apprehension.

'Thank you for coming so promptly, my lord,' she said. 'This is Doctor Cooper and he has grim news for both of us.' She flitted towards her dressing room. 'I'll leave you alone so that he can divulge what he has found.'

'What ails you, Betty?' asked Lord Plumer but she had already vanished into the adjacent chamber. He turned to Doctor Cooper. 'Well?'

'The lady requires treatment, my lord,' explained

the doctor. 'Not to put too fine a point on it, she has the French disease.'

'Well, she caught it not from me!' exclaimed the other.

'Perhaps not, my lord, but she would certainly have given it to you.'

'How do you know, man?'

'Because it's a virulent strain that I recognise,' said Doctor Cooper, 'and it is highly infectious. If there have been intimate relations between the two of you in recent weeks, there is no way that you could escape contracting the disease.'

'The devil take her!'

'Mistress Malahide deserves compassion rather than reproach.'

'The wanton will get no compassion from me,' snarled the other, pacing the room in agitation. 'If she did not catch the disease from me, then she caught it from another man. Betty has both infected and cuckolded me!'

'That's a private matter between the two of you, my lord. Fortunately, we have caught it early and I have a cure that will restore the both of you to perfect health.'

'What sort of cure?'

When the doctor explained in detail, Lord Plumer was so shocked that he had to sit in a chair to recover. He agreed to present himself later that day so that the first stage of the treatment could begin. The doctor left him to reflect on the consequences of his doomed romance with Betty

Malahide. He was still basking in remorse when she came back into the room. Her manner had changed completely. Hands on hips, she was now angry and vindictive.

'I curse the day I ever met you, my lord!' she yelled.

'I am the victim here, you harlot!'

'I offered you my love and you infected me in return. The French disease is a poor reward for all the efforts I made in this very room to pleasure you.'

'What are you saying, woman?' he demanded. 'You are the villain here. While swearing that you were true to me, you grant favors to another and let him pass on his hideous infection. I caught it from you in turn.'

'How can that be when no other man has touched me?'

'Do not lie to me, Betty.'

'You are the liar, my lord,' she accused. 'This condition from which we both suffer was picked up by you between the thighs of some common whore. Admit it.'

'I'll admit nothing of the sort,' he said with righteous indignation. 'Unlike you, I kept my vow of fidelity. In all the time that we were together, I never looked at another woman. I swear it, Betty! I'd take my Bible oath.'

Betty Malahide could see that he was telling the truth. It put a malicious glint into her eye as she came forward to confront him. She produced a cold smile.

'What about your dear wife, my lord? Did you not sleep with her?'

He flicked a dismissive hand. 'Ariana does not count.'

'Oh, but she does. In view of what Doctor Cooper told us, I think that she counts for a great deal. There is the root of our trouble,' she urged. 'It's my Lady Plumer who is to blame for all this. Your wife infected you and you passed on the disease to me.'

'Dear God!' he said, clutching at his throat. 'Can this be so?'

'It is so, my lord. And that raises another question. Who gave it to her?'

Lord Plumer gulped. A day that had begun so well had ended in disaster.

Christopher Redmayne had never thought of his brother as a tactful man but he was proved wrong. When the two of them called on Lady Plumer, Henry was both suave and politic, passing on the information with a degree of charm and wording it in a way to upset her least. Henry had recovered from his brush with her husband. Wearing his new suit, he looked as resplendent as ever but his serious manner counteracted the impression that he usually gave of being a decadent fop. Christopher also admired Lady Plumer's poise. She did not falter for a second.

'I am vaguely acquainted with Sir Beresford,' she said, 'and I'm sorry to hear that he was injured

278

in a duel with my husband.' Her voice hardened. 'I'm even more sorry to learn that Roger disgraced himself by shooting a pistol in that way. Yet you tell me that Sir Beresford will recover?'

'Yes,' said Henry. 'My brother has just been to see him.'

Christopher took over. 'Sir Beresford was badly wounded but the surgeon managed to save him. What he needs now,' he said, 'is a period of rest. His wife has been a tower of strength to him. When he feared that he was about to die, he confessed his sins to her but she was a true Christian and forgave him, provided,' he added, 'that her husband did not go astray again.'

It was a polite hint to Lady Plumer that the affair was over. In view of the trouble that it had caused, Sir Beresford Tyte was eager to abandon his relationship with her and, while he had not, in fact, confessed all to his wife, he had resolved to commit himself to a period of fidelity. Though she gave no hint of understanding what Christopher meant, Lady Plumer was, for her part, quite content. Since her husband had learned of her clandestine romance, it could not, in any case, continue.

She was grateful to the brothers for confiding in her. What they told her gave her a lever to use against her husband. Even someone as ruthless as Lord Plumer would not wish his friends to know that he had broken the unwritten laws of duelling so brazenly. Knowing the truth about what he did would purchase her freedom once more. Of the two brothers, she thought Christopher by far the more handsome and appealing but she sensed that he was too responsible to become involved with a married woman. She dismissed Henry as a possible lover because of his resemblance to Sir Beresford Tyte. In time, she would have to look elsewhere.

'I thank you both for this intelligence,' she said, smiling at Christopher.

'We felt that you had a right to know,' he replied, 'even though Sir Beresford was only a distant acquaintance. But your husband must be warned, my lady. The duel was interrupted by two constables. Had they managed to apprehend my Lord Plumer, he would have been arraigned on a charge of attempted murder.'

'Goodness!' she cried, secretly wishing that he had been.

'It might be better if he were to quit London for a while.'

'I'll insist upon it, Mr Redmayne,' she said. 'When he returns home, I will have a great deal to say to Roger. The time has come for stern words.'

'Do not be too harsh on him, my lady,' said Henry, suppressing a grin.

'No,' said Christopher. 'You may find him in a weakened state.'

★   ★   ★

Lord Plumer could not believe the severity of the cure. Stripped naked in the doctor's private chamber, he was forced to sit in a hot tub from which mercury vapour rose to invade his eyes and ears. It was agony but it was also the only known way to deal with venereal disease. If this first ordeal did not work, Doctor Cooper had warned him that he would have to endure isolation, semi-starvation, enemas, ointments and pills, each involving the hateful mercury. Lord Plumer felt as if he were being boiled alive. The worst of it was that he did not know whether to blame his wife, his mistress or himself. His dilemma was an impossible one. He could not challenge his wife without revealing that he had caught the disease, yet he could not sleep with her for fear of contracting the infection again. All that he could do was to grit his teeth and suffer.

'No!' he howled as the doctor added more mercury. 'I am burning in Hell!'

Jonathan Bale had been so helpful that Christopher felt he deserved an explanation. They met at the architect's house in Fetter Lane, one of the few buildings that had escaped destruction from the fire. It was so much larger and more comfortable than his own house that it always made Bale slightly uneasy. Christopher told him about his brother's folly in agreeing to represent another man in a duel though he did not disclose

Tyte's name or that of Lord Plumer. Bale's sense of duty pricked him.

'I should, by rights, arrest your brother and this false friend of his,' he said.

'Leave them be, Jonathan. Thanks to your prompt arrival, the duel did not, in fact, take place. You prevented the crime. But you inadvertently set off another. Henry's opponent did not behave like a gentleman.'

'Neither will I when I call him to account. Who is the rogue, Mr Redmayne?'

'A man who has been truly chastened.'

'He deserves to be locked up in Newgate.'

'Have no fear,' said Christopher with a chuckle, 'he has suffered worse than mere imprisonment. He has been deprived of his peace of mind.'

Christopher did not dare to tell him how they had employed an actor to play the part of Doctor Cooper or paid Betty Malahide to collude with them. Lord Plumer had been given a fright and that was the object of the exercise.

'You talked about a comical revenge,' recalled Bale.

'Yes, Jonathan. It's the title of a play by George Etherege.'

'You know my opinion of playhouses. They are dens of sin and iniquity.'

'They are also places of entertainment,' said Christopher. 'And they excite the mind as well. It was only because I once saw Mr Etherege's play that I was able to arrange this comical revenge. I look upon it as a fine piece of architecture.'

Bale was mystified. 'How is this play linked to the punishment that has been inflicted?' he asked, scratching his head.

'The Comical Revenge has a significant sub-title.'

'Oh? And what might that be, Mr Redmayne?'

Christopher smiled to himself. 'The Tale of a Tub,' he said.

COLIN DEXTER

BETWEEN THE LINES

17 Bridgnorth Street
Kidderminster

10 August

Dear Ronald,

I was sittin' only a coupla feet away on the night Big Jimmy was shot through his underachieving brain . . .

That's my opening gambit. No – that *was* my opening gambit.

Remember how our guru gave us those three guidelines? First, grab 'em all with that first sentence of yours. Second, don't get too worried if you find yourself writing a load of crap. Third (this is it!), if you want a short cut to 'ideas', just take any situation you've experienced recently, doesn't matter how pedestrian and trite, write it up as quickly as you can, and then just change one of the incidents in it, just the *one*, and see how your story suddenly leaps into life.

So please read my entry (enclosed) for

our competition. How I need that prize money! There's not much 'grab' about the new opening, but plenty of 'crap' in the rest. I'm not bothered. It was a *third* guide-line that struck in my underachievin' brain, and you'll soon spot that one fictitious incident in the story. Forgive me! Here goes.

There were twenty-three of us on that trip, with me the youngest but one. Mistakenly, I'd never expected things to live up to the brochure's promise: 'Ten days amid the cultural delight of Prague, Vienna and Budapest, with a unique mix of travel, guided tours and group seminars in creative writing. Travel is by rail, coach and boat. Each of our experienced guides is fluent in English. The leader of the seminar is himself a published author with four acclaimed novels to his name.'

I fell for him a bit from day one, and once or twice I thought he might be vaguely attracted to a single woman about ten years younger than he was. So I was disappointed when it was another man in the group who came to sit beside me as we travelled on the long train journey from Prague to Vienna. It happened like this.

The first-class carriage into which the group was booked was already uncomfortably full when the porter finally lugged my large, over-packed case up from the platform and told me it would have to be stowed away in the next carriage. Not a problem really. Since I was determined not to let my precious case out of my sight, I decided to leave the rest of the group and move along into the next carriage myself; and in truth I almost welcomed the thought of being alone and of concentrating my mind on that glittering short-story prize. I had already taken my seat and was reconsidering my opening sentence . . .

But I got no further.

'Mind if I join you?' (Did I?) 'I thought you'd probably be a bit lonely and—'

But before Ernest Roland, one of our group, had any chance of continuing, the automatic doors opened and two latish-middle-aged women made their way breathlessly into our comparatively empty carriage, each dragging a vast, wheeled case behind them. For a few seconds they stood beside us, glancing indecisively around, before pushing the two cases into the empty space on the carriage floor across the aisle, and finally settling down into the vacant twin-seats immediately in front of us, their backs towards us. From the window seat she had taken, it was the larger of the two ladies who spoke first: 'Well, we made it, Emily!'

Emily was a much slimmer, smaller-boned woman with a rather nervous-looking face – a face I could see quite clearly slantwise, for a slightly curious reason. Throughout the carriage the backs of the seats were designed in such a way that an opening left running down the middle, fairly narrow at the top and the bottom, but with a bulbous swelling in the centre, some four to five inches wide, the whole gap shaped like an old-fashioned oil-lamp. From my seat therefore, also by the window, my view of her was pretty well unrestricted, as was the view of the broad adjustable arm-rest in black leather which separated the blue-upholstered seats. The whole design was light and airy: a comfortable arrangement for passengers' comfort, if not for the passengers' privacy. Indeed, we could follow the newcomers' conversation quite clearly since we each spoke English, albeit with an odd transatlantic twang that almost sounded *un*-American. Very soon we learned that the window-seated widow (?) was named Marion; and it was Ernest who turned to me, eyebrows lifted, as he pointed to Marion's chubby right hand on the arm-rest, the middle finger displaying one of the largest solitaire diamonds I have ever seen. And I was wondering what beautiful brilliants bedecked her other hand when the connecting doors opened behind us. 'Listek, prosim.' Then with a change of gear to a moderate semblance of English, 'Teekits, please.'

Ernest managed to explain that we were both members of the . . . he pointed back over his shoulder.

The ticket collector nodded and moved a pace forward. 'You English also as well?'

'No,' Marion, 'we – are – from – Quebec – in Canada. You understand?'

The man shook his head and both women were now dipping their hands into their hand-luggage.

'Don't worry, dear,' said Emily.

But Marion's fingers continued to scrabble around the bottom of her bag, trawling a collection of brochures, tour-guides, papers, documents and whatever; and was placing them all in a pile on the arm-rest beside her when Emily gave a sotto-voce squeak of delight. '*I've* got them – *both* of them!'

The man checked and clipped each ticket, and moved on a few paces before turning around and eyeing the cases.

'Yours?'

'Yes.'

'I am sorry but . . .'

'You want them moved?' asked Marion belligerently.

'Next stopping per'aps many people . . .'

'We understand,' said Emily.

Ernest grinned at me: 'I think per'aps, er, we ought to . . .'

'So do I.'

We both stood up and joined Marion, who was already out of her seat and staring fecklessly at the luggage when Ernest laid his hand gently on her shoulder.

'Why don't you sit down and relax. *I'll* move the cases to the luggage place at the end of the carriage. They'll be fine there – it's where my friend here has left hers.' He smiled sweetly; and Marion expressed her gratitude equally sweetly as she sat down again – as did I when Ernest insisted that he could manage well enough – better, in fact – without any help from me.

Quickly the cases were stowed; and with my companion back beside me I had no opportunity of developing a second dazzling sentence that would follow my daring murder of big Jimmy. In any case there was soon a further interruption.

Two uniformed Czech soldiers stood beside us, asking in good English to see our passports. Ernest and I were immediately cleared. As was Emily. But Marion was once again scrabbling away in her bag in a state of incipient panic.

'Don't worry, madam. We'll come back.'

They moved along the carriage, and a

flushed-faced Marion turned to Emily. 'It's in my wallet. I *know* it is. But where *is* the wallet?'

'Didn't you see it when you were looking for your ticket, dear?'

'I just can't remember and then you found my ticket and . . . I'm going mad . . . I just—'

She broke off, very close to tears now as, for the second time, she began piling up the bag's contents on the arm-rest, and as a kneeling Emily was spreading her small hands over every square inch of carpet around them. And we joined her. With no success.

'I had it when . . .' bemoaned Marion. 'I just wonder if . . . You know those sort of zip-up things on the side of my case? Yes! I'll just . . .'

She got up and walked to the luggage area, only to return almost immediately, her face betraying disappointment.

'Do you know exactly what else was in the wallet, Marion?'

'Not exactly.'

'How much money?'

'About a thousand euros – more, I should think.'

'As much as that?'

'You don't have to rub it in, Emily!'

A knight in shining armour now rode upon

the scene in the form of a dark-suited middle-aged man who had been seated further along the carriage and who spoke excellent English, albeit with an obvious German accent. 'Excuse me for intruding, ladies. My name is Herr Steiner. I just wonder if I may be of some help to you?' He explained that he worked with the Canadian Consulate in Vienna, and that he couldn't help over-hearing about the wallet, containing pass-port, money and (surely?) plastic cards as well. (Marion nodded.) Above all the good lady should be worried about the cards, because even without a PIN number the thief would for a while have unlimited access to the big stores in the major cities.

For the first time Marion seemed aware of the full implications of her loss: 'I shall have to cancel the cards, yes.'

'That's where I can help you, if you wish it. You have a mobile phone?'

'My good friend here—'

'It's not charged, dear,' confessed a contrite Emily.

'Do you have any details about your pass-port number, card numbers . . . ?'

Temporarily at ease, Marion produced the sheet of A4 which we had already observed on the arm-rest.

Herr Steiner perused the sheet carefully: 'My goodness Passport number, copy of your photo, card numbers – even your PIN number. You really shouldn't let anyone see *that*, you know. But it won't be difficult to sort out the passport and cancel the cards. And if you would like me to do it for you . . . ?' The offer was gladly accepted; and very soon we heard Herr Steiner back in his seat, reeling off strings of numbers in German into his mobile phone.

Ten minutes later all arrangements had been made: cards cancelled, and the address given of the consulate offices in Vienna. Herr Steiner was back in his seat resuming his reading of Heinrich Heine's biography. Marion and Emily were now conversing almost normally. Ernest and I were swapping our assessment of the tour so far, and promising to send each other a copy of our short-story entry.

After crossing the Czech-Austrian border, it came as no surprise that we were subjected to a further passport inspection with (we had been warned) the Austrian police somewhat more officious and perhaps a little too efficient than their Czech counterparts (who, incidentally, had not reappeared). The two men considered our passports carefully, like scrutineers at some electoral recount; then moved on to the Canadian travellers, and it was Herr Steiner who came forward and encored his guardian angel act. He took the A4 sheet. Marion handed to him and showed it to the policeman, itemising the information given in rapid yet quietly spoken German. After some note-taking, and some discussion, their faces impassive, the policemen passed on up the carriage and Herr Steiner translated their instructions to Emily and Marion: when the train reached its destination in Vienna, both of them must remain in the carriage where the station official would meet them.

And that was about it really. Well, no – it wasn't.

Just before we reached Vienna, our group leader came through to ask us to join the main party for a short briefing. Ernest fetched my case and the pair of us left the carriage, bidding farewell to the Canadian ladies, but not to Herr Steiner, who must have been temporarily elsewhere since Heinrich Heine was still lying on his seat.

And what of Marion's wallet? Well, it will perhaps surprise my readers to learn exactly what had happened to it because I know the full truth of the matter.

It is easy enough to make a couple of intelligent guesses: first, that the wallet was not lost, but stolen; second, that the theft occurred on the train, and most probably in the very carriage in which Ernest and I found ourselves. Again, motives for the theft are variously obvious: in themselves passports are valuable items for much criminal chicanery, particularly for falsifying identities or legitimising bogus immigrations; the possession of other people's credit cards, especially with PIN numbers presented on a plate, can be extremely profitable – at least in the short term; and the attraction of a thick wodge of banknotes . . . Need I say more?

But *who* was the guilty party in all this?

Plenty of suspects. The Czech police would be the obvious ones, since anyone finding the wallet would probably give it to them, and they were on the scene from the start. The Austrian police? If they'd had a little more opportunity of finding the wallet itself, they'd had ample time to note down its key contents, so obligingly set forth on the sheet Marion handed them. But why, if they were the guilty party, did they bother to arrange a meeting with the 'station official' in Vienna? If, in fact, they had done so . . .

But no! Cross all four off the list, as well as the ticket collector – no, I'd not forgotten him! I know that in detective stories it is frequently the unlikeliest who turn out to be the crooks; but in real life it is usually the *likeliest*; and for me it was that smoothie of a 'diplomat' (ha!) who had moved into the top spot. Was it really necessary for him to spend so long studying Marion's sheet when he'd phoned – if in truth he was talking to *anyone*? And where was he when he left the carriage? Not in the toilet or the buffet-car because he would have had to pass us if he'd visited either. And he didn't. And incidentally, *he* wasn't the thief either.

So what we needed was a sharply observant detective like Poirot, say – or someone like me. For *I* was the one who observed the thief bend down to pick up a deliberately dropped Vienna guide from the dark blue carpet at the side of the aisle and to pick up something else at the same time – the camouflaged wallet, also dark blue, and casually slip both into what he called his Fisherman's Bag. That person was Ernest my companion.

How he profited from his theft I do not know, and have no desire to know. But it was a sad day when he came to sit beside me on that journey. The saddest recollection of all, though, is a small thing, yet one I always shall remember. As the train was slowing down at the outskirts of Vienna, Emily got down on her knees and felt along the whole carpet once more. I could have – should have – told the poor dear that she was wasting her time. But I didn't.

Finis

Well, there it is Ronald. Sorry I couldn't think of a decent anagram of your Christian name: 'Roland' is far too weak. But your surname came to the rescue, tho' I've never been too fond of 'Ernest'. Do read the story and let me know what you think.

Fond regards,
Diana (Duncan-Jones)

P.S. No Brownie points for guessing the 'one incident' that's changed!

29 Emmanuel Road
Cambridge

14th August

Dear Diana,

Thank you for your story – much enjoyed – although the last two paragraphs were a bit painful, to tell you the truth. I understand why you had no joy in trying to anagram Ronald, but I trust I've done better with you! I haven't got your skill as a writer since (until your dénouement) you describe the sequence of events with accuracy and economy and you quite certainly took our leader's injunction to heart about just changing one of the incidents. I've decided not to enter the competition myself but I've girded my loins and written an ending which relates far more closely to the truth. Ready? I begin with 'So what we needed . . .'

So what we needed was a sharply obser-vant detective, like Poirot, say – or someone like me! For I was the one who had noticed Nadia bend down on the pretext of retrieving a deliberately dropped guide-book and picking up the wallet with it and nonchalantly slipping both into her capacious handbag. I cannot believe she was sufficiently street-wise to understand the full potential of the wallet's contents. But I do know (she had told me on the tour) that she was getting uncomfortably short of ready monies. How she profited from her theft I have no desire to know but it was a bad day for me when I went through to join her on our railway journey. I said nothing to Nadia who looked as if she'd been stuffing her stomach with the most expensive meals in the most expen-sive restaurants in Prague – probably at the expense of the emaciated Emily.

Finis

Now listen Diana! For *me* the saddest thing of all is that we should both have come out of this with our reputations tarnished at least on the printed page since clearly neither of us has a particularly high opinion of the other. I must admit though that I took a bit of a shine to you and I think I still would have but for our time on the train together. What a pity things have ended like this! I shall put to paper no more about that strange morning since I am not such a big fan as you are of the 'changed incident' guidelines. But as you will have noticed I *have* changed just the *one* little thing: I did not actually see you pick up the wallet. I *did* however see the wallet in your handbag and I *did* see you push it down deeper so that it was no longer visible.

On a final and more constructive note let me congratulate you on your much more economical use of dashes and let me congratulate myself on using not a single comma in this letter to you.

Ronald Sterne

Extract From a Diary

Feb 5th 2005

I've only a few weeks to live, they tell me, and tho' I was brought up as RC I've never been into a confessional to tell of the sins I've committed. In any case I've no real regrets for any of them. My only confidante in life has been you, dear diary, and this will almost certainly be my last entry.

Marion and I were in the same class in secondary school; but after leaving we had exchanged only a few perfunctory letters over the years. So it came as a surprise when she wrote to me early last year informing me that her (second!) husband, a bigwig with a BA, had died, and inviting me, a life-long spinster, to join her on a fortnight's Hapsburg Holiday, dividing our time between Prague, Vienna and Budapest. An additional carrot was Marion's promise of an upgrade to Club Class (thanks to her late husband), and it was that which swayed me. I felt fairly sure that I could, in spite of my deteriorating health, just about cope with the travel, and almost everything else really – and I accepted the invitation.

Marion had always been a big and bouncy and bullying girl at school, and I had been hurt deeply (we were only seventeen) when she had robbed me of the only boyfriend I've ever had in my life, one of the sixth-formers a year ahead of us: Jonathan. And it took a very short time for me to realise that her boisterous nature had blossomed over the years (thirty-five of them) and developed into a selfish bossiness that I found well-nigh intolerable on occasions.

Increasingly I found I had no real say in where we went, what we ate, at what time we did whatever she'd decided to do. I won't go on.

At one point tho' things did become intolerable.

Many times when we were sitting together over a meal or over drinks, we spoke of our school days; and the evening before we were to catch our train from Prague to Vienna she asked me a question quite out of the blue.

'Did you ever keep in touch with Jonathan?'

'No.'

'He was very sweet on you, you know.'

'Not as sweet as he was on you.'

'I don't know about that. After you'd left school and gone off to Shropshire – and after things cooled down between us—'

'Yes?'

'He asked me if I had your new address.'

'Which you did have.'

'Of course. But he would have been no good for you, Emily dear.'

'Did you give him my address?'

'No, I didn't. He was a bit of a wimp, you know, and I thought you'd got over him by then – like I had.'

'Don't you think that what *I* thought was more important than what *you* thought?'

'To be truthful, Emily, I don't, no.'

That was it – virtually verbatim, I swear it. I didn't want to murder Marion, not quite, but I desperately wanted to hurt her. How? I'd no real idea, but someone was smiling down on me the morning we boarded the Vienna-bound train.

Seated immediately behind us were two youngish things on a group holiday; he, Ronald by name (we could hear all they said) seemed a pleasant enough fellow, with a diffident manner, in sharp contrast to his companion, named Diana, who sounded a selfish little bitch, openly flirting with her beau and equally bemoaning her shortage of cash. But both of them got up to help Marion when the ticket-man told us to move our luggage. So I was left alone for a couple of minutes, and all I needed was a couple of seconds. My opportunity! I took Marion's wallet from her bag and through the gap at the back of our seats I pushed it down into Diana's open hand-luggage. A lightening impulse and so risky. If the girl had told us of her great surprise at finding the wallet in her bag, who could have done the deed – except me? And I have never in my life felt so relieved as when we finally reached Vienna without her saying a word about the matter.

Marion soon bounced back of course

from this slightly distressing experience. The station official at Vienna was charming and helpful; the consulate had already made arrangements for the passport, all cards had been cancelled; the insurance company later coughed up not only for the euros but even for the wallet. This last information I learned when she rang me a few weeks later, but we have not communicated since. My one remaining hope is that she will not hear of my death and turn up to shed a perfunctory tear at my funeral. I mustn't be too hard on her. At least I enjoyed flying Club Class.

Just one thing I'm vaguely curious about: I wonder whether Diana and Ronald kept in touch after they reached home, and if so what they said to each other. At least *he* would have had knowledge of her address, surely so – which, alas, is more than Jonathan had of mine.

ANNE PERRY

LOST CAUSES

The court was so packed they had had to close the doors on more people trying to wheedle or push their way in. But of course I had known it would be, how could it be anything else, in the circumstances? Alan Davidson was being tried for the murder of his brother. I was sitting in my appointed place, very smart in my black skirt with high-necked white blouse, single pearls on my ears, and my wig itching like a hat that didn't fit.

My name is Judith, and some of my friends call me Jude, very appropriate – St Jude is the patron saint of lost causes, and if ever there was a lost cause, defending Alan Davidson was it!

What on earth had made me accept?

Counsel for the Crown, Sir Peter Hoyle, was questioning the police witnesses who had found the battered body of Neil Davidson on the living room floor of his house. They were making a good job of the horror of it. It was all quietly understated, no melodrama, no playing for effect, and above all, no exaggeration for me to find fault with. Not that it would have made any difference.

303

It would alter none of the facts that mattered, and they were all there in hideous detail.

As I sat increasingly uncomfortably, I remembered the message asking me to go to Lord Justice Davidson's office. At the time I had had no idea what it was about. I did not connect it with the crime in every newspaper headline. My first thought was that I had committed some solecism of legal behaviour of which I was unaware, and I was preparing a suitably profound apology. After all Lord Justice Davidson VC was one of the most senior judges in England, a man renowned for his wisdom, his heroism and his justice, even toward those who had been his enemies. And he certainly had those! Success such as his breeds envy.

And it had come to him young. During the darkest days of the war in 1942, aged barely twenty, he had taken a German gun position almost single-handed and saved the lives of a score of men. He had won the Victoria Cross for it, one of the highest decorations in the world for gallantry on the field of battle.

From then on it had been up all the way. Even his wife was a legendary beauty! And he had had two fine sons, and a daughter, by all accounts a beauty also.

I had knocked on his door five minutes early, and been told to enter straightaway. I had only ever seen him in the distance before. A couple of yards from me, in his late fifties, he was still one of the handsomest men I have ever seen. Many a woman would have paid a fortune for a head of hair like his, or eyes! Even the dark hollows around them and the ashen pallor of his skin could not mask the vigour of life within him.

'Yes sir?' I had said haltingly, only beginning to realise that whatever it was he had called me for, it was to do with him, not with me.

'As you will know, Miss Ashton,' he said gravely, 'my elder son, Neil was murdered four days ago. This morning they charged my younger son, Alan, with the crime.

'I would like you to defend him.'

For a minute I had had no breath to reply, no words evening my mind. My awe of him vanished, the distant, excited respect I had felt ever since I had been called to the bar was obliterated by my overwhelming human pity for him as a man, a father who in one terrible blow was losing both his sons.

'I . . . I . . .' I had stammered, knowing that I sounded like a fool.

'Please?' he had said simply.

I am a good barrister, sometimes very good, but there are still a score of people better than I, longer established, and with far more respect within the profession. He could have asked any of them and they would have been honoured to accept.

I had drawn in my breath to say 'why me?' but I hadn't said it. I had been flattered. I wanted to do it. He must have heard something about me, some brilliant defence I had made, perhaps of the

Walbrooke boy last spring. I was proud of that. Maybe this was my reward?

I had not argued or made excuses or protests of mock modesty. I had simply accepted, and promised him I would do everything I could to help Alan.

Of course that had been before I had met Alan Davidson, or knew the facts of the case.

Now here I was listening to Peter Hoyle asking the police surgeon to describe Neil Davidson's injuries, and watching the jury's faces as the pity and revulsion spread through them, and then the anger. I saw how they looked across at Alan, sitting motionless, his face frozen in misery. He refused to defend himself even by a second's shame or remorse in his expression, or the softening in the angles of his body. He sat as if already condemned, and I have never felt so helpless in my life.

I hated looking at Lord Davidson where he sat on the front row of the public seats, his face stiff and pale, his shoulders hunched. Beside him his wife had her face turned away from me.

The surgeon was waiting for me to say something, but what could I ask? The facts were incontrovertible. Someone had beaten Neil Davidson to death. There were bruises and abrasions all over his body, and one final blow had broken his neck. He was a strong man, not yet in the prime of his life. His knuckles were bruised and raw. Whoever had done that to him had to be badly marked themselves. And there was Alan with the scars on his cheek and the purple not yet faded from is brow and jaw.

'Miss Ashton?' the judge prompted and I could hear both the impatience and the pity in his voice.

'No, thank you, my lord,' I declined. The last thing I wanted was for the surgeon to say anything further!

Peter Hoyle glanced at me, and called his next witness. I have never liked him much, and at that moment I suddenly found him almost intolerable. He looked as if he were secretly enjoying all this misery.

Of course I understood now why Lord Davidson had chosen me. He would not embarrass any of his friends by asking them. No matter what passions of rage or love tore through his heart, the lawyer in his brain would know that there could be no defence. Perhaps only God understood the reasons why Alan had killed his brother, but the facts were being unrolled relentlessly in front of us as I sat there, and I was helpless to argue against any of them, or even to reinterpret them in any kinder light.

'And was there any evidence whatever of forced entry?' Hoyle was asking.

'No sir, none at all,' the police sergeant answered.

'And was there anything missing, as far as you could determine?' Hoyle pressed.

'No sir. According to the insurance records, and they were pretty detailed, there was nothing of value taken. All his ornaments and pictures were accounted for. His coin collection, which is very valuable, was all around in glass case, and untouched, and there were nearly two hundred pounds in notes in the desk drawer.'

'Then it would be reasonable to conclude that robbery was not the intention of his murderer,' Hoyle said with a glance at me, and then at the jury. 'Thank you, Sergeant, that is all I have to ask you. But perhaps Miss Ashton can at last think of something?' He left the rest unsaid.

I only wished I could, but every time my brain scrambled furiously in the jumble of facts, I remembered Alan Davidson's white face and blank eyes filled with fury and despair, but no will to fight. No matter what I said or did, or how I pleaded, he would barely talk to me. Even the little he did say was of trivia, small duties he wanted done for him, as if he expected to die and needed an executor rather than a defence. They were waiting for me . . . again. Not only could I not help Alan Davidson, this was likely to be the end of my own career. Memory of this would wipe out all my past successes.

'No thank you, my lord.'

There was a faint titter somewhere in the body of the court, stifled almost immediately, but I heard it and I knew what it meant. It was a mixture of nervousness for the reality of the pain, and pity not for Alan, but for me, because I was a failure.

Hoyle next called the elder of the two friends

who had gone to the airport to meet Alan on his return from abroad. 'And what date was that, Mr Rivers?' he asked politely.

'The twelfth, sir,' Rivers replied. He was a tall man, a little thin, although that might have been exaggerated by the pallor of his face and the pinched look around his mouth. I would have guessed him to be in his middle thirties, but today he looked more like fifty, and yet also oddly vulnerable.

'At what time?' Hoyle enquired.

'Half past eight in the morning. It was an overnight flight from New York.'

'Alan Davidson had been in New York?'

'No. He'd been doing botanical and ecological research in the Amazon Basin,' Rivers corrected with sudden asperity. 'He simply returned via New York.'

'I see,' Hoyle said, as if he saw nothing at all. 'And you met him at one of the London airports?'

'Yes, John Eaves and I met him at Heathrow.'

I looked across at Alan, but as almost always, he avoided my eye.

'Will you please tell us where you took Mr Davidson,' Hoyle asked.

Rivers clenched his jaw. Even from where I sat I could see the tightening of his muscles. He was obviously loathing every word he was forced to say, but there was no escape for him. Oddly enough, the transparency of his emotion made his evidence the more powerful.

'To the hospital at St Albans,' he replied.

Hoyle opened his mouth, a slightly sarcastic expression flashing across his face, then he changed his mind. 'Why was that, Mr Rivers? Did he ask you to?'

'Yes.' His voice was so quiet the judge directed him to raise it so the court could hear him. 'Yes!' he repeated, staring directly at Hoyle with such misery in his eyes that for the first time since the trial had begun I had a sense of some real and intense personal tragedy far deeper than sibling rivalry turned so sour it ended in murder.

'And the reason?' Hoyle pressed.

Rivers looked once at Alan in the dock, then spoke quietly but every word was distinct. 'He was very close to his sister, Kate. He'd been abroad for a long time with no way to send letters from where he was, or to receive them, I suppose. Almost the first thing he did was to ask after her.' His voice shook a little. 'He didn't know . . .' he stopped, blinking his eyes several times, and looking at Hoyle with such loathing I had a sudden vision of how he would look at me when I failed to do anything to help his friend. I dreaded that day, just as I knew that it was inevitable.

'And you answered him?' Hoyle said after a moment.

'I had to,' Rivers mastered himself again. 'He had to know. I just wish to . . . to God . . .' he took a deep breath, 'that I'd done it later! Or stayed with him . . . or something.'

In spite of himself Hoyle was suddenly gentle. 'What did you tell him, Mr Rivers?'

River's whole body was tight. 'That Kate had . . . had some kind of mental breakdown. Nobody knows what caused it . . . and . . . and she was in the hospital, and there was no real hope of her ever coming home.'

The court was silent. Hardly anyone moved, even in the public gallery. I knew the story, of course, but told again like this it was still horribly jarring. It was so easy to imagine the joy of home-coming, the reunion of friends, and then suddenly everything had changed, broken. The heart of it was gone. I could see their faces as they turned to look at Alan sitting blank-eyed in the dock.

Lord Davidson put his arm around his wife and she moved a little closer to him.

Rivers went on with the story, how he and Eaves had taken a shocked Alan to the hospital in St Albans and waited for him, pacing the floor, talking in snatched sentences, drifting from desperate hope into silence, then fractured words again, and more silence.

It had been nearly two hours before Alan had emerged, ashen-faced, walking so blindly he stumbled into the doors. They had taken him home where he had asked them to leave him, and reluctantly they had done so, not knowing what to do to help. Of course Hoyle made the most of Alan's state of mind, making him appear to have been planning murder even then.

'I thought he needed time alone,' Rivers said in an agony of apology. It was Alan he looked at, not Judge Davidson or Barbara beside him, her face at last turned towards me so that I could see her features, still exquisitely chiselled, her hair barely dimmed from the russet beauty of her youth, only a little softer, like autumn leaves as the year fades. I could not bear to see the pain in her, it was palpable, like a storm in the air. In a sense she had lost all her children, but in a slow and hideous fashion, worse than disease.

The following day Hoyle called more police witnesses to show that Alan had tried to cover his crime. When questioned he had denied any guilt, then when the net inevitably closed around him, he had fled, making him both a liar and a coward.

As I sat watching Hoyle close his case, without offering more than a token resistance, I felt utterly beaten. I have never prayed to saints for miracles. It is not part of my faith, and to be honest I did not think any form of intervention, divine or otherwise, would help Alan Davidson now. There was no shred of doubt, reasonable or otherwise, that he had gone straight from the hospital in St Albans to his home, and a few hours after Rivers and Eaves had left, he had gone to his brother's house and fought with him so savagely and relentlessly as to leave him dead. To escape so lightly himself he had to have taken Neil by surprise. He had not been larger or heavier, simply possessed by a rage which lent him superhuman strength.

Hoyle rested his case. Thank heaven it was too close to the end of the day for me to begin. I had nothing but character witnesses, for any real good they would do.

I left the courtroom. I had to see Alan and try one more time to persuade him to speak to me. I could not argue with the facts, I must try the reasons behinds them, if only he would trust me. There had to be more than the few bitter details Hoyle had brought out.

He was alone, staring at the small square of sky through the high, barred window. He turned as he heard the door unlock and the very slight squeak of the iron hinges.

He stared at me as the warder locked us in.

I was there for nearly an hour and an half. I tried every argument, every plea I could rake out of my imagination. I begged him, but he would tell me nothing. He just sat patiently on the stool waiting for me to exhaust myself, then spoke in his quiet voice, denying me anything at all. I left again with not a single weapon in my hand to defend him, and I had to begin tomorrow morning.

I thought of Judge Davidson and how I would face him when it was all over. I felt that the largest, most vital part of my life was also going to be consumed in this apparently meaningless tragedy.

And yet I had spent some hours with Alan and

had had no sense of a psychotic personality, and perhaps that was the most frightening part of it. Where *was* my own judgement? I used to think I was good at understanding people, that I had a sensitivity, even some kind of wisdom!

It was that moment that I decided to go to the hospital in St Albans for myself, and see if I could learn anything more as to what happened the night Alan had gone to see his sister. Of course I had questioned each of the witnesses Hoyle could call, but all they did was prove that Alan had been there, and had left white-faced and almost as if walking in his sleep. It hardly seemed possible he could hate. Neil so passionately simply because he had not told Alan of Kate's illness. He had been in the Amazon jungle and unreachable to anyone except by the most primitive means. And that was not the sort of message you give except face to face, and when you could be there to explain all you knew, and assure them that everything was being done for her. He could not have helped, and a fractured wireless communication would hardly make him feel better.

Perhaps they had not handled it in the best possible way, but it was a genuine mistake, not worth a quarrel, let alone a murder!

I took the train, and sat thinking about it all the way. It was not a very long journey, just under an hour on the express. By seven o'clock I was in a small side room where one of the doctors patiently explained to me that Kate Davidson would not be any assistance to me as a witness, even were she able to leave the institution and appear in court, and that was out of the question.

'I am afraid nothing she said would carry any weight.' He shook his head ruefully, pushing his hand through his hair and leaving it sticking up in long, wavy strands. 'She's completely delusional. Sometimes she is very depressed and we have to restrain her, in case she were to damage herself. At other times she simply sits and stares into space. I'm sorry.'

'But when she does talk?' I insisted.

'I'm sorry, Miss Ashton, but as I said, she is delusional. She wanders from past to present. She's very confused even about her own identity some of the time.'

I had nothing else to cling to. 'May I speak to her?' I asked.

He looked doubtful, his tired face puckered with lines of strain. 'She doesn't know about her brother's death, or that Alan has been charged with killing him,' he answered me. 'I'm afraid that news might be more than she can deal with. I'm sorry.'

I refused to give up, I don't really know why. I had no clear ideas. 'If I promise not to tell her?' I insisted.

He still looked dubious.

'You can be there with me,' I went on. 'Stop me, throw me out, if you need to for her sake. I'm at my wits' end, Dr Elliot. I have no idea how to defend Alan Davidson, and I have to start tomorrow. She and Alan used to be very close, she would want me to try everything I could, wouldn't she?'

He stood up slowly. I thought it was a refusal, but he opened the door and said 'Come on, then,' almost over his shoulder, and I followed his white-coated figure, a little stooped, sleeves too short, all the way up three flights of stairs and along what seemed like miles of corridor to a sunny attic. Inside a young woman sat stitching a piece of white linen. There were two other women there, also working at something or other, but no one needed to tell me which was Kate Davidson. She had the same beautiful hair, except that her face was marked with grief of such an intensity it caught my breath in my throat, and evening the doorway I almost wished I had not come.

'Kate, I have someone who would like to see you,' Dr Elliot said gently. 'You don't have to speak to her if you'd rather not, and I'll stay here all the time, if you wish.' That was a statement rather than a question, as if he already knew the answer.

She raised her eyes from her linen to look at me, and I felt a sense of her mind as sharply as if she had reached out physically and touched me. I did not see insanity, and certainly not any kind of foolishness, only a pain and a fear so profound that she had to shelter from it by removing herself from reality.

'Kate?' Dr Elliot asked gently.

'If you wish,' she said, her voice low, a little husky. Looking at her I had an overwhelming sense of what Barbara Davidson must have been like thirty years ago, and why the judge had fallen so passionately in love with her.

'Thank you.' I walked in and sat on the chair opposite her. I had already changed my mind about how to approach her. All idea of treating her like a child had been swept away the moment I met her eyes. It was not a retarded woman who faced me, but one hiding from an unbearable wound. Only one question beat in my brain – did I need to know what that wound was?

By the time I left three hours later I knew at least what she had told Alan the night he visited her. I was not certain whether I believed it myself. Surely it was too bizarre, too dreadful? But the only question that mattered was had Alan believed it? If he had, it would explain both his actions and his silence now.

I left her weeping quietly, but I thought with some kind of inner peace beyond the pain, because I had listened, and I had seemed to believe her. Or perhaps the truth was that in spite of its horror, its apparent impossibility, in my heart I had believed her, and she knew that.

Dr Elliot walked with me as I stumbled into the street and the glare of the lights and the noise of the traffic.

'What are you going to do, Miss Ashton?' he asked me.

'The only thing I can,' I replied. 'Try to prove that Alan believed her.'

'You won't succeed,' he said, biting his lip. 'And she can't testify. She was more lucid with you than I've seen her with anyone else. You might not find her like that again for weeks, maybe months. I wish I could tell you she was getting better, but she isn't.'

'I haven't got weeks or months,' I answered. 'Anyway, they don't call me Jude for nothing. It's what I do – increasingly often lately.'

He looked totally confused.

'St Jude – the patron saint of lost causes?' I explained. 'My name is Judith.'

He smiled, making him look younger. 'I got there rather before you,' he said. 'With the lost causes, I mean.'

I smiled at him, and thanked him. I had a lot of work to do and it would take me all night, and I'd be fortunate to be ready for the court to open in the morning.

My first witness for the defence was the Davidsons' cook. I had dug her out of her bed in the middle of the night, but I had asked her only the briefest of questions. She had very little idea why she was now on the stand testifying, and she kept glancing from me to Lord Davidson where he sat on the public benches. I could hardly blame the poor woman for being unhappy. She was confused and her loyalties were torn.

'Mrs Barton,' I began. The room was totally hushed. I don't really think anyone imagined I was going to get Alan Davidson acquitted, but they were all curious to know what I was going to try. The mixture of embarrassment and pity was about equal. 'Were you employed as cook in the house of Lord Justice Davidson on September ninth last year?'

'Yes, ma'am,' she said steadily, staring at me as if I were trying to hypnotise her.

'Was Mr Neil Davidson living at the house then also?'

'Yes, ma'am.'

'What was the state of his health, do you recall?'

There was a slight stir in the court. Lord Davidson shifted in his seat.

Mrs Barton swallowed. 'That weekend he was taken very poorly with the flu,' she replied.

'Was the doctor sent for?' I questioned.

'Oh yes, and he came. But there really isn't much you can do for it. Just stay in bed, and drink all you can.'

'Did anybody look after him?' I pressed. Please heaven she was not going to go back on her testimony now!

'Yes, ma'am,' her voice dropped to barely more than a whisper. 'His valet did, and then Miss Kate, his sister.'

I let my breath out slowly. 'How do you know that Miss Kate did?'

'Because she came into the kitchen and cooked

something for him herself. Seemed Mr Neil asked her to. Said she was the only one who could cook egg custard just the way he liked it, and would take some up to him on a tray.'

Hoyle rose to his feet. I knew he was going to object that this was all irrelevant, but in the event he did not bother. With a patronising smile he shrugged and sat down again, as if nothing I could do would harm his case anyway and he might as well be generous to me.

'And did she cook the egg custard, and as far as you know, take it to him?' I asked.

Judge Davidson stiffened.

'Yes, ma'am' Mrs Barton replied. 'She certainly left my kitchen with it.'

'Thank you.' I turned to Hoyle and invited him to question the cook.

He stood up and spoke with elaborate weariness, adjusting the front of his gown very slightly. 'Mrs Barton, has this touching story of sisterly affection nearly a year ago got anything whatsoever to do with Neil Davidson's death . . . by any stretch of your imagination, or ours?'

'I don't know, sir,' Mrs Barton answered. 'That was the night Miss Kate was took ill herself, an' I never saw her again.'

Suddenly the courtroom was alive. The ripple passed through the public benches like a shock of electricity before a storm. Davidson looked startled. Beside him Barbara was close to tears. In the dock Alan was rigid, glaring at me with panic in his face.

Hoyle for once looked as if he had bitten into an apple and found a worm in it.

The judge leaned forward. 'Miss Ashton?' He did not put words to a question but it was there in his face.

'I have no redirect, my lord,' I replied.

He sighed and sat back. I had not answered him, but he had understood that there was a story I was going to draw out, and he was prepared to wait.

I called Neil's valet. This was going to be the most difficult. He was a lean, dark young man with a troubled face, as if anxiety sat heavy on his shoulders, and he never once looked toward Lord or Lady Davidson.

'Mr Clark, were you valet to Mr Neil Davidson while he was living in his parents' home last September?' I began.

'Yes.' I already knew what he had done, and why, from the few words we had exchanged in the small hours of this morning, but this was still going to hurt, and I was sorry for that.

'Do you remember his illness on the ninth?' I asked.

'Yes,' he answered very quietly. For a moment I was afraid he was going to lose his courage.

'Of course,' I agreed. 'It is not something a competent manservant would forget, far less a good one, and as close as a valet. Did you look after him during this time, fetch and carry for him, help him in every way he needed?'

There was only one reasonable answer he could give.

'Yes,' he agreed.

I smiled and nodded. 'And were you there when his sister Kate brought him the dish of egg custard she had prepared for him?'

Now he looked confused, but if anything, less frightened than before. 'No.'

I knew he had been on duty that night. I did not want the trouble of having to call other witnesses to prove that. But if at this last moment his nerve failed him, I would have to. I could not succeed without him. I raised my eyebrows as if mildly surprised. 'You were off duty that evening? I must have misunderstood my other witnesses.'

His eyes narrowed and he turned even further away from Barbara Davidson. 'I was on duty,' he said miserably. 'I just wasn't in the room when he asked for her or when she came.'

'Do you know who was?' I said quickly.

This time his hesitation was so long that the judge intervened. 'Mr Clark, you must answer the question.'

'Yes,' he said at last. 'Lord Davidson.'

'Both times?' I pushed him. 'Or just when Neil asked for her?'

'When he asked for her,' he said grimly. 'It was he who told her to go.'

I felt a fraction of the ache ease inside myself, and a different kind of pain take over. 'Did you see her go in with the custard?'

'Yes.' Now it was a whisper, but in the utter silence of the room everyone must have heard him, even though they had no idea what they were waiting for, I prayed that none of them knew how much I also was feeling my way.

'Was anyone else in the room then, apart from Neil himself?'

'No.'

'And when she came out?' That was the question on which it all turned.

The man was ashen, and there was a sheen of sweat on his skin. Now at last he looked at Lord Davidson, but Davidson was sitting with his body forward, staring at Alan as if he recognised him for the first time.

Barbara looked at her husband, then at her son, then at me, and I was twisted inside with guilt for what I was going to do to her, but I could not pull back now.

'Mr Clark?' the judge prompted.

The valet stared at a space on the wall somewhere ahead of him. 'Yes, I was there.'

'Would you please describe it, please?' I requested.

'My lord . . .' Hoyle began. 'Miss Ashton is an actress of considerable skill, not to say ambition, but the tragedy of Lord Justice Davidson's daughter is not part of this trial, and ordinary decency requires . . .'

The judge was miserable.

Davidson himself had not said a word, but his

distress, and that of his wife, was a presence in the court so powerful there can have been no man or woman unaware of it.

His voice cutting like acid, the judge adjourned the court and requested me to see him in his chambers immediately.

'Miss Ashton,' he said the moment the door was closed behind me and I stood in front of him, 'I will not permit you to exploit the tragedy of Katherine Davidson's illness to divert the jury's attention from her brother's guilt. For God's sake, have you no sensitivity at all to her family's agony?'

I had been expecting him to say something of that sort.

'My sorrow for their grief does not allow me to conceal facts that are relevant to a murder case, my lord,' I answered. 'No matter how much I may regret the additional pain it causes, it isn't right to judge between one person and another, whose feelings may be spared and their sins hidden, and who has to have their wounds exposed.'

'You say that so easily,' he replied, and for a moment there was a flash of anger at what he saw as my blundering ignorance. 'You're what – thirty? Have you any idea what Davidson, and men like him, did for this country?' He leaned forward over the desk. 'You have no concept of what we endured during the war, what fear there was under the masks of courage we put on everyday, or what that cost. Davidson's heroism gave us hope, and belief in ourselves and the possibility of victory, if we could just hold on.'

I did not interrupt. I knew he needed to say it, and it was probably true.

'You look at him now with honour and prosperity, and you assume it was all easy for him,' he went on, now thoroughly consumed in his own emotional memories. 'But Barbara was married to Ernest Upshaw when she and Davidson met. It was passionate and total love at first sight, at least for him. He saw her across the street, and from that moment on he could think of no other woman.' There was a softness in his eyes, as if vicariously he tasted the fire and the tenderness of that long ago love story.

His voice dropped. 'They had to wait. In those days you did not divorce. It ruined a woman.' He was staring, soft-eyed, far beyond me or anything within the room.

'Ernest Upshaw was a hero too, in the same regiment as Davidson. He was seconded to a raid across enemy lines. He didn't come back. As soon as a decent period of mourning was over, Davidson and Barbara married.' Suddenly his eyes focused sharply on me again. 'They've lost their eldest son, but I will not have you drag their daughter's tragic breakdown into public. Do you understand me, Miss Ashton?'

'Yes, my lord, I understand you,' I answered without wavering my gaze from his. 'I am sure you will not allow me to overstep the boundaries of the law, but within them, I am going to do everything I can to help my client—'

'Your client is beyond help, Miss Ashton!' he said bitterly. 'You know that, and so do I. We'll go through the motions of the law, as we must, but he is guilty, and we can't redeem that. I will not permit you to crucify his father as well by exposing that poor young woman's mental or emotional collapse for the public to pore over and speculate about, and the newspapers to make money out of.' His face was hard, his lips tight, exaggerating the deep lines from nose to mouth. 'No ambitious young lawyer is going to save her own career, or rectify the mistake of having accepted an impossible case, at the expense of one of our greatest families, which has already suffered more than its share of tragedy.' It was not even a threat, just a statement of fact.

I felt a flicker of real fear in the pit of my stomach, like an awakening sickness, but I had believed Kate Davidson, and I still did. It was belief, it was certainly not knowledge, and that doubt was like a needle in my side. I knew that I was risking. But to back away now, to run from the battle because victory was not sure, would be cowardice that would cripple me forever.

'Of course, my lord,' I said steadily. 'If the case could be heard in private it would be the easiest, but since there is no question of national security involved, I don't think that will be possible.'

A dull flush spread up his cheeks. 'Are you attempting to mock me, Miss Ashton?'

My knees were suddenly barely strong enough to hold me up. 'No, my lord. I deeply regret the fact that evidence I may elicit from witnesses will be distressing to the Davidson family – and that is not just words – I do mean it!' I did, more than he could know. 'But my feelings are not the point. The truth is, and the nearest to justice that we can come.'

'Then you had better get on with it,' he said grimly. He seemed to be about to add something else, then changed his mind.

We returned and I resumed questioning the valet. The judge reminded him that he was under oath, and faced me with a spark of hope in his eyes. I killed it immediately. I hated doing it.

'Did you see Kate Davidson when she came out of her brother Neil's room?' I asked bluntly. He must have seen in my face that I knew the answer and that all the power of emotion in me was bent on dragging it out of him, whatever the cost to either of us, or to anyone else. He did not even look at Lord Davidson for help, or to the judge, and I refused to look at them either, in case it robbed me of my courage.

'Yes,' Clark said very quietly. But there was no a sigh or rustle in the room and every word was as dense as a scream.

'Describe her,' I ordered. 'Tell us exactly what you saw, what you heard and what you did, Mr Clark.'

He was a man defeated by a weight too vast for

him and finally he surrendered to it. He spoke in a tight, almost colourless voice, as if to add emotion to it would be unbearable. 'I heard Mr Neil shouting for me and the dressing room door swung open so hard it crashed against the wall, and he stood there in a rage like I've never seen him in before. His face was red and he had scratches on his cheeks and one eye was already swelling up. "Throw that garbage out!" he shouted at me, gesturing behind him.'

Lord Davidson started up in his seat, and then stood frozen, staring first at me, then slowly and with horror darkening his eyes, at Alan.

Barbara looked as if she were confused, like a lost child, growing more and more frightened with each moment.

Clark rubbed his hands slowly up over his face, digging the heels of them into the sockets of his eyes. I did not prompt him to go on, I knew he would.

Even Hoyle was silent.

'I didn't know what he meant,' Clark said hoarsely.

I was afraid for an instant that he was going to break down, his voice was so thick, so choked. But he mastered it, lifting his head a little and staring at me, as if I were the one person in that whole room who already knew what he was going to say, and somehow that reality helped him.

'Then I saw Miss Kate lying on the floor. Her hair was over her face and there was blood on her clothes. Her skirt was torn and up around her waist . . .' He took a deep, shuddering breath. 'And I knew what had happened. God . . . I wish now I'd done something different!' The pain in his voice was so sharp it cut the mind. 'But I was a coward. I was afraid of him, and . . . what he would do to me. I did as he told me. God forgive me, I put her out.'

I was sorry for him. He must have been in hell, the real hell of guilt. But I could not afford pity there or then.

'You knew she had been raped by her brother, and you picked her up and put her out? Is that what you're saying?' I asked.

He looked at me as if I had struck him, and that he deserved it. I admit even now that I can still feel the twist of guilt in my stomach I did at that moment.

'Yes,' he whispered. 'I did.'

I gave him his chance. 'Why? I asked. 'Why did you not help her? At least tell her father and mother what had happened?'

His voice was not much more than a whisper. 'Because a couple of months before that I had taken some money from Neil's dresser, just a few pounds. My mother was ill. I got something special for her, to help. Neil knew, and he told me he would fire me if I said anything about Kate. My mother's worse now. I can't afford to be without a job. There's no one else.'

'So you were blackmailed?' I wanted the jury to be sure of that.

'Yes. She locked herself in her room for several days, until they broke the door and the doctors took her away,' he said hoarsely.

It was even worse than I had expected. I don't know why. I had believed Kate when she told me. At least I think I had. I looked across at Alan. He sat in the dock with his head bowed and his hands over his ears, as if he could not live through hearing it again.

I meant to look at Lord Davidson, but it was Barbara's face I saw as she stared up at him, and in a dawn of horror more intense than anything I could have imagined before, I realised that he had known! I saw it just as she did. It opened up an abyss in front of me. It must have hurled her into one so deep she felt as if she would never escape the darkness again. He had known and he had done nothing!

She was so white she looked as if she must be dead! Perhaps in that moment something inside her did die.

I thought of the great love story of their meeting, her first husband, Ernest Upshaw, in Davidson's regiment – sent on an impossible raid – to die a hero! So his exquisite widow could marry Davidson?

Was that also the understanding I saw in her face as she stared at him now, as if she had never truly seen him before?

Lord Justice Davidson VC looked at the judge, then to the dock and the son who had avenged his sister because no one else would. Then at last, slowly like a man mortally wounded, he turned to his wife. I can't ever know, but I believe that in that moment at last he began to understand himself, and what he had done, what manner of man he was, and what it had cost him.

His elder son also felt that if he wanted a beautiful woman badly enough, then he could take her. He was cut from the same cloth – handsome, passionate, selfish at heart. The world had loved his father! Why not him too?

The court was still silent, like people who have witnessed something too terrible for speech. I don't know how much they understood, but they felt it.

Davidson turned to me. I expected to see hatred in his face. No man could ever forgive what I had done to him! And I had done it in public, in a courtroom, the realm where he was all but king.

But it was not hate that brimmed his eyes, it was the first white dawn of understanding of what sin truly is, and the hunger above all else in existence, to tear it from his soul.

Defending Alan from conviction was a lost cause, it always had been, he would have to serve something, even if the court accepted my plea for him of diminished responsibility – but perhaps I had saved another cause no one had even known was lost, until that moment? The path back from such a place as Lord Davidson had gone to is very long indeed, but it is not impossible. It takes more courage than facing an army's guns because the enemy is within you, and there's no armistice.

Thank you St Jude, for the miracle after all.

I turned back to the judge, my voice hoarse, but all uncertainty fled away.